Louis and the Ghost

By Henry G. Brechter

First published by Dog Ear Publishing
4010 W. 86th Street, Ste H
Indianapolis, IN 46268
www.dogearpublishing.net

ISBN: 978-1-4575-2334-2

This book is printed on acid-free paper.

Printed in the United States of America

For my ancestors
and my descendants,
and especially for
Kristen, Henry, Louis, and Karoline

PART I

CHAPTER
1

*I*t was Moving Day and the bright afternoon sunshine was clearly visible through the large muntined windows of Louis' new room. Finally, with this new house—an old house really but new for Louis and his family—the five-year-old boy had a room he could call his own. There'd be no more teasing from his big brother, Charley; no more telling him what to do back in Westbridge, in the shared space of what Charley had called "his" room. Yes, finally, all three of them—Louis, Charley, and Baby Thankful—each had their very own room. And that was probably the best thing about this new place down South, this place that was so far from home, so far from Massachusetts. Now all three kids could do what they wanted, he thought. *Well, maybe not Thankful.* At fifteen months, she was still kind of small. She was still just a baby.

Of course Mom and Dad ruled over the whole family. And they had their own room too.

For as long as young Louis could remember, Mom was always there for him. She was a lot more than a parent. She was his best friend. Mom, or KC as nearly everyone else called her, was so special. With her pleasant features and warm manner, Mom was the heart and soul of Louis' family. And while his dad was a loving father to all, he was always busy with something and oftentimes stretched too thin between work and family.

Rooms were all assigned by the time the family pulled into that long, twisted gravel driveway, on the sunny south side of the house. It was a bucolic setting but not quite in the sticks. The mailbox was still nearer the house than the road, with a creek—a "crick" as the locals called it—which marked off the property line on one side. Stone walls—unusual for this patch of Virginia—bounded two sides of the six acres that surrounded the old but lovely edifice. Truncated from its former lands many years ago, subdivided and sold away with no living memories of those times, the residence showed a cheery front yard that was wide open to a mostly empty street. That roadway would soon enough serve as the starting point for Dad's commute to his new "dream job" at the nation's capital.

Box after box crossed the main threshold of the Federal-style house with the unusual construction, and crowned by a sparkling white cornice. There were eight grand rooms and a huge breezeway, adorned with authentic posts and beams, which would serve nicely as a ninth room, a large carriage house, and a more modern, though smallish, garage. How the structure stood like a monument to the past, atop a small rise in what was mostly flat surrounding landscape. There was so much history here in Fairfax, but no one knew much about it these days. For almost 200 years, the house stood in place, with two strong chimneys guarding its flanks like tall stone sentinels. And now, on Memorial Day weekend of 2006, the great red sandstone welcomed a new family.

For Louis, there'd be plenty to do this summer here in Northern Virginia. And he'd have plenty of room to do it in, inside and out, before he started school in the fall, when a new chapter in his young life would begin.

As he sat in his room that first day, Louis was both bored and excited: bored of sitting alone in his very own space, without Big Brother needling him; excited to do new things, and some old familiar things, with minimal intrusions from Charley and the parental units, as Charley sometimes called Mom and Dad. There were boxes to unpack. *So many boxes.* There was stuff to set up. And how did he want to arrange his room? Was a five-year-old even allowed to arrange his room? The boy thought and thought. Then, with a finger placed on one dusty corner of the bare wooden floor, Louis began to draw a line over to nowhere. Then he drew another one. "Perinpedicular lines," he said in a soft voice.

If God didn't teach you how to breathe, you'd never be alive.

After all his five long years on Earth, Louis looked forward to school in the fall. He knew he was growing fast. Just like everyone said, he was either growing *so* fast, or *too* fast. He was riding his bike already *and* swimming in the pool. Well, the pool was back home in Westbridge, Massachusetts. There was no pool here at this house. There'd be no pool parties at this place. Here, he could still ride his bike though. There was the driveway and a country road right outside.

As Louis moved about his room and absentmindedly opened and closed the many boxes that were scattered about the floor, his big round blue eyes moved to the four pale blue walls. Then they moved up to the bright white ceiling above. Unlike the other rooms of the house, Louis noticed there was no big old plaster medallion with little angels adorning his ceiling. And he also saw that up above him was a narrow piece of unpainted wood that looked like a small door. "A door on the ceiling?" Louis thought aloud. "How wild is that?"

The house had an attic too, clearly visible from the outside, but one that no one thought much about until a few minutes after Louis first noticed that door high up in the ceiling of his new room. He also noticed there was no knob, but there was a strap of sorts—more like a cord—and he thought that if he could just reach it and pull on it, he could see if this thing really was a door that opened up to another place.

Among the many boxes and the few scattered pieces of furniture, Louis discovered his purpose. There'd be no more poking around. The boy stood up and sharply focused on the task that lay ahead. He moved, lifted, and then stacked three boxes, one on top of the other. Then Louis started to climb up toward the pull-cord. If he could just reach that pull-cord and pull. But another box was needed.

"Yes!" He stretched. *If I can just reach that cord.*

Louis scanned his surroundings and spied a smallish box that could be carried and placed at the top of his cardboard mountain. Wobbling occasionally, with his heart jumping and knees unsteady at times, Louis finally came within reach of the strap, which he grabbed and pulled with great purpose. As if by parachute, the boy floated gently downward, holding onto that rope cord now with both hands, as the tower of boxes tumbled away from his feet. Sud-

4

denly a narrow ladder came into view, sliding smoothly and rapidly down toward the floor, nearly taking the boy's young adventurous head with it. Then, releasing the cord, Louis just as quickly found his footing and flipped the folds of the ladder down several times, one end resting now on the wide pine floorboards at his feet and the other pointing the way through the trapdoor to the brightly illuminated attic above.

Ascending to the top of the ten-foot-high ceiling, little Louis poked his head through to the world that rested above his very own room. He was ready for something but he didn't know what. Neither Mom nor Dad had mentioned anything about the attic in this house. Finally Louis had a place to explore—a place to satisfy his rampant curiosity.

As he hoisted himself fully onto the attic floor, the little boy quickly positioned himself and looked around in all directions. Dazzled and comforted in this place, he saw there were boxes and more boxes, and ancient-looking steamer trunks. Batteries of fogged windows on three sides of the attic did not diminish the brilliant sunlight. A couple of old faded pictures in frames dangled crookedly off pitched rafters. And there in one corner, near a chimney and next to a large antique mirror, a man sat. He smiled and held a dark brown pipe in one hand that rested on his knee.

"Welcome, *mein Liebster.*"

The words were clear and soothing. Yet the man's mouth did not move.

Here was a pale black-and-white outline of an unusual man with lively gray eyes. Slightly transparent. As Louis' own eyes widened, the image and richness of the man grew. Color seeped into his form, though slowly.

"Do you know who I am?" asked the man.

The boy thought for one long moment and looked the man over, head to toe. He looked at the chimney, and at the pipe, and then back again to the man.

"Santa Claus?"

The man's laugh quickly gave way to a cough. A smoker's cough of sorts, not unlike the rattling sound he occasionally heard from his own grandmother.

"I'm Opa."

His visage glowed.

"Should I...know you?" asked Louis.

"Not yet, I suppose. But you will, *mein Liebster.*"

The boy took a long look at Opa. He smiled at the man and slowly turned away. Then, turning back to the man, Louis politely excused himself.

"I've gotta go, Opa." Pausing, he added, "I'll be back."

The man smiled, having never left his perch atop one of the old vintage wooden chests.

CHAPTER
2

"What a weekend to be moving. It is so hot and there's still so much to do." It didn't seem as though Dad was directing his comments to anyone in particular. Not to KC, who at the moment was outside. Not to Little Thankful, who sat cheerily for the moment in her adaptable car seat / stroller on the wide-open spaces of what would soon become the family's living room. Dad apparently was not talking to Charley either, or to the moving men who traipsed in and out of the house without a pause. He did notice Louis, ah Louis, came down the stairs and went into the foyer. His Number Two Son was "*Louis Quatorze,*" as he sometimes referred and so proudly pronounced as if he were French, or even the King of France. Oh, how Dad loved to articulate that name as the French would articulate it. He had, after all, insisted on the French pronunciation at Louis' baptism and since then, whenever else he spoke to or about his beautiful son, his intelligent and very articulate son.

"How's your room, honey?" Dad focused his deep-set eyes down onto his boy. "Are you all done unpacking already?"

"Not yet, Dad," answered Louis.

"What's taking you so long, kid?" Dad asked with a smile.

"I was talking to Opa upstairs, way upstairs in the attic."

"What?" asked Dad.

"I was talking to Opa." Louis started to look as if he were in trouble.

Dad lowered the box he was holding and approached his boy. "You mean somebody's up in the attic?"

"Ye-aaah," answered Louis.

"Who?"

"Opa. I told you. Opa, Dad."

"A mover?" Dad put a hand on the boy's small frame. "A moving guy?" He didn't wait long for an answer. "Answer me!"

"I don't...think so." Louis could see trouble in his father's deep, sea-green eyes.

"KC. KC!" Dad screamed now as he grabbed his son and practically threw him outside the house, followed quickly by little Thankful, still cheerful, who napped now peacefully in her comfortable car seat / stroller. Dad slammed the door behind him. Everyone was outside now and out of danger.

"KC: Call 9-1-1! Now! There's somebody in the house." He was very animated.

KC, vivacious and the anchor of stability in an oftentimes chaotic household, was just plain "Mom" to everyone in the family but Dad. "What are you talking about?" she asked as she went to his side. Nothing would surprise her. What a crazy couple of months it had been. Her husband's new job in Washington came right out of the blue one day, setting off a chain of events that carried her family five hundred miles south to a charming old house—a dream house really—with modern amenities that comfortably coexisted with deep wood grains and wainscot.

"Louis saw a guy in the attic. Call the cops, now!" Dad was in a frenzy. "Where's your cell phone? Wait. I'll call the cops myself."

"No, no. I got it. I'm calling now." KC calmly asserted herself into what was a very scary scenario. *Someone in the attic? How could that be?* she thought. *Is this dream house really too good to be true?*

Dad kept the movers at bay while KC made the call.

"Charley! Charley! Find me a baseball bat. Now!" demanded Charley's father.

"But, Dad. I told you," pleaded Louis. "It's Opa. He's nice. Really, Dad."

"Some friggin' squatter living in the house is not a nice person, Louis." He looked down at his son, at his trusting and innocent young son, and added, "I'm sorry, honey. I didn't mean to use bad words." Too often Dad was foul-mouthed around the kids and just as often apologized for it.

"But, Dad—" Louis started.

Suddenly Charley appeared, as if out of nowhere, grabbing Louis from behind, as he so often did. The feisty nine-year-old was the family jock, an avid sports fan, and sometimes, but not always, loud and annoying like the sportscasters he mimicked. Charley, too, was a beautiful boy: tall, thin, and very handsome, with a great smile that captivated everyone who saw it. Charley carried no bat for Dad.

Had he not heard his father's command?

"What's going on, Dad? What's wrong? Dad?" asked Charley.

His dad didn't answer Charley. Louis did not say a word, and an uneasy calm descended. Everyone was on the front lawn and, so it seemed, out of harm's way.

Within minutes PFC Will Lee and his K-9 partner, Jade, were on the scene, followed within a few more minutes by a team of motorcycle officers. It seemed the house and the whole neighborhood were abuzz with all kinds of activity. Police lights flashed, dogs, both Jade and the local dogs, barked and howled. The movers, there were three, sat under the shade of an old oak tree and casually took in all the action.

While Dad, Mom, and Charley stood nervously near the front door, only a few steps from the covered porch, a portico, really— the kind that protected the main entryway to the house—Louis was off to the side of the house and was interviewed first by one of the motor officers.

A thorough search of the house revealed nothing. There was no sign of forced entry anywhere, and no obvious sign of a squatter's presence, either in the attic or anywhere else in the house or its adjacent structures. There were no signs of any quick exits either. Louis' account to the officer only confirmed that he had in fact been upstairs in the attic.

"There's no one in the house," said the K-9 officer to Dad, Mom, and Charley after he briefly conferred with his associates. Then, he gestured over to Charley and politely asked for some private time with his parents. PFC Lee turned away from Charley, and the three adults walked under the shelter of the portico.

"There are no signs of life…other than y'all and those three guys under the tree. There's no one in the attic, and except for your boy Louis—gosh, how that name fits that little guy so well—it looks like no one's been up there in months…maybe even years."

Dad stood in stony silence as the officer continued with his verbal report on the matter.

"Smells real nice up there though. It reminds me of my dad and his pipe. Not stale at all. Fresh. Aromatic."

"Officer…Lee. I know you're trying to comfort us," said Dad. He knew. His own father had been a policeman. He knew and mostly admired the tactics and manners of the profession.

"You know, that boy, he's so smart. He's so articulate. I think Louis may just have a bit of an overactive imagination. Was he like that back North?" Officer Lee stood over six feet tall. He was handsome and courteous to the core.

"No. Never," said his mom. "Not anything like this."

"Nope," added his dad.

"No imaginary friends?" asked the officer.

"No. Never," the somber parents proclaimed in unison.

"You know, at his age kids don't always know what's real and what's not real. I'm a parent too. My kid's right about Louis' age—my boy Darrel's six—and sometimes he just doesn't really know what he's supposed to believe and not believe. You know, with moving and all, maybe the little guy just needs a little extra love and attention right about now."

"May-be," said Dad. "Officer Lee, I really appreciate your coming down here so fast and checking the place out. I—" He looked over to his wife. "—We really appreciate it. We'll have a little talk with our son, and we'll let you know how we make out, if that's okay?"

"No need, sir…ma'am." He tipped his cap to KC. "That little guy is something else. I think he'll be famous someday. He may be a lawyer. Like F. Lee Bailey."

"May-be," said Dad.

One of the motor officers then approached the group and gave a long look at Dad and an obvious-to-all once-over in the direction of KC—an undeniable beauty at just over forty. In a somewhat thick southern drawl, the officer pronounced, "The young'un says he knows what he saw up there. Consider that the boy may require some professional attention."

"I think we can handle this, Officer," said Dad. "I think we'll all be okay once we settle in."

The motor officer turned again to KC, bowed his head slightly. "Ma'am." Then, with a look over to Dad and a quick acknowledgment to PFC Lee, the tall man, with his dark uniform and sergeant's stripes, high boots and helmet, bid "Good day, y'all." And with a slight glare and a grin, he turned and walked away.

"Don't pay him too much mind," said PFC Lee. In a sincere and comforting tone, he added, "Sergeant doesn't always get it right. He isn't always mindful of what he says or does to others."

A few minutes later, the police had all left, and the adults' moving routines uneasily resumed. Charley and Louis played together down by the creek, and Thankful returned to her nap back inside the house.

CHAPTER
3

L ouis had no doubt of what he saw, and was saddened, even shocked, that no one seemed to believe him. He was five years old and getting ready to start school. His family just moved into this very classy old house with the steep pull-down ladder and the narrow trapdoor that led to the attic that belonged to Opa. And no one believed him. He whispered, "Some people might even think I'm a crazy person."

And why wasn't Opa there when those police people went looking for him?

Louis was convinced though, and he rather liked the old guy, brief as their introduction had been. Now, alone again in his great big room with those pale blue walls that matched his big round eyes, Louis looked up again and in the direction of that trapdoor.

It approached nightfall, so if he were going to do it again, now was the time for it, he thought. How best to get back up there? There, standing in the corner was his fishing pole. That pole never caught a big fish, but how he loved it. Now, he had an idea to use that little old pole to snag that strap up above his head and reel it in, or rather reel it down, to get that ladder to slide to him.

Would it work? Louis really didn't want to use a pile of boxes again, or another ladder to get to the ladder. Mom would go crazy if she caught him trying to go back up there, and he had to be careful that Mom or Dad didn't move him out of this very awesome room, just to get him away from that attic. Yes, he'd give his fishing pole a try.

Moments later, as his little heart pounded, up into the attic he went.

Louis peeked his head through the entryway, and it wasn't long before he saw Opa over in the same place. He smoked his pipe, thoughtfully it seemed. Clearly the man was not surprised to see him. In fact he acted as if he had expected him all along.

"Louis." A brief pause, then the man said, "Ludwig."

"Where were you when the police came by?" Louis asked innocently enough.

"I was here, *mein Liebster.* Those men…the men just didn't see me." The words had fallen this time right from Opa's lips. The pipe's smoke filled the attic with sweet air. The aroma tantalized Louis, just as the smell of gasoline always had. Though it was a totally different fragrance, the pleasure was much the same. The natural light that had flooded the attic earlier in the day receded steadily, yet the boy's surroundings were as comfortable as before.

Downstairs KC was busy in their new, modern kitchen. She unpacked box after box of supplies, canned goods, utensils, and gadgets. Her thoughts ran wild now, alongside her few moments of much-needed alone time. *What a day it had been!* As the family took up residence in this elegant home, the work of settling in promised to be as massive as the great house itself.

And what would the family do for dinner tonight? she thought.

Dad was busy in what would be the family's study, sandwiched between the soon-to-be family room and the main downstairs bath. There were boxes of books all over. Hundreds—perhaps over a thousand books—each in need of its own niche on the dark mahogany shelves of the built-in bookcase that occupied two walls, from floor to ceiling. His massive desk was already in place, and faced out toward the northeast, with a full-length country porch that sat between his old piece of furniture and the lovely backyard that ended at the creek: the creek that barely flowed in the summertime. *Not exactly Bull Run.* The creek that he was told would flow considerably during the wetter seasons. Back inside, other furnishings still needed to be positioned or situated better than where

13

the movers had left them. The kids' computers also needed to be moved to the room next door, and set up there.

Dad's mind darted next to Tuesday and what would be his first day of work at *the* National Archives—a lifelong dream that just popped back into his life one day, as if out of nowhere, and hit him smack in the middle of his face. Never had Dad, at fifty-two, imagined such a major career move at this point in his life. The relocation from the South Shore of Massachusetts to this area was totally unanticipated only a few months ago. Back home were all the relatives and the friends, and the jobs both he and KC so suddenly left behind. Yes, these would all be missed, but his new job, the family's new life, and their new home—practically a southern mansion—would fast become the family's sources of new pride and focus. There had been virtually no time to consider the downside to working in D.C., and the huge changes that that entailed. But the job—and with it the pay, the benefits, and all the trappings of a U.S. Government bureaucrat—offered him a new life start, to pursue a new career as the Assistant Deputy Research Director for the Archives' Civil War Records' Branch. The job description was about as close to perfect as he could ever imagine. And while he never considered himself much of a salesman, he had somehow managed to sell KC and the kids on the idea of leaving their beloved home in Westbridge.

"KC," Dad called. He was hungry. What a long day it had been. "KC," he called out a little louder, but still there was no answer. He forgot for the moment that he was not back home in their smallish Cape with the thin walls and the limited space. *God, how we all loved that house, and everyone could hear everyone else without a problem.* Dad decided to just take a walk around the new place and find his wife without yelling and yelling until she heard him. That might take some getting used to, he thought, but this was, after all, a new home and a new beginning.

CHAPTER
4

*O*ver the next several weeks, adjustments to life in Northern Virginia were not so easy. Nine-year-old Charley was challenged to finish up third grade at his new school. He sorely missed his many friends back home. Dad was totally immersed in his new job at the Archives, and was barely seen during the weekdays. Usually buried among old books and records within cavernous rooms and vaults where he often worked, Dad was generally happy there and engaged in ways he never experienced in over twenty years in the health-care industry. But Dad's presence at home was sorely missed. Mom had her hands full with her toddler Thankful and the boys, while she somehow managed to handle all the other household affairs. She remained especially concerned for Louis. It seemed he spent way too much time on his own, and usually tucked away in his room. And that creepy story about the guy in the attic continued to trouble KC, although whenever she brought up the subject with her husband, he just shrugged it off as a kid's overactive imagination that was mixed up with the craziness of a major relocation. The attic had been checked and rechecked, he said. No one ever found anything up there to suggest a squatter's presence.

Maybe he is right, KC thought to herself. *Louis seems so happy and content, and so normal. He never talks about that first day—Moving Day—anyway, and it's no big deal if he does have an imaginary friend. Lots of kids do. Louis just ought to spend more time outdoors.*

* * *

Louis *was* spending a lot of time upstairs. It seemed he was hardly ever in his room compared to the attic, anyway, and when he was up there, it always seemed that time moved so very slowly. Mom never seemed to miss him. Whenever she came looking for him, he always seemed to be where she looked. Louis couldn't tell time real good, at least not with the round clocks with the arms that moved. Digital time was okay though. He could read the digital clock in his room, and it hardly changed from the time he went up to the attic to the time he got back. And the round clocks barely moved at all. Yes, that was strange, as was the whole idea of an old man living up above him in the attic.

And the ladder seemed light as a feather whenever he hoisted it back into place.

And why wasn't he scared of the man? That first day he saw Opa, he was kind of gray, like a newspaper picture. Vague was the word that grown-ups used. And the more he saw Opa, the better he looked. He looked healthier, he guessed. He thought Opa was very interesting and, at times, even exciting. And yet there were times it seemed they'd talk about nothing. And that didn't matter. Why would any of it matter? The two of them had such a strong connection already. The truth was that for the first time ever, he felt that he had a real friend. A friend to be loved and a friend he loved to have around.

CHAPTER
5

"*S*o if you're not Santa, who are you?"

"No, I'm not Santa. And you know Christmas trees were still a bit of a novelty where I was born...when I was born."

"Did I ask you that out loud?" Louis remarked. He studied the man with a careful eye, and then slowly scanned his broader surroundings. Still troubled, and even shocked at times, that on that first day no one believed his story, Louis looked very closely at Opa. *There's no need to bother people with stories,* he thought. *Not Mom, Dad, or Charley.* Everyone was busy these days, and no one seemed to have time for each other anyway. Even dinnertime, a time the family always used to catch up with one another, was barely a family event these days. Some nights Dad didn't even get home till bedtime, just in time to read him a short story before going to bed himself.

"I hear your words." Opa smiled. His face and his clothes had color. He wore a faded flannel shirt, it seemed, and some very old-looking jeans. There were black shoes or boots on his feet, neither with much of a heel, and they made no sound at all when Opa walked over what were for Louis very creaky floors.

"You're weird." Young Louis smiled. "What kind of a name is Opa, anyway?"

"I'll answer that question with a question," Opa shot back. "Do you know where you came from?"

"Massachusetts."

"That I know, *mein Liebster*."

"And what's that mean?"

"Let me just start in the beginning, Louis. For me, the gift of life started in the Year of Our Lord one thousand, eight hundred and twenty-three. I was christened a Catholic—"

"I'm a Catholic too," interrupted the young boy.

Opa smiled politely, nodded, and continued, "—three months later, on February 8, 1824. I grew up on a farm in a district—the Donaukreis—that was surrounded by God's glorious world. The blue sky reflected on our river, the handsome blue Danube, which shaped the western boundary of our farm. The high mountains and the rich forests of Upper Swabia are to the south." Then, as if he had heard the boy's question, Opa quickly added, "It's 'Upper' Swabia because we were closer to the Alps. Do you know the high Alps, *mein Liebster*? The mountains?" Louis seemed absorbed but did not say a word. "'Lower' Swabia is in the north. Bavaria lay to our east and in those days was still a fair ride by carriageway. Bodensee—Lake Constance is also to the south...like the Alps."

"We had a king back then, the King of Wuerttemberg, a good man who worked very hard for the people, and our family was among his more fortunate subjects. We had our land, our health, and each other...for years. There were fifteen of us by the time my parents, Philipp and Maria, finished. There were thirteen kids, as you call them, of which I was the third. Sadly, my mother was only thirty-seven when she died, only a few months after my sister Josepha was born."

"What was it like having a king?" Louis wasn't sure if he spoke those words out loud, but it didn't matter. Opa had heard him.

"Wilhelm—Willy we called him. The Good King Willy ruled our little country for almost fifty years. Before him was his father, named Friedrich, or Frederick. Frederick was the first king of Wuerttemberg and was known as 'The Big Belly.'"

"The Big Belly? That's funny." Louis giggled and smiled at Opa. He looked deeply and lovingly into the man's sparkling gray eyes, which were framed squarely within his thick, straight, salt-and-pepper hair and dark, bushy moustache.

"Yes. Big, fat, and tall was old Frederick. People could also call him 'Fritz,' but everybody—"

"Called him the Big Belly," added Louis. The two laughed in unison. Opa's hoot was followed with an acute, though fairly brief, coughing spell. He continued after that.

"Well, did you know that Big Belly helped Napoleon fight the Prussians?"

"The Russians?" asked Louis.

"Well, them too. But the Prussians, you see, were different. They were Germans, just like Big Belly was. Just like my father was…and my family. My father was just a boy about your age at the time when Big Belly—that big, fat, and tall king—took the throne."

"I thought you said you were from Slobia."

"No, *mein Liebster*. Swabia. We were Swabians. A lot of people from Wuerttemberg are called that. The Prussians were Prussians, but Swabians and Prussians were, and are, also Germans."

"So there were different kinds of Germans?"

"*Ja wohl!* And there still are, just like there are different kinds of Americans. I think you know: you are in Virginia now, but you came from Massachusetts. People who live here…and where you came from, are Virginians and…and whatever you call people from Massachusetts. But they are all Americans. We are all Americans, I should say."

"Oh—kay," a slightly uncertain Louis responded.

He looked at the expression on the young boy's face and asked, "How about Napoleon? Do you know who Napoleon was?"

"I don't think so." His innocent eyes invited Opa to go on. "But I've heard of him."

"It was long ago and Napoleon was the Emperor of France. He was a little man with a big dream, and people like the Big Belly lent Napoleon a hand in fighting against their own kind. Now, as I said, my father was just a boy when the Big Belly ruled over Wuerttemberg—Swabia is part of Wuerttemberg—and he was very, very happy to see Fritz go when he did. You see, my father's brother, my uncle Nicolaus, was sent to fight in Napoleon's army, and died in Russia because of that man. My father hated him. The traitor! One of Big Belly's daughters even married a brother to Napoleon, a fellow named Jerome.

"When those wars—the Napoleonic Wars as they are called—were not going so well for old Emperor Napoleon, the Big Belly first thought that he would follow that man back to Paris, but then decided instead to change sides...again. So Fritz marched his troops alongside other Germans and allies, in pursuit of Napoleon, not long after the man had passed through our green valley headed east, and chased Napoleon and his once-great La Grande Armée back into France. So in the end, Big Belly saved his skin and ended up on the winning side. You might say, I suppose, that that man even hastened Napoleon's demise."

"Wow," said Louis. The boy could see Opa's faded clothes had gained color and substance, and his cheeks and hands were practically the same color as his own. "What's demise?" Louis added calmly. "What's hastened?"

"Not important, son, not now." Opa looked lovingly at the boy. "But it means that it ended sooner. Now at that time, and like you, I wasn't on this Earth, but we all came to know Big Belly from those people, like my father, who lived in those days. Big Belly's son, Willy, became king a year later, and things began to get better." Opa arched his back a bit and continued. "Yes, Swabians got real happy once the Big Belly was gone. He was responsible for a lot of the pain and suffering of his own people—my people." Opa's eyes, now as rich and gray as a house mouse's fur, fixed again on young Louis, and he added, "And your ancestors. Do you know the word 'ancestors'?"

Louis was enthralled. He had so many questions, so much to say and to ask. But instead, he sat there and let the man continue. He nodded in agreement.

"Willy, his son, was different, a lot different. He even married a Russian girl. She was his first cousin, Catherine. And a beautiful princess she was."

"A Prussian girl?"

"No, this time it is Russian. A Russian girl. There's a big difference, *mein Liebster*." Opa smiled.

"You never told me what that meant." Louis looked serious.

"It's like when the people of Northern Virginia call you 'honey chile.'"

The boy nodded in agreement. He recalled the old black lady who called him that just the other day at the restaurant.

"So...anyway, I knew so much about those times from my father and his stories. Oh, the stories he told us, every night it seemed." After a brief pause, Opa added, "So my father told us."

"My dad tells me stories too." Louis recalled the night before, when he asked his father to wake him up when his story was over. *What was it again?* The boy couldn't remember. It was a famous story, his father said, about "a heedless young fellow" named Jack. He could see Dad reading in the dim light that reflected off the pages of the old book. He just smiled and kept on reading, and Louis couldn't recall whether his dad ever woke him up. They weren't always the best stories he told, but it was always nice to have Dad nearby at bedtime.

As if waiting for Louis to finish his thoughts, Opa appeared pensive himself. Then, once he sensed the boy was ready for him to resume his tale, he spoke.

"Now I was here, in America, when our Good King Willy passed." Opa rose slowly and Louis noted for the first time that this man who stood before him was no more than his mother's height, which he knew was good for a girl but considered short for a man. "I almost met my maker before King Willy did, but that was not meant to be. I was at death's door in this very house, and in this very attic space. The sickest of us were put up here to be closer to God, so they said, and for His taking. I was right over there." He pointed. "For four months I lay there with others like me. But the end was not to be. Not then."

CHAPTER
6

*C*harley was in his room when the shouting started between Mom and Dad. He was trying to do his homework and was very happy to jump off his bed and run downstairs to determine from where the distraction was coming. On the broad stairway landing, Charley listened and it seemed as though all the commotion was coming from downstairs in the study.

"I can't tell you more than what I know. Louis was—is—so happy." KC raised her typically deep voice quite a bit to Dad, who pressed her about the "return" of Louis' imaginary friend. It was not as if that friend had gone anywhere. It was just that ever since Moving Day, Louis had not said a word about the man in the attic.

Charley expertly opened the study's door a crack to secretly get the most from his parents' argument, if that was what it really was. It seemed so. He could see that Dad was clearly upset with all the stuff Mom was telling him. A moment of uneasy silence quickly ended when Mom added, in a somewhat sarcastic tone, "You would have thought he spent the last two weeks in the library." Charley was thoroughly captivated until Mom noticed him at the doorway and tersely said, "Charley: leave your father and me alone...and close the door. Thank you."

The basic truth was that it *had* happened again. And it was still happening. Louis told his mom about the man earlier that day, after she, always the warm, kind, and understanding parent, casually invited the discussion. Then, with a gleam in his eyes and a broad smile on his face, the boy told his mother he saw his friend Opa regularly. Mom was totally torn by the disclosure. She put a brave face on for her son, while she privately lamented and agonized when or even whether to tell her husband.

KC opted for a full disclosure and took Dad into the study when he returned home from work that evening. The kids had already eaten. Louis was playing outside on the lush green grass with his little sister, and Charley was in his room with some homework. School would end in a few days.

Louis said he and Opa "hit it off" quite easily. He said they met often—almost every day, since the first day, and sometimes more than once a day—and that the old guy said he was close to the family. As she heard her son speak, so eloquently at times and with such certainty, she knew this went way beyond the initial panic over a home invasion. No, she thought this was far more disturbing. The complexity and content of his words did not match his young voice.

The last two weeks had settled down quite a bit for KC. She was in regular contact with her friends and family back home—for her, Massachusetts was still home—while she quickly made new friends and acquaintances in Fairfax County, one of the most affluent communities in the whole country. But that was just the way KC was: always a magnet for friends and a great communicator. It didn't matter where she was. KC was someone who people wanted to be around and in touch with. She was so likeable and extremely pretty, with her stylish, bobbed and bleached blond pixie-cut hair, her bluish green eyes, her small build and heavenly shape—in spite of, and in addition to, having brought three beautiful babies into the world.

The family's one-month anniversary in their new home rapidly approached. But now this. *This…again.*

With a gentle smile and a great big hug, Mom gave Louis a pat on his bum and sent him outside to play. This place was such a nice, pretty, and safe locale, not really a neighborhood, because the neighbors were few and distant, but pleasant enough and certainly private. While the quiet street connected all the neighbors' properties—and there were only four families in the immediate area—the lots were expansive and not conducive to quick hellos or cups of borrowed sugar.

Just ignore it, KC thought at first. *It's harmless. Imaginary friends are harmless and oftentimes fill an important void in a young person's life.* She had been to the library and had quietly read up on the subject, both online and in town, after the events of Moving Day. "Pure childhood fantasy," she said half aloud. "It has to be." Then with a look of puzzlement, KC muttered, "How radical, though. And just when I was ready to discard all this newfound knowledge to the dustbins of history." Pacing the kitchen at times, as she prepared dinner for the kids, the mother mused, "But how many five-year-old kids' stories are so damn sophisticated? 'The Congress of Vienna?' Come on now!"

Dad's immediate reaction to what KC told him was shock ("What?"), then anger and selfish disbelief ("I can't believe this is happening to me!"), followed by just plain anger ("Fuck this shit!"), then impulsiveness ("Let's ignore it, brush it off, and it'll take care of itself."), and finally an admission that something needed to be done.

"I think the kid needs help. I'm concerned, really concerned." Dad didn't look so good. It was Saturday and he had been up since 5 AM, working in the study on his various work-related projects. He absolutely loved his work, but there was so much of it, it was hard for others to imagine why that was so. "With this move, then the heat, this friggin' neighborhood with no kids around, and with kindergarten starting for Louis right after Labor Day, and with Charley telling him bad things about school, I think the little guy just has a screw loose that needs to be tightened up a little bit." Dad took a deep breath. "That's all. A little tune-up." He seemed to have convinced himself of this course of action only as his words left his mouth.

KC didn't disagree. She was visibly saddened with her husband's reactions but was resigned now—now that she had spoken with both Louis and with her husband—that some action other than no action needed to be taken. She'd do some research and find someone somewhere who would listen and offer opinions. She'd look at a number of options: child psychologists or psychiatrists, family therapists, licensed clinical social workers, and maybe even some nontraditional alternatives.

"I wish we were back near Children's Hospital. They'd know what to do. I know they would." Dad was so distressed. He needed to keep talking. "Whatever it is to a five-year-old, it's really just an overactive imagination. You know he's gonna grow out of it. But just to be on the safe side, let's take him somewhere…as soon as possible. Okay?"

"Okay, honey." KC would do this now as much for her husband as for Louis.

CHAPTER
7

*L*ouis was certain that what he heard and what he saw were real. There was no doubt about it. The bond between him and Opa was unquestionable, and growing stronger by the day. He loved being around the old man, and the comfort and sense of belonging there in the attic with him in no way lessened his own place within his own family. It all seemed to make a strange sense to Louis that things should be the way they were. Louis could clearly see how Opa's form had gotten livelier since they first met. The man had strengthened to more brilliance in color and substance. He appeared in multiple styles of dress, though always old fashioned—often with the looks of a farmer, and at times he looked more like a soldier.

Louis could tell Mom and Dad were real worried about him. The other night Charley told him that they had a fight over him and his "imaginary friend." And since then it seemed that whenever he walked in on his parents, they'd act weird. They'd cut short their soft talk and look at him like he caught them doing something. It never used to be that way. Well, Louis didn't want to cause them any more concern. For now he'd pretend that Opa was not real and that he was nothing more than just that imaginary friend they believed he was. Yes, for now Louis would keep his stories—Opa's stories—to himself. There'd be no harm to carry one little secret for a while. He'd continue to see Opa, yes. The old guy sounded like a talking chapter book, and

Louis felt so cozy, so safe, and so welcomed when they were together.

KC wanted to be sure she'd be doing the right thing. A little more research and she'd be ready to make some calls. She had to be very careful not to make things worse.

Insurance was no problem. The Feds offered quite a deal for their new employees, or at least for people at her husband's level. She didn't know for sure and she didn't really care. There was hardly a copay for behavioral health services, and everybody seemed to be in-network. All were fairly local. There was a doctor specializing in preschool-age kids. He was a PhD actually, a psychologist. Then there was also a child psychiatrist, but that course seemed too harsh for this particular situation. A softer approach seemed warranted. Social workers and childhood nurse clinicians were also available, and they were all over the place. The truth was that she just needed to decide where to go. She had to make those calls.

CHAPTER
8

"*S*o you must be pretty old?"

"You could say that, *mein Liebster*." The boy could see that, barely visible beneath his gray moustache, the man's lips were still not moving.

Imagery projected between the spoken and unspoken word, and even at times onto a blotchy old mirror which stood upright and was tucked neatly in a nearby attic nook. With increasingly colorful descriptions of his early life, Louis learned that Opa came from the land of storybook castles. "You know, Good King Willy had a brother named Louis, a name like your own, only Ludwig was our way—"

"The German way of sayin' it?" asked the boy.

"Yes...Ludwig." He winked at the young child, and with a slight cough, he added, "My mother tongue."

"So was Louis—Ludwig—related to you?"

"No, no, no, *mein Liebster*. We were not royalty. We were farmers. We planted in the spring. We harvested in the fall. All of us."

Opa's manner of speaking was mostly in the vernacular of a twentieth century man. While his accent, though usually slight, betrayed a certain foreignness, the man's words, whether spoken or unspoken, were generally easy for his young listener to follow. And even when he hadn't heard the words before or the complex thoughts behind them, he absorbed much of what was said to him.

"It was my father's farm. There was no doubt about that. There was also no doubt among us that the farm would someday belong to my brother Martin. You see, Martin was the oldest son, and the tradition was for that to be his right of inheritance." He paused. "Do you know that word, *Lieb*?"

"Whatever it is, it doesn't sound fair." Louis' eyes were wide and riveted.

"There are many things that are not fair. You know, my sister Theresia was only twenty when our mother died. I was just seventeen. Theresia assumed Mother's roles and cared for the children of our family. Josepha was the baby of our house, and she was quite frail. But Theresia was strong and gave to all of us as if she were our own dear departed mother. So her life passed on into middle age with no husband and no family of her own. Theresia's life only grew in sadness."

"Did you have horses?"

"A few, yes. We had dairy cows mostly and lots of pasture. Oh, how in the springtime the cattle grazed in those pastures. We had many hectares of land on which our animals lived in full view of God's great forests of ash and elm, of oak and pine. Not far to the south were His glorious snowcapped mountains. We also had pigs...chickens...geese. Ah, the piglets were as playful as pups. And we had crops. We grew potatoes...lots and lots of potatoes and barley...and wheat...and rye."

As Opa spoke of his life on that land, Louis rose from the soft pine floor and looked through the aged glass of one nearby dormer window. There was the road and the driveway, neighbors' houses, spots of Virginia farmland, and more houses that stretched out toward the southern horizon. As his eyes drew back to his more immediate surroundings, Louis saw the mailman approaching the mailbox, which stood on a short post back from the road, about halfway to the house. He thought it odd that the mailbox stood where it did, but what was remarkable was that the postman looked as if he were barely moving. He walked in what seemed to be an eternity of slowness. Startled, the boy looked quickly over to Opa, who smiled and, without words, said, "Time stands nearly still when you're here with me." There was no fear and the boy understood.

29

"At the time I was just about your brother's age, in those days already considered a young man, and our lives had been quite good. They had been so for years. There was always a market for our goods. *Zollverein* saw to that." Somehow the boy understood that word. With a brief pause for a suck on his pipe, the man continued. "Yes, we were happy. Then sickness and injury claimed two of my brothers and two sisters over four short years. When Little Hansy drowned, he was only three. Our family was strong and somehow we managed our grief, right to the time Mother died, about five years later. After Mother's passing things were never the same. She was the heart of our family, and she died on her own birthday—April thirteenth." Louis seemed surprised by the date. That date was his birthday too. "Yes, *mein Liebster*," added Opa with a wink and a nod. His kind face glowed richly, in stark contrast to the reddish chimney stones behind him. Then with a smooth motion, Opa reached for his pouch of pipe tobacco, which was tucked away on a small shelf under an attic eave.

"Mother had not been well since Josepha's birth. Oh, my little sister. How she ruled that house." There was a cough from deep down in the old man's chest, and then a smile at no one and nothing in particular. "Not one of us—there was Father, Theresia, Martin, Genofena, Anastasia, Victoria, Elisabeth, Johann, and Konrad—ever faulted Josepha for Mother's death. And it was as if she were our little angel. She was wise, beautiful, and fragile. She was all of these things and more." He flashed an arch of his right eyebrow and added, "She could be extremely demanding, but was always polite. Her young life ended after only eight years on this Earth. Fortunately, I did not see my sister die."

"Why not?" asked Louis. He was riveted and now seated Indian style at the feet of the man.

"By that time, I had made my way to the Free City of Bremen, many, many miles to the north and worlds away from the farm."

"Why were you away from home?"

"It was no longer my home. You see, about five years after Mother died, I found a wife. Together we had nothing but the love between us. Theresia was her name, the same as my big sister's name. We married at our parish church, the same church where we both were baptized, and within a year we had a beautiful son. His name was Longin."

"So isn't a parish close to home?" Louis remembered this word from church and from his brother's schoolwork. Charley often did his homework in close proximity to his brother.

"Yes, but once Longin was born, our young family went east, to Munich. I was sure it was there, in that great city, where I would find my future. There was no future for us on the farm, and the cities offered us hope. An industrial revolution gathered full steam, and I aspired to work in the factories, or the breweries. Theresia wanted for us to go to Ulm or to Stuttgart, well-known places in Wuerttemberg; places where we both had family. I, however, insisted on going to Munich, which is deep in Bavaria and was, and still is from what I know, the loveliest of cities."

"Wow." Louis yawned.

"Longin was christened in March, in Munich, our new home. March 14, 1847. We were near the trains and nearer still to *die Wies'n.*" The man smiled broadly and continued. "We were a happy young family. King Louis, yes, *mein Liebster*, Ludwig of Bavaria, tried his best to keep things reasonably good for his subjects. He even lowered the price of beer. But then, the very next year, terrible riots erupted in the city. All over Europe—Paris, Berlin—there were disturbances and upheaval. It was 1848 and the Old World, and Germany especially, was awakened to the calls of liberty and liberalism."

"What happened, Opa? Did something bad happen to the Old World?"

"My wife and son were killed in the unrest." There was a long silence. The boy and the man locked their eyes in sadness, and finally Opa's words were heard again. "I took flight. For months I traveled from town to town and city to city, as if in a dark dream world. There was more sadness at that time than I had ever known."

"Gosh, Opa. All that death."

"Yes, *mein Liebster.*" Again there was silence. His mouth did not move, but then the boy heard, "The ships of Bremen took me to America, where I started a new life."

CHAPTER
9

*I*t was 8:30 AM. The waiting room for Dr. Tuttle's practice was already full with parents and kids and lots of noise. To KC's right sat Louis, who fidgeted quietly with a small plaything he had picked up off the floor. She looked around at the other kids who were all about and thought, *There are a lot of behavioral issues here.* Her son didn't belong at this place. She was sure of that now—well, no, not really *sure*, sure—that she had made a wrong decision. But perhaps a nurse, maybe that CPN or that MSN out by Providence Park, would be more suitable for her son.

KC had certainly considered a lot of people for this first encounter and had chosen a full-blown PhD, a childhood psychologist who was very well regarded, so she was told on his website and by her new health insurer. Thanks to a last-minute cancellation, it had been only a few days since she first called for an appointment. She'd see how it went and then consider her next moves. *Hey, the problem may already be solved,* KC hoped. *Louis admitted he made the whole thing up, didn't he?* And he hadn't said a single word about that man in over a week. But somehow Louis just wasn't that convincing.

KC's mind raced all over the place as she worked to complete the new patient profile for her son: a full questionnaire with demographics, medical history, the reason for the visit, insurance information, and more. The world—her world—hadn't stopped because of Louis. Quite the opposite, it seemed. Well, at least third grade had finally ended for Charley. Still, there was so much else going on and so much more to do. And that husband of hers! After insisting on "professional help" for their boy, he couldn't even make it to this, their first appointment. After so much equivocating, last night he finally said he just couldn't miss work so early on in his brand-new career.

"Mom," Louis said softly.

There was no answer from Mom.

"Mom," a little bit louder, he asked.

"Honey? Yes, honey?" Suddenly awakened from her daydreams, KC looked at the source and met the big blue inquiring eyes of her beautiful son. She thought how those eyes perfectly matched the color of his shirt. She thought of the joy of having such a wonderful boy, such a wonderful helper around the house and especially with little Thankful. She lamented how, in only a few short weeks, this would all end with kindergarten.

"Can you tell me again why we're here?" Louis had asked that question before.

In silence, KC looked at her son with a small smile on her roundish face. Taking a deep breath and saying nothing, she thought, *How out of place my poor boy looks.*

Finally, at about 9:15, a young woman in street clothes—with only a crookedly placed name tag to betray her employment—entered the waiting room and called for Louis. *Impressive. As the French would say it.* Then, after a number of people stirred in response, the woman went on to totally mispronounce her boy's surname. That gaffe, along with the obvious HIPAA privacy breach, was an all-too-predictable annoyance for KC. Now she feared that here, in another part of the country, it would morph all over again. That in spite of slower speech patterns, she'd hear new people butcher her married name similarly. *What was so difficult about a two-syllable German name? Cultural differences, perhaps?*

With some reluctance and a touch of resignation, KC rose and took Louis' hand.

Dr. Tuttle's office was full of degrees on the walls, books on the shelves, and whatnots scattered all over what was a warm and welcoming atmosphere. There was a large couch and a fine desk that was lighted by an ornate and authentic-looking banker's lamp.

Two cushiony chairs were fixed in position opposite the desk, and these KC chose for herself and her precious young son to take. Crossing her left leg over her right, KC politely smiled to the doctor, who was seated before them. Hidden from his view were the shapely legs beneath KC's small black skirt, which rose tantalizingly close to her thighs. The truth was that KC preferred to dress up almost every day, just like she was still working in Boston.

Behind the desk sat a smiling man in his fifties or early sixties, clad in a white lab coat with a name badge placed perfectly over its pen-filled chest pocket. With hearty and sincere gestures, Dr. Tuttle welcomed his two visitors. He smiled and opened with the customary small talk, followed by a "Why are we here?" The doctor then provided ample time for the predictable and rehearsed response by Mom before he offered the dreaded clinical-speak that she had already heard and read about *ad infinitum* over the past month.

Focused now on the boy, Dr. Tuttle asked, "Who's your best friend, son?"

Louis took the question at face value and thought for a moment. "I don't know. I guess it's...Mom."

"Did you leave friends behind in Massachusetts?" he asked.

"No. Not really. It's pretty much the same here. There's Charley—"

"Charley's our oldest," offered Mom.

"And there's Mom and Dad," Louis continued. "Thankful's just a baby."

"She's our youngest." Again Mom felt she needed to interject. *And how thankful everyone was when she arrived safely.* "We have three kids."

"I see," said Dr. Tuttle. "So are there other kids close by, around your age?"

"No," started Mom.

"Not really," agreed Louis. "I haven't started school yet. I mean I have my cousin Maxxwell, but he's...a lot younger than me. And he's back home."

"Is school where you're supposed to make friends?" asked the psychologist.

"Yeah, I guess," said Louis.

"And back home? Do you mean Massachusetts? Is that where Maxxwell is?"

Before Louis could respond, KC offered, "There really weren't any kids Louis' age in Westbridge...Mass." She looked briefly to her son, then back to the doctor, and continued. "Around our house, that is. Maxx lives a few towns over. And here in Fairfax, our area doesn't really have a lot of kids either. No kids Louis' age, I mean." She thought briefly of the young babysitter she consigned for that morning. KC was uncomfortable with her defenses. She knew where the conversation was headed.

Dr. Tuttle looked to the boy and then asked, "Why don't you tell me about what you do at home all day, Louis?" After a pause and no answer from the child, he added, "I mean at home in Fairfax."

"Why?"

"I'd like to hear it. You want me to help you, don't you?"

"No-oh," shot back Louis. "I don't need your help."

"Calm down, son," said the doctor.

"He's not...uncalm," KC said sternly. The comfortably lighted office seemed unaccustomed to loudness or shouting.

Turning to KC, Dr. Tuttle looked as if he had made some remarkable discovery. His blue eyes were wide with excitement. His brow was furrowed. Then, he turned back to Louis and calmly said, "I don't mean 'help' in a sick sense, son. You look like a fine, healthy young man to me. I mean that I need to understand what it is you do, to see what we," gesturing to himself and KC, "can do to make things better."

"I don't need 'better,'" Louis responded. "I'm...good."

"Of course you are, son."

"I'm not your son."

"Louis!" his mother admonished.

"Mom!"

"Doctor Tuttle. You can see I have a very bright young boy who just hasn't made a lot of friends...yet." KC was powerfully crisp and clear with her words for the doctor.

"He has no friends outside the family," the doctor responded dryly, and looked KC squarely in the eyes.

Suddenly KC sounded exasperated. "Can we get past that and talk about..." Her eyes were weak with worries.

"Talk about what?" the doctor asked.

After a pause, KC said, "Oh, I don't know."

"Mom? Are we in trouble?"

"No, honey." It was obvious to Louis that Mom held back tears. She turned back to the psychologist and asked, "Doctor, would it be all right for Louis to wait outside in the waiting room?"

"Mom!" Louis protested.

"Please, Louis. This will only take a few more minutes," she pleaded.

"That will be fine," said the doctor. "But why don't we ask Louis first about his friend?"

Turning to his mother, Louis proclaimed, "Mom. I told you: Opa's not real."

"Opa?" repeated the doctor, as if to make sure he heard the word correctly.

"That's the name of the man," KC said.

"Ma-ah-m," Louis whined.

"Just a minute, Louis." KC reached over and squeezed his left hand.

"I told you, Mom. He's not real. Come on, Mom. Let's go home."

"Does Louis have his grandfathers? Living, I mean?" asked the doctor unexpectedly.

"Yes. Well, one. Why?"

"Louis, is Opa your granddaddy?" Dr. Tuttle asked enthusiastically.

Louis thought for a brief moment and said, "I don't...think so." Turning to his mother, Louis continued, "Mom? He's nobody. I told you."

Doctor Tuttle reached for his desk phone and asked for a person named Margaret to be sent into his office. He looked at KC and then to Louis and said, "My assistant is coming in and will take you downstairs for a great big hand-dipped ice cream treat. Sound good, Louis?"

"I guess," he answered blandly.

A short moment later, Margaret, an extremely bubbly and matronly black woman, entered the room and made instant friends with Louis. KC assured her son she would only be a few more minutes, and the two left the office as planned. Once the door closed KC turned back to the man behind the desk.

"Do you think Louis is missing his grandpa?" She looked vulnerable. "Why?" Another pause. "My husband's father died years before Louis was even born." While eager to sort this out, KC's anxiety level rose far greater than she had imagined possible. "You know, Louis did say Opa was an old man." She noticeably chipped away at a broken fingernail and then continued. "But he can't be Louis' grandfather. Opa is…from a different time…and a different place. He's old like centuries old and…from…Europe."

"You know that in German, the word 'Opa' is an endearing term for grandfather."

"No. I didn't know that." KC was smart and freely admitted what she did not know.

"How about your husband?" Adjusting his glasses, Dr. Tuttle added, "I can see here that your name *looks* German."

"No. I think I would have known if he had made a connection."

"Imaginary friends are often made up in childhood. They're usually used to fill voids in a young one's life, sometimes for a needed friend or a confidante. Sometimes an imaginary friend is used to fill the space left by a loved one—oftentimes, but not always, for a departed relative. The companion can also be a teacher—a tutor—someone who in your boy's case might be preparing him for school."

"All this makes sense. I've read up on this subject. But his stories—Louis' stories—are so sincere. And the detail!"

"Well, you said, and I can see, Louis is a very bright boy."

"Yes. Yes, he is." KC ached for something else to say. "He can spell…chrome." Her eyes were sincere. "He plays school with Charley, his older brother, and he shines at it. He wants to be a doctor…but not a surgeon. No. He says, 'There's too much blood, thank you!'"

"Ma'am, it's not uncommon for this kind of psychological phenomenon, where these kinds of interpersonal relationships take place in a child's mind rather than in the real world. These characters can have very elaborate personalities, and they can reveal the child's perceptions of the real world."

"What should I do?" she asked. "Should I be worried?"

"I suggest you keep your boy occupied and enjoy that little fella before he heads off to school. I believe you said he told you he made Opa up."

KC remained fully attentive and nodded slowly. While she appeared a bit tired and drained, she remained engaged, and wholly attractive.

"I'd ignore the past and focus on the here and now with the boy. If he brings Opa back up again, I'd listen to discern what might be driving this behavior, and try to figure out which of these characters Opa—and there may be others—might be."

"I'll do my best, Dr. Tuttle."

"I know you will. But watch the little one for signs that would suggest fear or anxiety, or worse, if his friends—as I said, there may be more than one—become indistinguishable from real people. In extreme circumstances these behaviors can be indications of an early onset of delusional psychosis."

"Oh my God!" she exclaimed.

The psychologist could plainly see the shock and pain on KC's face. He quickly added, "That's worst case…and very rare in children. I honestly don't think this is the case, and please don't pay it much mind."

KC arose and Dr. Tuttle could see she was slightly unsteady. He moved from behind his desk and put a hand on the woman's shoulder. As he led her toward the door, the doctor added in a comforting and conciliatory tone, "Don't worry, ma'am. You have a beautiful and bright young boy. Enjoy him while he's young."

CHAPTER
10

*I*t would be a few hours before her husband arrived home from work, and KC mulled over the day at the doctor's. *Delusional psychosis.* She could not get that term out of her mind. Dr. Tuttle had, however, zeroed in on the stark facts about her son and his relationships, or rather his lack of relationships. These were the real problems and the real challenges. *Weren't they?* She must find Louis some friends now. She could no longer just wait until school started.

Louis was upstairs, to change his clothes for outside. It had been such a long day: first the appointment, and then all the errands. He'd been such a good soldier for his mom. And there was still so much to do before her husband got home. KC knew of a playground not too far away from the house and the library where she planned to go beforehand. It was just a short drive over there with Louis and Thankful. Charley was already outside in the yard and would come along too, although he would probably resist. Their oldest was independent minded and so mature for his age. *Oh, how he protested the babysitter this morning!* At that thought the middle-aged blond pixie ran fingers through her lustrous hair. She slowly tucked a hand under her chin, took a deep breath, and headed up to her son Louis' room.

Shock and disbelief greeted KC as she stared at the outstretched attic ladder. By the base stood Louis, with the proverbial look of the kid with his hand in the cookie jar. The boy had barely been upstairs for five minutes. Lying on the floor nearby was his fishing pole.

Louis' eyes followed his mom's eyes to the rod and then back again to him and the ladder. The boy could plainly see the pain in his mother's face as he tried to speak reassuringly with his eyes. That was not working. He saw anger too. Mom turned away, as if to leave, and then turned back to face the ladder again. Without a word, she entered her boy's room and climbed the stairs to the attic entryway.

She poked her head through the opening and looked around. She could see nothing out of the ordinary. There was certainly no man up in this place, unless he was well hidden. There was, however, a strange, sweet aroma hanging in the dense air that was not unlike a pipe's tobacco. She thought suddenly of Officer Lee. He'd noticed it too. It was a very delicious smell indeed, and one that left KC's senses as soon as she returned to the room below. There, Louis waited. Precocious but never pretentious, the wide-eyed child simply stated, "Mom, we have to talk."

And they talked.

It was seven o'clock before Dad got home. Not too late by the standards of the day. Louis' new disclosures to Mom, hot on the heels of their appointment with Dr. Tuttle, would all be thoroughly discussed once Dad got settled. What frightened KC now was how Louis spoke so reassuringly of Opa. But she could not believe her son's stories. How could she? No way. They were so fantastic. She would listen to what her husband had to say, and together they'd figure out next steps.

In the security of the normally quiet study, the parents first met in private. In between the more emotional moments, and when Dad had calmed down sufficiently to speak softly, KC and he decided it was time for the couple, together, to have a candid discussion with Louis about the man. In truth, Dad was very concerned for his son. While it was late, he preferred not to wait till after dinner to talk with their son. The kids were together in the nearby family room. From the door of the study, the parents called Louis in unison.

Invited to speak, Louis spoke of Opa with a gleam in his eyes and happiness on his chubby young face. How that man continued to draw the boy's imagination. That was obvious. "He's really, really cool." The boy splayed his little arms. "You know he's kinda old though. He's probably older than you, Dad. But he's *really* cool. He used to live where those big castles are...with kings and princesses. And he talks sometimes without moving his mouth. Like one of those...um..."

"Ventriloquists?" Dad offered stiffly.

"Yeah, Dad. I think so. A trenquilotrist. But he had to leave when his wife and little baby died in the city. They went there for a job, but he had to leave after that. He said he couldn't live there anymore."

Dad listened with an uneasy mix of shock and amazement. He stared at his boy, quietly and without expression.

"It was very sad, Dad. He left the city."

"Where did he go?" asked Dad.

Mom quickly added, "What did he do?"

Louis was very animated and eager to resume his tale. "Well, Dad, Mom, Opa took the train—the Bavarian Ludwig Railroad they called it!" With much emphasis on the "Ludwig," the boy paused and regarded his parents. "Isn't that funny?" Dad was frozen in position with his wife at his side. "Ludwig's like Louis." Both adults were visually glued to the little boy who stood before them. Yet neither looked at anything of their son's in particular. "Now Opa didn't have a lot of Gulden, so he had to walk a lot too. So anyway, he took the train and then the boat. He walked along the roadsides and rode on farmers' carts. In the end he came here...to America." Louis dazzled in his rendition. "There was a lot of disunity and stuff, so it wasn't that easy to get around in the Old World. Opa had to work on a river barge for a while. He helped on farms and worked in factories...in a couple of places. He rested by streams. Opa went hundreds of miles north, from city to city. He hitched rides on wagons. He rode horses. Finally he got to a place called Bremen."

"Bremen? Louis! Till we moved here, you didn't even know Virginia was part of the United States. How the hell do you know about Bremen?" The whole thing sounded eerily familiar to Dad. He thought of his family tree and his forebears who came from

Bremen 150 years ago by steamship, on what was a weeks-long transcontinental ocean voyage. *Tidbits of history embedded since childhood.* "What are you reading? What about Bremen?" he asked.

KC stood by without a word. She always seemed more inclined than Dad to take a levelheaded look at things. He was always the more emotional one. With an occasional "Easy does it," Mom always seemed to work her magic when nerves frayed, to mediate and tone things down whenever necessary. She prepared to step in.

"It's on the water, Dad," offered Louis.

"Louis!" Dad shot back.

"That's all I know so far." His eyes were truthful.

"So far?" Dad's voice rose, in contrast to his prevailing stone-faced silence—that paralyzed look of total amazement with all his boy's revelations.

Then bursting into the study without any kind of warning, Charley suddenly exclaimed, "Mom: when are we going to eat?"

"Your father and I are discussing something with Louis," KC calmly stated. Then, in direct response to the hungry eyes of her growing and gangly son, she added, "And the answer is, 'soon.'"

"It sounds like you're fighting." There stood Charley, tall and still covered in the soiled clothes and sweaty self of one very active and healthy nine-year-old.

"We're not fighting. It's just your father talking loudly." Given the thick horsehair plaster walls, gumwood doors, and the general space between everyone in the new house, it was a little hard to believe that their discussion had breached those formidable barriers. "We're discussing...something." And with the faint echo that hung on her words, it suddenly seemed that the walls were cold and bare, and unforgiving. It was time to get things wrapped up for now, she thought, and try to finish up later.

With a little edge, Dad added, "We'll be just another minute." He glared a bit at his son Charley. "Go get changed for dinner. And get washed up!"

"What are we having?" Charley asked.

"Go!" demanded Dad. "Go! I can't believe you're still in those filthy clothes!"

With the kids hungry and Louis starting to cry—and God knew when he'd be telling his tales to Charley if he hadn't started already—the couple sent Louis to join his siblings elsewhere, and hastily talked things out on their own.

First there was the unquestionable fascination with Louis' knowledge and sophistication. When did he get so smart? And that *was* actually kind of a nice problem to have, they supposed. But the real problem, whatever it was, was not going to go away on its own. It was then mutually agreed to seek a second opinion against what Dr. Tuttle had offered. Perhaps therapy or treatments would be considered. But where and by whom? These were all open questions, and it was decided that KC would resume her due diligence in the morning.

"Louis's crying in the living room," Charley suddenly proclaimed from the hallway.

"I'm not crying! I'm screaming!" Louis protested. "Mom. I need you!" he cried.

"What do you need, honey?" called Dad before Mom could form a response.

"Mom," answered Louis.

"And Thankful looks really hungry," Charley interjected. "She's practically chewing on the furniture. She's gonna hurt herself, Ma."

For now and for everyone, it was suppertime.

CHAPTER
11

*I*t was bright and early in the morning. It was not too early to start with the phone calls, though KC hadn't slept all that well last night. With her husband gone from the house for several hours already, and the boys playing out in the yard, chasing one another with balls and Wiffle bats, she was determined to screen a few more behavioral health providers. She'd pull a few more names off the Internet while Thankful napped. *And why is it so difficult to get mental health treatment for children?* "Half these places aren't taking new patients," she said softly to herself, "and the other half is booked out for weeks, some for months." She faced north and looked out a kitchen window. *How lucky we were*, thought KC, *to have gotten that appointment with Dr. Tuttle when we did.*

After what seemed a zillion phone calls, KC managed to book a couple of appointments, one with herself and Louis, and the other for herself, alone. She hoped her husband could make both meetings, but she wouldn't count on it. Both were with pediatric nurse specialists. Both, it seemed, had impeccable credentials. There was someone else though, a licensed ontologist, she noticed. And how could she not notice Dr. Oona Neeci on that splashy website? *Wow! Ontology: the study of existence.* Now here was an untraditional option to consider if all else failed. Maybe she would give that woman a try. Licensed, but licensed by whom? What credentialing body would license such a specialty? *An Msc.D?* She'd need to do more research for sure. But perhaps all that was really needed was a little professional advice on how best to nudge her boy out of this imaginary friend phase. But where was Louis getting all his knowledge? He always liked libraries and had been reading since he was four and a half. That was a whole half a year ago. And for what it was worth, the "industry" consensus seemed to be that the business of imaginary friends was, just as Dr. Tuttle had said, not uncommon. The smartness thing though, that was the interesting twist. It was as if Opa was a tutor to her son.

KC took a moment to think back to the night before. She hoped that she and her husband had not traumatized the little guy. He did seem fine that morning. The threats to move Louis out of his brand-new room, or to nail the attic door shut, were voiced only between KC and her husband. Those were extreme measures that KC was not prepared to support at this time anyway. Those were her husband's remedies. Those were Dad's threats and Dad's solutions, and fortunately they had *not* been shared with their dear boy. And with what she thought she had heard earlier from Louis—before they had spoken with his father—when he said that he wouldn't lie or exaggerate, she knew the problem with this "promise" was that the little guy was still not offering up anything new or different. And if he had to keep his promise, she feared he might have to internalize his world even further. *And that deafening silence from his dad last night.* KC preferred it to her husband being cynical or mad or insulting or nasty, as he sometimes would be with the kids. Remarkably, he had not asked Louis to renounce his stories. He had not demanded obedience. He mostly listened. And these were all good things, she thought. And Louis' promise was his promise. And that was a good thing too. There were neither denials nor apologies for anything in the past. *Now it's just about going forward, isn't it?*

*A*lone now. The place was anything but a crowded clinic's waiting room. There were office hours in the evenings and during the weekends, at any time really, but by appointment only. It had been a week since KC made the call and arranged for Dr. Neeci to first meet alone with Louis, and then together with herself and her boy. This "ontologist" was probably the most beautiful woman KC had ever beheld. She was raven-haired, with large black marble eyes and a full mouth with cherub lips not unlike those of Louis. The website could not nearly disclose the presence of that young woman, and she was very young, or the deep aromatics and overall atmosphere of her office. KC imagined there were many things about Oona Neeci that were not listed on her CV.

This doctor was, in fact, a powerful sorceress and medium, a seer of ghosts and spirits and a metaphysical whirlwind, true to the memory of Mamie, her beloved grandmother and famed New Orleans *Voodooienne*. Oona Neeci's magnetic eyes bespoke twenty-four years since her marvelous blend of female humanity entered the lush world of St. Catherine Parish in Jamaica. This doctor was also an incredibly charming enchantress who could use hypnosis and even cast spells to affect her subjects.

KC saw that her surroundings resembled more a Tarot card or palm reader's establishment than a clinic space. What with the candles and fragrant incense, she half expected a mambo priestess to appear waving a sanctified chicken. KC also mused that since that night a week ago, when she and her husband had those talks with Louis, it seemed their son had once again backed off of his earlier stories about the man in the attic. Was this just a ruse? A tactic? Or had Louis finally come clean on all this business and, in his own innocent way, admitted he'd made the whole thing up? Oh, how KC wanted to be sure. Every hour of every day she thought about it, and she knew right now how much she wanted this doctor's professional opinion.

When the door finally opened, a mildly dressed Dr. Neeci appeared and motioned for KC to enter the dimly lit room behind her. As she approached, KC could plainly see her son inside, in a high-back red velvety chair, with his feet dangling and swinging freely a few inches over the floor. The room was, strangely, quite comfortable. Books covered three walls, leaving one for shelves with what looked like glass jars of herbs and specimens, as if they were on display in a shop or a museum. There was a round table off to one side where a group of six people could convene. There were dark maroon drapes over the full-length windows that betrayed the grand antebellum structure of which this "office" was one corner part. The plush, billowy, and velvety treatments exuded an air of comfort rather than creepiness.

Louis turned to greet his mom as she approached him and the vacant chair to his right. With his cheery though shy wave, Mom knew in an instant her boy was at ease. Then, with the slightest detectable French accent, KC had no doubt whose speaking voice would control their meeting. Locking eyes for one long moment with KC, followed by a quick glance over to Louis, Dr. Neeci smiled radiantly and took the chair behind her desk.

"Your son Louis is at a tender age when make-believe and reality are often blurred. You have no doubt heard from the many sources that speak of imaginary friends, fantasies, and normal versus abnormal." The doctor paused, smiled, and continued. "Some things are just things, aren't they? And not everything has a name. Why must they?" There was another pause. The ontologist examined KC with her eyes, then for an instant appeared blank and distant but no less beautiful. Louis suddenly rose from his seat and turned to make an exit. Before KC could question her son, the young doctor added, "How that name fits your boy so well. But why must there be a name for everything?" Louis reached one hand onto his mom's shoulder and then headed for the door. As the two women watched the five-year-old take his leave, the doctor remarked, "Louis will wait for us in the reception area."

With a small smile and a hint of exasperation, KC met the charcoaled eyes of the stunning beauty. She was a doctor of what, really? With a touch of wonderment, but before she could ask, the woman softly spoke,

"I am a doctor of ontology. I am many things to many people. And please call me Oona."

"Your practice is…impressive."

"You are curious about my qualifications?" Her statement seemed more like a question.

KC nodded politely.

"I was seventeen when I entered Harvard. There I majored in metaphysics, with a specialty in ontology, the study of existence, as you know. I earned my advanced degree at age twenty, an MS in metaphysics with my specialty…in ontology. Upon graduation from Harvard, I returned to my family in New Orleans, where I stayed for two years, engaged in research and other professional and spiritual activities, before relocating here in Virginia. I recently earned my PhD in ontology from Georgetown. I wrote my dissertation on the categories of being." Oona reached out in the direction of many wall-hanging frames with what looked to be her degrees and citations. "I studied under the great metaphysicist Brisbane Turner."

"Very impressive," KC acknowledged. She was intrigued, really. She also thought back to her own years at Suffolk U, her MBA and her career, before the children started arriving. KC had more to say, but for now she wanted to get back to the subject of her son Louis.

"Trust your son. Believe in him." Oona smiled lovingly. "Do you wonder, 'Where are the books? Where is the library from which this boy is drawing all his new knowledge?'"

"We do have a library nearby," KC announced. She conceded there was no hiding Oona's sensuality. For anyone who'd appreciate beauty, there was Oona's long, wavy—almost kinky—ebony tresses that glistened now in the low artificial light of the office lamp and which cascaded gently down over her shoulders and onto her very ample bosom. Perfect for her was a well-defined jaw-line.

Again, Oona smiled and nodded. "I can help you understand what you believe to be strange goings-on in your home." Her eyes spoke as fully as her lips. "His denials are transparent and inno-cent, and yet still very clever." At times like these Oona betrayed so many of her charms. "Your son paints a very reasonable picture. He is thoroughly dazzled by Opa's tales, and finds these times even more entertaining than his father's bedside reading."

KC smiled in return and remained intent on listening to the soft-spoken words of the doctor. Nothing could have prepared her for the utter intensity of this alluring creature.

"Opa is always leaving off where another story begins." The two women exchanged broad yet seemingly shy glances. Oona slowly swept her long-lashed opal eyes from side to side. Their eyes met again, and they smiled for each other.

"It's as if you know Opa." KC was thoroughly captivated and also believed she and Oona were fast becoming friends.

CHAPTER
13

*L*ouis felt oddly refreshed and renewed from the day's events. There he lay in bed, staring at the attic door. *Oona called it a portal.* Someone *really* believed him. Then rising out of the comfort of his bed—it was 10 PM and everyone in the house was asleep—he decided to go on up.

There, Opa sat. His clothes were gray and lifeless and matched the deeper gray of his eyes. A veil of sadness quickly lifted as Opa seemed to draw on the boy's energy. It was early July—the holiday had already passed uneventfully—and minus the warm yellow sunlight, the attic space was really quite cool for Louis. In contrast, as the boy drew closer to Opa to take a place at the man's feet, he was greeted with the radiance of mild, sultry warmth.

"Opa. What do you do up here when I'm not around?" Louis loved meeting Opa whenever he could spare a moment. And it seemed a moment was all that he ever needed.

"I've been here a long time, *mein Liebster*. There's boredom and extreme loneliness."

"I visit you every chance I get." The boy's innocent, loving eyes locked with Opa's. "Why does it seem that when we're together, it's like regular time, you know? But when I go back downstairs, it's like the clock hardly moved." The boy smelled a slight scent of something pleasant. The air moved gently around him.

"Time works differently up here, Ludwig." He smiled that warm smile of his that meant so much to the boy.

"Why don't you just leave?"

"That's not possible, *Lieb*. Not now. Not yet."

"So what do you do? Do you read stuff, like a newspaper or something?"

"I haven't read a newspaper in 150 years."

"You're funny."

"The Messengers keep me current with the news of the day. Thank heavens for the Heavenly Messengers." Opa's body was now visibly strengthened. His eyes were as rich and as gray as the thick dark fur of a Maltese cat. His clothing showed various shades of soldierly blue.

"Are you from Heaven?"

"No. I've never been to Heaven."

"Not even just to visit?"

"No one visits there. Once you're in, you're in, as you say." Opa sometimes spoke quite freely in the Modern English.

"So who's up there?" Louis asked.

"There's a whole heavenly hierarchy from what I hear. There's the Almighty of course, saints and angels of various degrees, and plebes that have some heavenly privileges. The Messengers are among a large group officially known as Heavenly Scribes. They do a lot of the work up there as well as here on Earth, *mein Liebster*. Scribes listen to the prayers of the faithful; they facilitate good events and relay petitions to the Lord for redemption. Ghosts and spirits are Earth-based. Ghosts of Purgatory, like me, use the Scribes for news of loved ones...and for news in general. It's through the Scribes that I can tell you something about Heaven. And for me, more importantly, it is through the Scribes that I have learned how to get there."

"So you're a ghost?" He emphasized the last word. Louis reached out to touch the man he believed he knew. His hand passed right through Opa's legs, as if it passed through a mass of steamy, rain-foresty air. *Thick air. Watery air.*

"I am a non-wandering spirit of a person no longer living and who survived the death of his body by maintaining his mind and consciousness here...at this special house in Fairfax, Virginia."

"Wow." Opa looked real enough, the boy thought. The man—the ghost—the spirit stirred all sorts of emotions for young Louis, and fear was never one of them. While he never knew real sadness till he met Opa, at most times he felt happy and real good to be with him. It was uplifting, like Mom said after she did her exercises. Then, as Opa rose from his usual place on top of the old trunk, the air moved and brought a slight coolness to Louis' cheeks.

Downstairs there was talk of developmental psychologists, diagnoses, meds, and remedies.

"It's been more of the same from the nurses," KC declared. "Only Dr. Neeci offered something different."

"And what's that?" her husband asked incredulously.

"She wants us to listen to Louis."

"You mean like, believe him?" His eyes widened.

"Believe *in* him. And listen." There was obvious stress in KC's words. Her eyes darkened with tears.

"This is madness!" he said.

"No. This is your son. This is our son. And Louis has probably been seeing ghosts and spirits since infancy."

"Who told you that? That doctor? That oncologist?"

"Stop it! She's an ontologist." KC recalled Oona's words, expressions, and manner. "Remember Louis cooing in that crib? Remember the times when his big blue eyes darted around the room? Remember?"

Louis' father remembered. He said nothing.

"And yes, it was Oona."

"Oona? One meeting and it's 'Oona'?"

"Well, yes. We're friends," KC announced, with an intentional measure of overblown pride.

"Oh, man. This is bullshit. Maybe we need a priest. You know, like a blessing—or an exorcism."

"You'd do an exorcism, but you won't believe that Louis is seeing something for real? This is not bullshit." Complete passion for her son and her family enlivened KC.

"I'll go check on him." Dad jumped at the opportunity.

"No you won't!" After another long day, KC was finally spent. "Well, don't wake him up. He needs his sleep." Her words carried a slight echo in the expansive surroundings of the family room. Its still-sparse furnishings were lingering evidence of the family's recent upheaval and relocation to this house with the long hallways, the large rooms, and *something* in the attic. Something that KC could neither see nor grasp. "I'll check on the others." With some sadness, KC realized that neither she nor her husband was sold on this odd business of Louis and his friend. Maybe he needed to meet Oona. Maybe she should visit their house.

"*Y*ou're still up, little man?" Dad's voice was usually comforting to Louis. "Did you brush your teeth?" He looked down at his boy and then took a seat at the edge of the bed. Louis' mouth was still filled with all his baby teeth. He was so pure. Dad put a gentle hand on Louis' cheek.

Louis smiled at his dad and nodded. He didn't say a word. He looked forward now, his head on his pillows, his covers pulled to his chest.

"I'll read you a story." Dad loved to read to his kids. All he needed was a flashlight. He scanned the room for one, and also searched for a suitable book. "You weren't up to any funny business now, were you?" The words just jumped out of Dad's mouth, and before he regretted his outburst, Louis replied,

"You can see from the time, Dad, it's highly unlikely I was in the attic."

Amazing choice of words! his father observed.

"I love you, Louis." Dad spied just the book he had hoped for. A rather old storybook that belonged to his own dad, one that had all the famous stories: The Brothers Grimm and all that kind of stuff. He rose and took a few steps to fetch the book from the shelf and the flashlight that sat atop the boy's dresser. Dad returned to his boy's side and reached over to turn down the light that rested on his nightstand.

"I never knew I had so many dead relatives, Dad, or just as many distant cousins." Louis was wide awake, evidently with a lot on his young mind.

"When did you get so smart?" his father asked gently. *The things this boy came up with.* "Before we moved here, you asked if they spoke American down here in Virginia. Do you remember that?" There was a bittersweet quality to his words, as if he conceded that some of Louis' innocence was lost now, and forever.

"Da-ad." And he smiled. "Did my ancestors touch those pages?" With his chin, Louis nodded toward the book.

"For sure," his father said. *How'd he know to ask that?* He flipped through the pages. "Now, I have a great one for you." Dad was almost there.

"Will you wake me up when the story's over?"

"For sure, Louis."

CHAPTER
15

JC led the way upstairs. Oona was early—7 AM—but not early enough to catch her husband before he left for work. Oona would circle back in the evening, she said, to make that acquaintance.

For now, there was important business with the delicious distraction that walked ahead of her. As the two women ascended the grand staircase of that antebellum house, Oona closely followed the shape that paced at eye level and only a few steps ahead of her. She studied the tight-fitting black taffeta skirt high up over her knees, the deep tan, and the white cotton blouse that lusciously wrapped the fetching mother of three. *Matching tans and strong tones.* Then, as the two women arrived on the landing at the midway turn, the gifted seer of ghosts and spirits and things past saw old wall murals that once shone prominently on both sides of the stained-glass insert. How this place reminded her of New Orleans and the beautiful Garden District house where she moved, at only one year old, with her parents and Mamie. Now, as she grew familiar with these surroundings and their history of great sadness, compassion, pain, and human dignity, she determined that this was once a well-known place called the Bornheim House.

The women continued up the stairs. There were more distractions. Oona recalled the great halls of academia—her years at the finest boarding schools in France and Switzerland, and her college days in America—where her brazen bisexual exploits, both on and off campus, were legendary. She recalled those times were not so long ago. And there was still no sex, shape, size, color, or manner of dress from which Oona's affections were immune. Yes, indeed, there were many distractions here in this place, and the fondness that preceded her up the staircase now was reminiscent of more than one brilliant seduction.

The stairs gave way to a spacious second story. KC turned right on the shiny hardwood floor that looked like new. Oona followed. They turned again and walked down the corridor that led to the boys' rooms. Louis' was the second door on the left and it was open. Both boys had already been up and about for almost an hour. Having had a quick but nourishing breakfast of Nutella toast and granola cereal, Charley and Louis continued their morning in the family room, and watched *SpongeBob SquarePants* on Nickelodeon. Only with Oona's arrival had Louis emerged briefly to greet her.

The house was alive for Oona. She stood at ease for a long moment while KC retrieved a stepladder from the master bedroom which would be used to access the fold-down ladder to the attic. Once KC planted it on the floor, she quickly retook the lead for their ascent to the attic. Thankful was still asleep in her own bedroom adjacent to the master, and their good old dog, Zupper, was slumbering on the floor in front of the baby's door.

"Don't mind my big butt." KC was both giddy and anxious as she turned to Oona, as if a great weight would soon be lifted from her shoulders. "I shouldn't have worn a dress for this."

"Not a problem," Oona said with a smile unseen by KC. *Firm buttocks.* Oh, the lovely distractions. *Toned arms and legs.* How, more than once, she'd landed in bed with a middle-aged married woman. *Not now though. No. Not here.* There was work to be done for this fine family. *Remain chaste.* "I don't mind," she added unevenly. Then, quite seriously, Oona took notice of the emerging attic space and the great clutter of information that hung in the air above her. She rose through the trapdoor and stood there momentarily. With her feet planted firmly to the floor beneath her, she moved her head and, at times, her torso, and the young ontologist took in more than one deep breath.

Oona seemed to inhale her surroundings as she began to move about the space. For one long moment she stood before the old steamer trunk. She whiffed the air again and moved her head slowly and thoughtfully. Next she moved to a large, finely carved upright mirror. She turned to KC and with a wink and a warm smile she said, "An old Black Forest mirror." KC smiled in turn. She was positioned near the south bank of windows, and obstructed only a small amount of the daylight behind her. She said nothing. Another wink from Oona was followed with, "You can get some money for this antique."

"Such an ornate frame," said KC. She felt very comfortable and at ease. She looked from it back to Oona.

"Yes, finely carved...walnut cartouche." Oona's hands moved slowly and purposefully across the surface of the wood and the glass. Then she whirled slowly, like a model at a photo shoot, her choice of loose fitting and colorful Caribbean attire in stark contrast to the businesslike clothing that KC chose for herself that morning. Next Oona sauntered to the stone chimney at the southeast wall. From that vantage she could plainly see the entire attic space. She let her hands glide lightly over each beam and rafter she passed, and the young woman paused now and then to regard what were clearly carvings and inscriptions in the wood.

"Have you noticed these, *ma chère*?"

Such a lovely voice. KC approached Oona and could see the very obvious writing and artwork, much of which was nearer to the floor than to an adult's eye level.

"Soldiers left these messages." She looked blankly past KC, as if at nothing, and she continued. "The sick, the dying, and the wounded: their places were all here. Berth after berth of tightly packed cots...so little space lay between them. Stifling heat of summer. The damp chills of winter. At times men were moved onto the floor to make room for new arrivals. Some left in life. Most left in death." Then, she looked deep into KC's eyes and placed her right hand softly to the smartly dressed mother's left cheek, and she whispered, "One soul is here now."

KC's eyes widened in an uplifting expression. With obvious and fearless amazement, she was utterly relieved by this doctor's declaration.

Oona left KC's side and made her way to the window that faced east. "Desolation," she said. There was a long pause with sobering effect. "There were no trees in sight of this house. Only stumps here and there, like the amputations that were carried out downstairs." Then, as if she noticed it only for the first time, Oona turned her attention to the old trunk and approached it cautiously. KC followed her. The aroma that surrounded the attic space was slight but undeniable.

"It smells like pipe tobacco here," KC offered. Oona nodded and got down on her knees. KC moved in close beside her, and the women poked and prodded and managed to open the trunk without breaking a fingernail between them.

Empty.

"Where is he?" asked KC. "Where's the soul?"

"He's here." After a brief pause she added, "If he wants to reveal himself...or if he can reveal himself, I think he will."

"Why wouldn't he? Why couldn't he?" KC was puzzled and intrigued.

"This may not be allowed. Not now. There are strange rules in the afterlife. Things we can't always understand." Oona approached the bank of windows facing the southwest. A gray haze hung over the glass, yet inside, everything seemed clean and bright. "This was beautiful country before this house was changed. The family fled south." The black-haired beauty pointed south for a moment and then turned to address KC directly. "They expected to return after a few months of war, but they never did. This place and its outbuildings—long gone from here—were used for a field hospital and convalescence. The soldiers came and took the roof right off the stone house. They built up this attic for comrades who could not be moved north." Oona resumed a seemingly casual tour of the space. KC was fixed on her every move. Finally Oona paused by one particular carving set deep in a rafter. An elegant letter "A" was enmeshed within the branches of a great leafy tree. She ran her hand over the carving and traced its grooves slowly with her fingers. Turning back to KC, Oona whispered, "His name is Anton."

CHAPTER
16

Dad arrived home much later than usual. His introduction to Oona was brief. Like the famous General Jackson, he just stood there in the vestibule like a stone wall as his wife practically begged him to grab a bite to eat and move along to the study. Oona was beyond words: drop-dead gorgeous he thought, like Shakira with black hair, so young and not at all what he had expected. *Flawless young skin.* Though oftentimes flirty in attractive company, it had been one very long day at work, and he was in no mood to socialize with this shrink or whatever she called herself. He could barely look at her anyway—she was so hot, while he was so hot and sweaty and just plain beat.

Oona easily sensed his demeanor, took her leave with a European-style kiss to both of KC's cheeks, a polite "Good-bye" to the boys, who had gathered nearby, and a firmly professional handshake for their dad. Zupper sat quietly and contentedly at Louis' side, her bushy tail dusting the polished floor from side to side, and she offered Oona a good-natured, farewell bark. The woman departed to the comfort of her shiny new Porsche Carrera.

KC pulled her husband along into the kitchen for some dinnertime leftovers, and then took her leave to check on Thankful. When she returned, she could see him, often an emotional and high-strung guy in his normal state, was particularly so this evening. A loving and committed father, no less, his extreme reactions were too often predictable. Nevertheless, KC insisted they talk about her day's events with Oona. Then, as they started to do so, her husband was suddenly and unexpectedly animated.

"Did you see the way she looked at us? That woman's a sexpot. I think she *really* likes you, if you know what I mean. Those kisses. That accent?" His words were strong—more than just playful banter.

"You're just trying to change the subject," KC protested, and flashed a half smile.

"I'm telling you, she's either a lesbo or she plays for both teams."

"You're sick. We're friends, and we—you and me—need to speak with Louis. We need to speak with our son now," KC said firmly.

"Again?" he whined. He knew that voice of hers, and the determination that went with it was palpable.

"Let's go to the study," KC insisted.

He followed KC with a half-full plate of cold chicken and mashed potatoes. The long days had started to take their toll. He loved his job, yes, but at some point he needed to step back a little. The Fourth of July had already passed, and the extra time off he had planned for never materialized. Now, he did not want to deal with Louis' problem. *Not now.* Work was one way to avoid it, but once again KC was persistent. He just knew that Louis had imagined the whole thing, and he was equally confident that his boy would grow out of his odd behavior by the time he started kindergarten. If only KC would be patient and give it a chance, by fall all the resettlement anxieties would wind down and go away once and for all.

In the study, KC described her time in the attic with Oona. He saw her lips move, but his thoughts were deep in air brushed imagery. There, in the attic, he imagined the two women upstairs and all alone. *It started with a touch on the shoulder, then a small kiss carefully placed on the back of her neck. The mysterious beauty, her olive skin glistening in the humidity of the warm, bright attic, offered unhurried and thoughtful kisses and caresses to his mildly resistant wife. With a hand on her breast and another on the small of her back, the women slowly sank to the welcoming pine floor. Soft murmurs grew in intensity, until finally, they peeled away each other's garments and made hot and sweaty oral love, each comforted with the knowledge that the thickness of*

the walls and floor were more than enough to muffle their cries of ecstasy.
What more could a married man ask for, he thought, if he couldn't
do that black-haired trollop himself? Then, as if suddenly awakened from a spectacular dream, he took pause at the mention of
the name Anton. As if he himself had seen a ghost, he froze in
shock for a moment before regaining his composure. He wondered
if KC had noticed anything. He looked at his wife closely. *Probably
not.* His wife continued to speak without interruption.

"I wish you had been here. Oona was unbelievable." Her eyes
widened with enthusiasm. "It's as if she saw things as they were a
long time ago. I guess that's what ontology is all about. You know,
break down the barriers of time and metaphysics and all that stuff.
I really wish you had been here."

It was as if the walls of the room had suddenly closed in upon
them. He struggled to put on a brave face, and then he quipped,
"And where is she from again?" He appeared subdued, though his
thoughts lingered on that name. *Anton.* His grandmother's grandfather was named Anton. It couldn't be. *It's too weird. It just can't be.*

"Oona's from New Orleans."

"She sounds French though. Like *really* French." Dad's visuals
estimated Oona was five-foot-eight. *How hot was that woman?* She
had about six inches on KC. "An affectation perhaps?"

"Well, she is. I mean her father is French. I think he's still alive.
He's a diplomat or he was one. Her mother is French and Haitian.
They moved to America, on assignment, when Oona was a baby.
She's really smart, you know. She has a PhD now and is
really…mystical. She sees things. I know she does."

"Grandma's grandpa," he mumbled.

"What?" KC asked.

"She looks young."

"She is. I think she's twenty-four. Now stop changing the subject. We need to tell Louis we're with him on this and that we
believe in him."

"I don't…believe him. I mean I love my son, but these are just
stories. Fantasies."

"Believe *in* him. He's our son. You know we need to encourage Louis to talk about this with both of us—we're the parents—
and to encourage him to talk about any other things that matter to
him, any time. We need to promise him that we'll always be there

for him, to listen. I'm telling you: I believe *in* him, and I believe him."

"That doesn't mean I have to believe." He turned away. "I think this is all bullshit."

"You think?"

"Yeah. I think."

"So you're not sure." KC glared at her husband.

"How can you be sure...of anything?" He regained a measure of combative comfort.

"Now *you're* being mystical. Philosophical." KC took a short breath, and as if slightly frustrated, she continued. "Look: Oona's come into the picture at a time when this family is under tremendous stress, and she's helped me manage this tremendous stress by helping me understand and come to terms with our house issues. Some stuff just doesn't make sense in the black-and-white world you live in. There's some soul named Anton up in the attic, and I want to get to the bottom of this."

"Oh, did you see him too?"

"Listen, asshole. Anton calls himself 'Opa' when he's with Louis. And you know what Opa means? Grandpa! And I think that deep down in *your* soul you do believe there's someone—something—in our attic. Get with the program now and let's deal with it."

There was silence.

"Now tell me," KC spoke with great strength of purpose, mixed now with a touch of sarcasm, "is there a guy named Anton in that precious family tree of yours?"

"Let's get Louis in here if he's still up." His eyes darted around the room.

"I'm sure he's still waiting." KC felt vindicated.

PART II

CHAPTER
17

"**S**o how do you know he's a ghost and not something just right out of your imagination?" Dad's eyes were deeply focused on his boy, as if searching for something. Searching for the truth, he guessed. He was not smiling and did not look happy. Seated and seemingly at ease in his favorite cushioned chair was Louis, a bit tired but so far not yet cranky, and looking ready for bed in his Incredible Hulk jammies.

"He told me, Dad."

Turning to KC, who stood by like a referee—ready for anything—Dad mumbled a not so quiet "This is bullshit."

"Watch your language. Ask your questions and listen." At this hour, KC was in no mood for childishness from her follically challenged, oftentimes impulsive, usually sarcastic, and always skeptical husband.

Dad took a deep breath, as if he struggled to go on with a charade, and then shot out, "But how do you really know?"

"Dad, old people don't live so long. I mean people don't live more than 150 years, do they?"

"No." There were no smiles. No humor from the boy's father.

"Besides, he told me. I told you, Dad. Opa told me."

"What? That he's a ghost? Come on, Louis." Dad looked mad but not mean-mad.

"Well, yeah, Dad." Louis remained calm and engaging. "He said he's a ghost of Purgatory...and a non-wandering spirit." Louis looked at his dad, as if waiting for a reaction.

"Bullshit!" said Dad. "Just because people tell you something, it doesn't mean that it's always true."

"But, Dad. He's not people. He's a ghost. I told you."

"Louis." Mom stepped in. "I think what your father means is that this is all so fantastic that it's hard for us to come to terms with it all. We believe in you, honey. And we love you and want to do what's right." Dad walked in a huff off to the side and rolled his eyes just enough to be noticed. It seemed that he struggled to stand still.

"Hold it right there!" said KC as she looked critically at her husband. Then, she turned back to her son and continued. "Oona told me that—"

"Here we go again with Oona," interjected Dad. He glared at KC, his nostrils practically flared.

"Shut up and get with the program," replied KC sternly, and she waved a pointed finger at her husband. "Louis, your father is just upset right now." Looking again at her husband, she added, "He'll come around…very soon. I know he will." She took a breath of renewal; then she picked up where she left off.

"Oona said that you've seen other ghosts and spirits—"

"Well, yeah, but that was when I was a baby." Louis paused. "How do you expect me to remember that? That was like two or three years ago! I'm like a grown toddler now."

Dad took another deep breath and appeared now to have regained some composure. He rubbed one hand over his mostly bald head and then rubbed his eyes with both hands. He looked like he was getting ready to wake up and get out of bed. "So what else did this ghost tell you?"

"Did he call himself anything besides Opa?" offered Mom.

"Well…no."

"You said he's an old guy?" asked Dad, innocently enough.

"Well yeah-eah! He's been around since the eighteen hundreds, Dad!" The boy took a moment to go on. With a quick look over to his mom, Louis then turned back to his father and resumed his response. "You know, he said that when he died, he was actually younger than you, Dad." Louis smiled and then cracked the gum he'd discreetly enjoyed all this time, as if for added effect. "He said his years of the flesh took a heavy toll."

Dad smiled wryly and looked at KC. Without a word, he turned back to his son and said, "Well then, what else did he say? He came from Bremen. Then what?"

"Well, he went to New York City and started to live on the Low West Side."

"Do you mean the Lower East Side? Manhattan?" Dad was amazed. His ancestors had in fact settled there. That much he knew. That and the Anton thing were kind of creeping him out, although that name—Anton—was from what's-her-name, and not his son. Still, with what he had said about Germany and whatnot, Louis couldn't be getting all this from the family tree. *Could he?* He was too young to use that software, and besides, he would never use his parents' computer without permission. *Would he? Could he?*

"Okay, Dad. That's it. He lived on the Lower East Side with a bunch of other Germans. He knew they were all Germans, even though they came from different places over there and were called different names."

"Yeah, right."

"Dad," Louis pleaded. "I coulda, woulda, and shoulda told you this stuff sooner. But I didn't want you to get mad. I did tell Mom some of this stuff though. You know. A lot of it I told her."

"Yup. I know, Louis. And I love you, honey." He didn't know what to believe or how to feel any longer. "Continue," he said. *This is all too weird.*

"Well, he met somebody named Maria after a while, and he married her in a church after he got to know her." Louis paused to snap his gum. "They lived in a ten-e-ment with a bunch of other people on the Low—the Lower—East Side."

"Germans?" Dad asked softly. *Jesus Christ*, he thought privately. One thing he *did* know about his grandma's grandpa was that Anton married someone named Mary.

"Well, yeah. I think so, Dad. You know they really didn't speak American yet, and they all had to help each other."

"I know." Dad even amazed himself as he engaged more freely with his son and followed the boy's story with greater interest. *But this kid is just way too sophisticated.* His words were so beyond his typical manner, he thought. His story was...so articulate. It was well beyond what anybody would expect from a five-year-old kid.

"Opa's house—his home, I mean—was only one room, Dad, and they all shared a place to poop and to pee."

"And when was this?" his father asked.

"Not sure, Dad. But it took Opa a while to get over here...from there. From—"

"From Bremen," offered Dad dryly.

"Yeah, Dad. That's right." The boy suddenly blew a medium-size bubble and just as suddenly popped it.

"Louis. Lose the gum. Now!" commanded his father.

"Okay, Dad. Don't get so upset."

"I'm not upset."

"No, he's not upset," said Mom suddenly. "In fact, your father is doing...quite well." KC winked at her husband with a small smile and then nodded for her boy to continue.

"Opa and Maria didn't have kids at first. Not that they didn't want them. They just couldn't for a while. I really don't know how that works, Dad. They finally did have a couple of kids."

"How many?" asked Dad.

"Two. They had one kid before the War, after Opa came over to America, and one kid during the War." The boy looked deeply into his father's eyes. "Maria was here, in New York City, when Opa got off the steamboat." The boy paused briefly, then added, "You know, Dad, to start his new life."

"I know, hon." Dad was trying his utmost to stay calm, but deep down inside, his anxiety level grew. With these latest revelations along with the boy's earlier stories, it seemed that there really could be some family ghost up in the attic.

"You know, Opa wondered if he was even meant to be a father, but then one day it just happened, and he had a boy first. Later on, during the War, he had a daughter, who we come from. Well, not Mom, but...you know what I mean."

"What was her name?" Dad braced himself for what he feared would come from the boy's mouth.

"Eva."

There was no disguising the obvious look of shock on Dad's face. KC watched his expression and knew Louis' story made brutal sense to her husband. *Vindicated once again!*

"But that's not even the good stuff, Dad. Opa was in the War. He marched in the mud and lived on the ground and did all these cool and gross things. When he tells me this stuff, I feel like I'm there. Sometimes I even see pictures of what he's talkin' about."

"What war?" Dad's mouth was left just a little bit open. His head was bowed and tilted slightly.

"I don't know the name of it, but it's really, really cool, Dad. Really."

"I...can imagine." Dad was frozen. "You see pictures, too?"

"Yeah, sometimes."

"Let me ask you, Louis, have you said any of this stuff to Charley? Be honest." He winked at his son. "I know you will. You know, like did you confide at all in your older brother?"

"No, Dad. Should I be doing that?"

"No. Not now. I mean for now, let's keep it between ourselves: you, Mom, and me. Okay?"

"Yeah. Okay."

"You know. Just while we try to sort everything out." Dad offered another wink to his son.

It was unusual for his dad to wink, and for Louis, it was oddly reminiscent of Opa. The boy nodded and smiled. Then, he finally removed the gum from his little mouth and added, "You know Charley knows some stuff."

"Like what?" Dad was curious but in no way alarmed.

"Well, you know. Like that you and Mom are fighting a lot about me and Opa."

"That's not really what I mean. That's no big deal, Louis. Everybody fights from time to time."

"And usually about nothing," Mom offered with a smile.

"I have a feeling we'll all be up in the attic at some point, soon." Dad's words trailed off gently.

"Wow. You mean it, Dad?"

"Ah...I don't know, honey. I really gotta think about all this shi—stuff." The man looked at his son with great fondness and asked, "What else ya got?" Not knowing what else to do or what to say next, and hating times like these, the loving father and husband decided to just go with the flow and egg the boy on a little further. "Come on. Let it out, son. Did he say anything else about his family?"

"I don't know. That was about it, so far I guess."

"So far?"

"Yes. So far." KC glared at her man.

"Well, actually Opa said he had three brothers named John, or Johann as the Germans call them."

"How could he have three?" Dad spoke softly at this late hour. A well-built man, especially for one in his early fifties, he normally held his back straight with his chest out. Before the move, he tried to get to the gym several times a week, but since Memorial Day weekend he hadn't even found a new gym, or the time, or the inclination to go anywhere. Now with his shoulders sagging and his eyes dimming, Dad was afraid he was showing his age.

"The first two died."

"A lot of death in this guy's family." Stoically Dad looked down upon his little boy.

"Yeah, Dad. That's what I said too."

Dad showed a weary smile and said nothing.

"First there was Little Yoyo. Isn't that a funny name, Dad? It's spelled like Jo Jo, but it's pronounced like the toy. Yoyo was like seven when he died." Louis regarded his dad briefly. His father's face was worn and he looked tired. "Then there was Hansy."

Dad froze at the mention of a nickname that had been used for his own Hansy, an uncle he never met and who died a young man, many years ago.

Louis didn't notice his father's reaction. "He was seven too when he drowned in the blue River Danube." Louis took a breath, then he pleaded, "But don't you wanna hear about the War?" Louis thoroughly enjoyed his parents' audience. And his mom was soaking everything in, with her eyes on Dad as much as on himself.

His father was still frozen.

"Dad. Don't you wanna hear about the War?"

He swallowed deeply. "Ah, yeah, but I don't think I can handle any more stuff tonight, Looster."

Louis loved it when people called him "Looster." He didn't know why he liked it, but he did. The boy remained highly animated and said, "You know—"

"I gotta get to bed and you do too!" Dad sounded adamant.

"You know, Opa made candy too. He was a candy maker."

"Just what I need to hear," commented Dad, who shook his head slowly from side to side as he moved away from his son.

Neither KC nor Louis knew exactly what Dad meant.

CHAPTER
18

*D*ad awoke in utter denial. *How could this shit really be happening?* He got out of bed. *Was it all a dream?* It was 5 AM and about the right time to start this day. KC was still asleep but had started to stir. *And why was all this happening?* There was time enough to get on the PC and check out the old family tree.

Dad loved the user-friendly family tree software and this personal link with the past. But for all the names and facts and stories, most of the stuff he had in the tree belonged to KC's side of the family. Her mom, especially, was a New Englander with more blue blood than she herself ever imagined, that went back to the earliest settlers in Boston, Salem, and Gloucester. *Salem. Witches.* There were so many of them in the tree: twenty-three to be exact. There were probably even more that he didn't know about. Relatives of his wife who were all accused of witchcraft at the infamous trials that began in 1692. Four were hanged. The closest of this cast of characters was a first cousin to the kids, eleven times removed, Rebecca Dike—fortunately a minor player. As for KC's dad's family, they came over much later. And so much less was known of them, as was the case with his own family. His mother's side came from Sicily in the early twentieth century. His dad's ancestors were all Germans. They came over around 1850, part of the first great wave of European migration to the United States.

For most of the time he was hearing his son, he was awestruck by the kid's choice of words, his knowledge and his sophistication.

The acorn doesn't fall far from the old tree. But this kid was truly amazing. His stories were amazing!

Yes, it was time to consult his family tree. He'd added quite a few names and stories since his own father's passing, but so much of the stuff he got from his mom before she joined him in the ground and, of course, up in Heaven. Dad never thought much of that family stuff when his father was plying him with information. No, it could always wait, he thought. But then one day, all of a sudden his dad was dead, and the things his father knew about his family were lost forever. What he took to the grave were things this dad struggled to piece together, with his mother's help for a while, till she died three years later. But the stuff they managed to collect was oftentimes spotty and flawed and riddled with error. He knew it was. God, if he had only paid more attention to what his father, and all his dead relatives for that matter, had been telling him when he was a kid. *Defeated? Perhaps.*

Dad knew some stuff about a guy named Anton Dietrich, his great-great grandfather. But for all the talking over the years, this was one guy nobody ever seemed to talk about. He had no idea even when or where the man died. Everything he knew, or thought he knew about Anton Dietrich he'd gotten on his own. He labored through the Mormons' LDS family files, a mess of vital records and a couple of U.S. censuses. There wasn't much on Anton at all, other than that he came over to the good old USA...from the Donaukreis: the old Danube District of Wuerttemberg. He suddenly grabbed a pencil and bit down hard for one long moment. He wondered if his own middle name, Anthony, the English version of Anton, had any connection to this guy Anton...the candy maker who married a woman named Mary.

"I'm gonna go to work today and do some serious research on Anton Dietrich. That war Louis is talking about just might be the Civil War." *Defeated? Not yet!*

CHAPTER
19

*L*ouis loved sharing Opa's stories about the War with Mom. It made him feel good. It was like the stories brought Mom and Opa closer together. Mom trusted him. She believed in him. And after last night, it seemed like Dad was getting closer to believing him too. But Dad wasn't convinced yet.

Louis couldn't wait to tell his dad about the War and what it was like being a soldier. He'd tell Dad about the marching and the fighting and all that stuff Opa told him. *But it'd be even better to get Dad and Opa to actually meet,* the boy thought. *After all, Dad did say that they might all go up to the attic. Yeah. That's all it would take to convince him. That'd be so cool…if it happened.*

The day's commute had been, so far, mostly uneventful. It started with the morning's Kiss-and-Ride drop-off at the Metro, followed now with the long ride home. Whenever he took the Orange Line to work, it was dependable and clean, and crowded with other professionals heading to the nation's capital for all manner of business. While he generally split his travels evenly between driving all the way into the city and taking the train, the sudden availability of "Rapunzel in short shorts," the cute Dutch babysitter, a lovely girl of fourteen named Trixi, allowed for a small measure of alone time with KC, with a ride to the train station and a free-parking moment for them once they were there. A little precious time to review plans and options among his wife, the COO of the family, and himself, its self-styled CFO. He planned to catch a ride home from a colleague tonight once they arrived in Fairfax. It wouldn't inconvenience anyone.

That morning he arrived at Union Station—it was not South Station and definitely not Boston. There were no skyscrapers in Washington, different architecture, but still two cities with many similarities, like traffic and commuters, great food, and cultural events aplenty. It was a fair walk to work from Union, and in the early morning it was never too hot. A few minutes of reflective private time passed before he walked past "The Past" on the Pennsylvania Avenue side of the Archives. It was a sculpture of an old Greek guy holding a scroll and a closed book, supposedly "imparting the knowledge of past generations" and "staring down the corridors of time." "Study the Past" was inscribed on the base of that statue. And these days, how prophetic was that?

After he reviewed his own calendar and emails, he embarked on the morning's "stand-ups" with staff, brief five- to ten-minute sessions to review various statuses and projects, and a little time to delegate a variety of new tasks and assignments to his small army of employees. Once that was finished, he quietly tucked himself into his office to start his own special project. Things he usually deferred or didn't care about could always wait, he believed, but with that realization he feared he'd become an apparatchik of the massive federal government, as well as the undisputed czar of his Records Division fiefdom.

First he pulled up an NATF application for Anton Dietrich… These days a textual archives request normally routed for several weeks before it landed on someone's radar, and before it queued up for a search that, if successful, ended when copies were mailed to the requesting party and the original records were returned to their places. For the here and now though, he'd requested multiple searches with oftentimes scanty information, but which had enough stuff to cast a wide net and get researchers started. Regimental records and muster rolls, veterans, census, pension files, bounty and land lists, discharge certificates, whatever he knew existed, he'd asked for. He was sure he'd find something. Fortunately the process would be greatly expedited. Dad had estimated up to three days before he'd have something back on this guy Anton. He had good people behind him. And where specificity was required on the forms, Dad's august position allowed for exhaustive searches without the use of all required fields.

CHAPTER
20

*L*ouis thought the knocks on the door belonged to Mom. Charley never knocked, and he still behaved like he did back home. *Wait. This is home now. Isn't it?* His dad wouldn't be home this early either. It was 6 PM. So with a burst of excitement and nothing to hide, Louis flew down the ladder's rungs to greet his mother. His confidence and happiness clearly showed as his mother entered the room on her own and without any fanfare.

"Mom!" the boy declared. Their eyes met for a warm moment. Then each of them looked in the direction of the stairs that led through the top of the high ceiling to the attic.

"What am I gonna do with you?" Mom asked as her eyes moved back to her little boy.

"Come on, Ma. Let's go up together."

"No, not now, honey. Dad'll be home soon, and we have too much to do tonight."

"Mom. Do you really think Dad'll take us all up to the attic together?"

"He might." KC took a deep breath and added, "I think your father is just trying to figure out how he really feels about all this stuff. " Mom's chin pointed briefly to the trapdoor above.

Now it was the boy's turn to take a deep breath. Then, the child began to spout like a fountain, as he described the things he felt would be so cool for his dad to hear: the braying of mules, the terrible stench of battle, the everyday life of a long-ago soldier.

Louis had no doubt his mother believed in him and Opa. But Dad needed to know this stuff too.

"Louis, when you go up there, do you ever notice anything besides Opa?"

"Yeah," he said. "I notice stuff, but I look at Opa most of the time."

"But like what?"

"I don't know. Like the mirror, and the trunk he sits on." The boy thought for a moment. "There's an old rocking chair, but he never uses it. There are a lot of windows, but only on three sides. They're kinda cloudy." He winced. "Well, some of them are cloudy."

"How about the smell. Do you smell anything?"

"Yeah." The boy's eyes widened immensely, just as they always had on Christmas mornings. "He smokes, you know. And coughs. Like Mimi." Mimi, his grandmother, had COPD. "It smells nice though. He's always smoking that pipe."

Mom delayed her response. "You know, on second thought, let's you and me go upstairs." Without hesitation, together they climbed through the opening. It was still light outside, but the pull of a string broadly illuminated their indoor surroundings. The smell was definitely there.

"So I think you said Opa sits on the trunk." Mom was hardly dressed for attic searching, but she was anxious for something to happen. "So where is he?"

"I don't know, Ma."

Louis was so handsome, more cute than handsome, really, at this early age, she thought. "Like when those policemen came, no one else could see him, right?" Mom wandered slowly about the space; she peeked through the windows and at the walls, at the stuff you normally find in an attic, and at the stuff that looked more peculiar. She looked back and forth to her son as she moved around. "You know Oona felt him."

"Like thick air, right?"

"Oh. I don't know. You've actually touched him?"

"Well, yeah, a couple of times. It's almost like moving your hand in the pool. Kinda. Only it's thinner...and dry."

Mom didn't know how to react. She was not afraid or concerned. She was clearly surprised, but hoped that she didn't show it. "And what about that pipe, Louis? Does he smoke it over by the trunk?"

"Well, yeah," the boy said. There was nothing in his voice to suggest anything out of the ordinary. The son and his mother then met at the trunk.

It's the empty trunk, thought Mom. Her eyes darted around the space. "It does smell nice here. It's a nice aroma." Dreamily, she added, "Old, but nice." *Ubiquitous.*

"He keeps it over there." Louis' eyes were open wide as he pointed to a small shelf tied to two rafters.

"What?" It was a harsh whisper, followed by a pause and a much louder "What?"

"The pipe, Mom." The boy walked where he pointed and reached behind a small piece of lumber. His small hand traveled between the rafters to an obscure place on the shelf. There he pulled out a dark smoking pipe and, a few seconds later, an old pouch. He handed both to his thunderstruck mother.

KC didn't know what to do with the objects in her hands: a soft cloth pouch that smelled divinely sweet—she dared not open it—and an ancient-looking briarwood pipe with a well-used bowl and a long, chewed-up stem. In shock she held the items, her mouth slightly ajar. Off in a distance she heard her boy talking...and talking. His words, for now, were not important.

They didn't know Dad was home till they heard him storm through the front door. Everyone was in the family room. Dinner was ready, he had called ahead, and KC and the kids were more than ready to eat. Whenever possible KC preferred waiting for Dad so everyone could eat like a family. Though Dad sounded okay on the phone a few minutes earlier, the noise of a slammed door behind him alerted her that something was up. She rose from her seat, motioned to her children to head into the kitchen, and left as well to greet her husband.

"What are you people doing?" he hissed.

"You people?" How KC hated that expression. And he only used it when he was either mad or upset or just wanted to piss her off. "What is it?" KC looked sternly at Dad.

"There's just too much shit going on." Dad's deep-set eyes looked darker than usual, but the green was still evident. "I'm trying to look into the Anton stuff and—"

"Your real job got in the way?" Mom offered. She knew her man so well. The hothead who, sometimes for reasons unknown, she happened to love so much. He looked like it surely had been a busy day. And what did it take for him to get home this evening at a reasonable hour? she wondered.

"Yeah." Lovingly, Dad motioned to KC to move on with him into the kitchen. "Honey, can you make me a drink?" He looked exasperated.

"If that'll get you out of your mood, I will." She smiled. "Kids, your father is home. Dinnertime!"

CHAPTER
21

*K*C couldn't wait to call Oona to tell her all about what happened over the last couple of days. Dad was "mentally preparing himself" to go with her and Louis, and possibly with Charley, up into the attic. *Oona too?*

They talked and they talked and talked as good friends do. She visualized Oona, tall like a model. *Statuesque.* Then finally, and only after Oona politely declined an invite to join them on the anticipated attic expedition, she suddenly said:

"We—Louis and I—found a pipe up there." This announcement was greeted with a soft silence from Oona. "Do you think it could be his?"

Still, there was only silence from Oona.

"There was a pipe and a pouch." KC's nervousness was clearly in her voice.

"Ahhhh" was Oona's only sound. It was light as a soft breeze.

"Oona. Either someone living is upstairs smoking that thing or we have a smoking ghost." KC was anxious. She hungered to hear something from her friend. "How can this be?" She paused. "Say something. Please say something, Oona."

"Strong ghosts *can* handle small objects," she finally said.

Instantly at ease with her response—any response would have done—though the thought was no less mind-boggling, KC considered Oona's every word.

"I have not encountered a pipe smoker in that part of our world...and I have no doubt Anton is one," said Oona.

"How can this be?" KC asked. How fortunate she felt to have found Oona Neeci.

"Strength depends on energy, *ma chère*. A ghost such as he can, I am sure, move and lift light material things; he may even drink a little water from time to time, beer perhaps. Any liquid really, if given the opportunity, but always in small quantities. I suppose this ghost can also open and close doors or small windows. This has always intrigued me, KC, the connection between material, physical, and metaphysical substances." She briefly paused, then added, "I am sorry we did not find these things when we were together."

"I didn't open it. The pouch, I mean." KC wanted instructions.

"That's perfectly fine, *ma chère*. You would not wish for someone you had never met to open your things. Would you?"

"Don't play with me now." She could practically smell Oona's French perfume. *As if she was here with me now.*

"Darling, your ghost is real and he's waiting." Privately Oona's heart ached. "You don't need me, *ma chère*. Your son is an exceptional seer." While occasionally drawn to older women, her attraction to them was never so powerful as it was now. *Play with you?* Yet the enchantress was resigned for now to bridle her desire for KC and save it for another time, another place. And she'd contain the urge and throw no tricks, no charms. No spells. She wanted this conquest to be totally real. Her strong will was palpable and inviting. So unlike her own mother, who did anything she was told. The thought cast an undeniable measure of self-doubt, and she questioned her own infallibility. She'd be leaving shortly for her holidays in Europe, and for now she'd rest content that she warmed her heart to that wonderful family and helped it come to terms with its uncommon realities. "Keep me posted, love."

"I will," KC promised.

There was a small flutter in her French voice before Oona closed with "Love you. Bye."

KC added her own good-byes and slowly placed the phone back on its cradle. She looked outside onto their yard and to a lovely mix of hickories and oaks, and hoped her husband would have something soon about Anton Dietrich, the man. Something—anything—that would inspire her man to take the plunge up into the attic.

CHAPTER
22

*I*t was a glorious weekend and Dad had something to share. After he tended to a few routine chores about the house, unusually cheerful for a time when he performed such routines, he gathered the family together. It was a bright Saturday afternoon, and it was time to sit down and tell everyone everything he knew about his grandmother's grandfather.

Charley seemed excited and terrified at the same time. "Opa means Grandpa?"

"Yup." Amid all the noise and excitement in the family room, Dad remained deeply focused as he recounted the details he remembered from Louis' stories with what was already known about Anton Dietrich. Then he calmly turned to KC, as if to seek her approval, and quietly asserted that the presence in the house was most possibly the great-great-great grandfather to their children. "From the time I was a little boy, I don't recall anyone in the family ever speaking a word about this man Anton. Nothing was ever mentioned. It seemed no one ever asked about him either." He took a deep breath and turned back to his children. "It was only over the last ten years that I learned anything at all about the man." He paused. "And what I did find was dutifully entered into our family tree." He smiled, pleadingly. His audience nodded in apparent appreciation. Thankful walked in uneven circles around Zupper, who rested nearby.

KC looked on approvingly as her husband repeated an earlier message. To a mixed reaction from his audience, he declared, "There is nothing to fear from a family ghost, if there even is one."

Louis was immune to that part of the discussion and, much buoyed in his beliefs, he added, "Opa lived in a tent for over a year!"

"Okay. I found two Anton Dietrichs at the Archives. I don't know if they're related; maybe they're even the same guy. You know, it's funny. I never thought to check army records for this person. I just assumed he was too old for the Civil War."

"There's only one Opa, Dad." Louis' big blue eyes sparkled in the sunlight.

"I know, hon. We will know more over the next week or so. There's still a lot of stuff to check."

"You know, Opa marched in the mud. He told me about his shoes, and the hard stones came up through his—Dad, what do you call those things on the bottom of your shoes?"

"Soles," said his father.

"Soles, Dad."

Souls, thought KC. She smiled to herself.

"He had a lot of pain in those shoes and because of those soles. And you know, Dad, Opa says whole battles were fought over shoes and soles and the places they made them, the factories. He said there were a lot of gray skies too, Dad."

He looked open-mouthed at his son. Here, as he prepared for the attic with some trepidation, his fear and anxiety were pleasantly mixed with anticipation and excitement.

CHAPTER
23

Dad awakened Louis early Sunday morning, and together they quietly climbed up to the attic. Dad didn't think that anyone else would mind so much that just he and his young guide would set out on a preliminary foray.

The attic already brightly illuminated from the east, Dad could see the crisp contours of the eaves and rafters, the worn, wide pine floorboards, and scattered pieces of attic junk that were left by past occupants. He saw nothing unusual. He felt nothing unusual. Nothing seemed to have changed since his first and last visit here on Moving Day. There was no hint of a squatter. *There's that sweet aroma, though. Still nice.* Then, suddenly a bright idea impelled him to grab Louis and abort their mission. Dad descended the ladder quickly. Louis followed. Then Dad called softly for Zupper. He'd enlist the extrasensory services of the family dog.

A drowsy Zupper answered the call, and a minute later Dad, with sixty pounds of extra weight in his arms, carefully ascended the attic ladder. Zupper jumped from his arms as soon as they arrived, and with the curiosity of a puppy, she sniffed all around the attic space. Her actions were totally unremarkable. Louis followed her around and she eventually rambled over to Opa's favorite perch, where she settled down and resumed her snooze, as if she were at an unseen master's feet. Dad remained on the sunlit side of the attic, where he observed the original architecture and the structural integrity of the place. A few feet above his balding head, Dad could plainly see the entryway up onto the black slate roof and the fenced cornice. *Look out.*

Off at the other end of the attic, Dad heard Louis, but his son was neither speaking to himself nor to the dog. With very mixed emotions and a slightly dropped jaw, he knew the boy was chatting away with someone or something else. *Opa? Anton?* Clearly torn by what to do or to say, Dad slowly approached the other side of the attic. His palms began to sweat and his heartbeat was elevated. Should he engage them or just observe from a safe distance? He didn't know what to do. He was anxious. Excited. Confused.

"Louis," he blurted out. He startled Zupper, whose dog tags jingled alive. "Louis," he said again, in a short burst of manly noise.

"Yeah, Dad?"

"Ah, what are you doing?" Dad struggled to be calm. He inched closer to his boy.

"Dad, I don't think you see him, but I'm talking with Opa." The boy was fully composed, and as best as any kid twice his age could do, he offered introductions. "Opa, Dad." His eyes locked with his father's as he said, "Dad, Opa is here." He pointed to the trunk. "He says, 'Hi.'"

Zupper remained at the base of the trunk and rested contentedly. Dad was clearly perplexed.

"Ah, ask him in what unit he served—in the Civil War." There, he had said it. He had asked a question, and while happy to get it out, he was at the same time saddened. Had he just encouraged supremely bad behavior on the part of his son? Was this insane, inappropriate, or just plain dumb-ass stuff? What would KC's take be on this little exercise in interlocution? His boy was at such an impressionable age. Might he be doing his son irreparable harm? He felt overwhelmed and confused.

"He heard you, Dad." Louis was composed and privately thrilled. "He says the, uh…" He paused and smiled. "The, uh, the twenty-ninth infanery."

Dad froze, swallowed, and softly said, "Infantry, son. The word is infantry." He remained frozen. It was real. This whole business was real. The twenty-ninth!

"He says he was nearby, Dad." There was a slight pause. "At Bull Run?" His young voice rose with those words, as the young Virginia resident was not yet familiar with that place.

"Yeah," Dad finally responded. "The Archives said Anton Dietrich served in the 29th New York Infantry Regiment and was at both battles of Bull Run." With one question, Dad had apparently confirmed the presence of a ghostly ancestor in their midst. Yes, now he was sure. Or was he? Louis was a sharp boy and an outstanding reader. *He, the boy, could have done some family research. Right? But at five—almost five and a half?* He swallowed deeply. *No way. No fucking way!* Dad continued to stand in his place, visibly stunned.

"Dad?" Then, with a measure of greater concern, "Dad?"

"Louis?" he said, as if suddenly awakened from a dream.

"Opa says he was in the fifteenth too." Louis grabbed hold of his father's arm. "But that was later, Dad. It was later in the War."

The boy's father felt a numbness and an intense love for his son, more than he had ever known before. *Such a blossoming young character to admire. Such raw strength and honesty.* "Yup," he offered in return. Now he believed. Oh, how he believed. While unable to see or feel Opa, Dad was now utterly convinced that this ghost was real. *The 15th New York Heavy Artillery.* So it *was* the same guy. *Got out. He reenlisted.* Both exasperated and excited, Dad was still not quite ready to meet this ghost face-to-face, this spirit of some sort, this ancestor that no one ever mentioned, this thing who for some strange reason spoke through Louis. *How is this shit happening?*

Dumbfounded, he slowly disengaged from his son's embrace, turned away, and ambled toward the exit way. *Why is this happening?* He ran both hands over the sides of his head, looked both ways, as if crossing a street, and stumbled slightly on nothing visible. He mumbled, "Why here?" *Why now? Why?*

Louis followed his dad.

CHAPTER
24

"Enough with the F-bombs, already," KC demanded. She hadn't ever seen her husband so scattered with his thoughts. He was like a teenager, nearly out of control. "Just tell me!"

"I tell you: he's real. No doubt. No fu—no doubt. I just can't see him, but I know he's there. Louis sees him and talks to him, and I don't know why or what this is all about."

"Settle down." KC was gorgeous in the morning hours. She always looked refreshed and natural. Her hazel eyes scanned her husband thoroughly. "I'm just glad we're both on board, and you know what? We'll get to the bottom of this…together."

"Well, I want to take you and the kids, and Zup of course, all upstairs. First, though, I want to get everything I can on this guy from the Archives. You know this guy is real. This is my grandma's grandpa we're talking about! I can't believe it! I mean, I really do believe it, but you know what I mean." He looked at his wife and could see the very fine lines of middle age around her eyes and mouth. She looked so…professional. *Looking like a CEO in Spandex shorts and an apron.* He had often referred to his wife as the family's COO. But it made little difference now with what she was called or how she was dressed. She stood strong and beautiful in their kitchen's easterly exposure. "You know, this must be something good… You know?"

"Yeah, I think so too." Relieved, KC had by this time pulled together the various elements of a Sunday morning breakfast that the family could enjoy before church. Big Sunday breakfasts were one of many traditions she exported from home to Virginia.

"I'm hotter than a bastard right now. Are you hot? Is the AC on? Uh, wait. We don't have AC, do we?" The father of three and devoted husband of one still behaved as if he were spinning out of control.

In time she hoped he would settle down and return to a more rational demeanor. "Ah, no. It's on our list though. This house is actually rather cool. Don't you think? It's a stone house, remember?" Off in the distance, she could hear the early morning cries of Thankful. In minutes the rest of the family, Charley that is, would wake up. "Get used to it, my man. It's only mid-July. And the attic must be most unbearable."

"Yeah." He made a deep sigh. "This week I'm gonna get everything I can on old Anton." He *was* settling down. "Then we'll go upstairs and meet this ghost head-on and ask him all kinds of stuff. You know, family tree stuff, being dead. You know. That kind of stuff."

"Why do you think he's here, honey?" She was an undeniably lovely woman: poised and, it seemed then, forever calm.

"Don't know, hon." He really didn't have a clue. He jutted out his lower lip.

"How strange is this?" She took a long sip of her coffee. "That we move into a house, and of all the people that ever lived…and died…your great grandpa is here too?" Then, after a brief pause, she added, "Weird, but not a bad kind of weird." There was no time for silence as she cracked a large brown egg on the side of a mixing bowl. "Get ready for one awesome breakfast."

"He's my great-*great* grandpa." His eyes glared for a moment. "How old do you think I am?"

"Of course, honey. Don't worry. You're not that old…yet." She smiled and prepared herself for the customary and sometimes venomous reciprocity from her other half, but there'd be none of that this morning.

For her husband, there was simply no time for it. "You know, of all the emotions I had up there, KC, fear was never one of them. Look: whenever time permits at work, I'm gonna get everything I can find on this guy. He was in twice! Not once. Twice he served this country! He must've gotten out and then gone back in again."

"Uh huh." She was busy at work, preparing breakfast.

"I'm sure that wasn't unique to old Anton. But it does make me rather proud. Like I said. Remember? I told you there were two Anton Dietrichs in the Archives. Remember?"

"Yes, yes, I remember. Don't sweat it, honey." Several more eggs cracked in rapid succession. "Stay cool. See what you can find, and like you said, we'll all go upstairs together when you're ready." With another sip of her coffee and a jerk on her flowery, old-fashioned apron, she added, "I'm just so happy right now. I don't want you to lose it over this, hon. I feel like a great weight's been lifted from our shoulders. Don't you? Isn't it a relief? You know, with Louis and all the anxiety it was causing us? Remember?"

"Yup." He looked like an out-of-control man who recently gained some measure of self-control. *Would coffee help or hurt?*

KC wiped her hands on her apron, turned, and then snuggled up to her husband. "Well, I don't want to start worrying about you over this business. I mean, I worry about you...all the time...but not over this." There was an unconvincing pause, then, "You know what I mean. It's as if we're moving on now...into a new chapter, so to speak."

"Yeah. I'll calm down. Don't worry." The glaze had worn off his eyes.

"Promise?" She kissed him on the cheek and drew back slowly.

"Yup. I will." He took a deep breath. "So whenever time permits I'll research the Civil War, at work *and* at home, and see what we have on Anton Dietrich's role in it and after it."

"Yup. You've said that. How many times now?" She flashed her beautiful smile. There was no wonder why so many people were so easily drawn to her.

"After the War, I mean." He rambled on. "There's not much...I know...yet." He was hungry now. His eyes moved over the counter space and a nearby open cabinet as he prowled for a quick snack.

KC would have none of it. "We'll be eating soon."

"I'm ready for a quick shower, I guess. And try to keep Louis out of the attic till we can all go up. Okay?" He smiled at his wife.

"Yeah, I'll try," she said with a small smile.

"I just don't wanna miss anything, you know." Finally he moved in for a cup of coffee. "He's still a little kid and, you know, he can lose some stuff in translation." He poured the steaming liquid into a colorful ceramic mug. "Right?"

"Right. No problem, hon." She turned and moved to the stove.

Something was baking inside. No wonder! This had contributed to the temperature in the kitchen, he fumed. *Stay calm.*

"We have a busy week coming up...out of the house anyway. I'll keep Louis occupied. Don't worry." She sipped her coffee and placed it back on the counter.

"I'm not worried, KC. I'm really not." He sounded unconvincing.

The couple parted to go about their separate business, and as they did, Dad asked, "Where *is* Louis anyway?"

"He's...upstairs." KC half smiled and then quickly looked away from her husband.

"Did he go back to bed?" Dad asked. The two locked eyes on one another.

How pleased she was that her husband and she were finally in sync on this very major matter. And how weird it all really was. Why was this happening? *How was it happening?* "Come on. Go have your shower...in the *downstairs* bath. Then, it's breakfast time!"

CHAPTER
25

"*S*o, Opa, did you guys look like the Blue and the Gray?" His eyes glistened. "Is that how you dressed in the War?" Leaving the man little time to respond, Louis added. "I've been reading, Opa."

"So you have." Opa winked and took what seemed to be a deep breath. "Yes, *mein Liebster*. We were covered in blue. Distinctive. Zouaves, they called us." There he sat rich in his own colors. A smile underneath his thick mustache was clearly visible. His words flowed but his mouth did not move.

"Zouaves?" asked the boy.

"Yes, in the beginning we were Zouaves." Opa made easy gestures and reached for his pipe and the never-ending supply of sweet tobacco that seemed to sit in the pouch beside it. "Zouaves were often quite colorful soldiers, many with red Chausseur pants and fancy braids; with sashes and tasseled fezzes, or even turbans." He jerked back as if he were about to laugh loudly. But he didn't. "Now, I don't expect you to know all these words, Ludwig. But colorful Zouaves were the fashion warriors' rage, first in Africa, then in Europe, and finally in America."

Young Louis easily visualized images of the colorful, sometimes comical, warriors, with their big and bushy moustaches and their gaudy outfits. Some of the men looked like clowns. His dreamy eyes sparkled in the natural light of the attic while Opa continued his narrative.

"Vincent van Gogh himself memorialized the 'Zouaaf,' though years after the craze had passed. And by then my time had passed as well. But it was a great privilege to serve as a Zouave. And I can tell you that they—we—made quite the picture at Bull Run. There were colorful Zouaves from the North and the South, from New York and Louisiana. We in the flank companies were mostly in blue: blue caps, very loose trousers—pantaloons—and a short jacket. With white...or light-colored knickers." Opa nodded and kept his eyes on his young descendant. He clearly enjoyed his own narrative.

Louis could see the soldiers quite clearly in his mind.

"Did you know there were two hundred different uniforms on the fields of Bull Run?" Opa didn't wait for an answer. "The confusion would have been comical if it had not been so...deathly." The man took a long puff on his pipe. "They were some of the silliest duty uniforms, those Zouave designs. But as with our other German-American regiments, those bright uniforms helped us recognize one another through the dense smoke of the battlefield."

This made perfect sense to the boy. He nodded.

"The Rebels matched the color of that smoke though, and bested us in those early days of fighting." Opa winked at Louis.

"So why won't you talk to Daddy, Opa?" He fumbled with his stubby fingers. "Why couldn't he see you?"

"I believe he will be seeing me soon, *mein Liebster*. Soon."

CHAPTER
26

*I*t was Friday evening. He sat in his oversized swan-back chair in the soft, dim light of the study. Surrounded with sadness and melancholy. *Smothered in emotion.* He thought of work and some things he'd seen at the Archives. Then, he rose from his chair and moved toward the family room, where he planned to stay till he was ready for bed.

The next morning the house was alive with great fanfare and excitement. The family would soon be ready, or as ready as they could ever be, for an attic outing. It was cool and a little cloudy at this early hour, and KC busily packed eggs and muffins, juices and coffee. She had a wicker picnic basket nearby, balanced on a tall stool. Thankful talked away in her highchair, and Charley asked a thousand questions. There were folding chairs to be brought up the fold-down stairs, along with the dog, kid toys for Thankful, a small cooler, and the camera and other things.

"We'll see soon enough, Charley," she said. "Daddy couldn't see him, but you know your father. He's sure and when he's sure, he's sure." She made a little laugh to herself. "I don't know what we'll see. I just don't know if we're going a little too far, with Louis being the go-between with a ghost. You know, I think it'd be much better if we were all involved. Don't you?"

Charley sat not too far from his sister. His dad was some-where, and Louis was in the bathroom. "What about that lady,

Oona, Mom?" Charley's eyes matched his mother's so perfectly. "What's she think?"

"Oona is summering in Istria. She's incommunicado." KC wondered what Oona *was* doing at that moment. *Six hours ahead of us? Probably on the beach.*

"What's that mean?"

"Incommunicado? It means she's away from phones and computers." KC thought of Oona, her friend. *Oona, the ontologist.* She smiled fondly and felt good.

"Where's Istria?"

"Somewhere in southern Europe, my son. Oh, my beautiful son." KC drenched her boy with loving eyes and lips, and in her deep, rich voice added, "Croatia, I think."

"Ma-ah!" he protested mildly.

"I believe it is very near to Italy."

"So when are we goin' upstairs?" asked Louis as he returned from the bathroom.

"As soon as your father is ready. I don't know where in this house he is, but he can't be far."

CHAPTER
27

"*I* have a ton of stuff with me, Anton!" Dad was alight with nervousness.

Young Louis sat on the floor with Thankful, who at the moment rolled around on a small blanket, and with Zupper, sprawled out on the sunlit floorboards a few feet away. Charley stood close by. He looked ready to pounce on something, anything.

KC offered a calm "Hello, Anton." She also stood and scanned the attic space. She prepared herself with a long, deep breath. "Well," she said, "I think we should start at the beginning."

Then she looked down at her boy. "Louis, can you ask Opa..." KC stopped in mid-sentence and then turned toward the ghost's trunk. "Never mind, Louis," she said. KC believed she faced him now, and then she said, "I'll address you directly." KC looked back down at Louis and said, "Right, hon?" How she wanted his extra encouragement to address this ghost directly. She got it without reservation.

The whole family had gathered about in a semicircle of sorts, in proximity to Opa's trunk. There was plenty of room for everyone. A picnic blanket was spread on the floor with two chairs on either side. KC took a seat in one while her husband was already in the other. Everyone was dressed for summer. The attic was warm but not yet oppressive.

"Why are you appearing to Louis? And why now?" Then KC rose from her seat, and with a deeper and steadier voice she added, "And why here?"

Louis saw how Opa changed once he heard these words from his mother. He was seated on his trunk, just as she thought. His colors deepened, his smile broadened, and he looked nearly opaque.

Opa knew they believed. He was greatly strengthened by that realization.

KC remained standing. "And will you show yourself to us now?" Her lips drew slowly back, revealing her perfect teeth and then a perfect smile. "Please."

"You're getting way into the weeds on this, honey," Dad offered anxiously.

Louis stepped in before his mom could respond. "Come on, Opa. We love you. We believe in you, Opa." Suddenly the boy seemed close to tears. "Please show yourself so Mom and Dad can see you. You look great, Opa."

Opa smiled at no one in particular. For a moment he looked to Louis like he was preparing for a great speech or a grand reentry. He rose and stood alongside the old mirror. His shirt colors were rich plaids and his pants were darkish blue. There was no reflection.

"You look almost real." Louis sounded very pleased. He tried to hold back his emotions. He waited a moment, and then added pleadingly, "Charley and Thankful can get to know you too. Please, Opa. Show yourself...to everybody."

Still, there was nothing visible to anyone but the young boy.

"Please, Opa. I want Mom and Dad to see." He paused and waited for the man, who said not a word and still stood by the mirror. Opa acknowledged the boy with a wink and a quick cock of his right eyebrow. But he did nothing else.

"Louis: If this is going to be too stressful on you..." KC intervened.

"No, Ma. It's okay. I think he's gonna do it." He smiled and remained full of emotion. "I really think he's gonna do it."

Everyone waited and still there was nothing.

KC looked at Louis imploringly. She said, "Maybe we should give Opa a little time to decide, and we can go downstairs and get ready for...something." Her honest eyes were fixed on her son's.

Louis always knew those eyes.

Dad interrupted, as if in a rush. "That's right, honey. We can just go. Don't worry about it. It's no big deal, Louis." His words ended in a whisper.

Opa still stood as if he waited for some kind of permission. Again he looked down to the boy. He showed a slight crinkle of his ghostly nose. His face was pale and gray, but with deep black lines that fenced in his broad, thick mustache. Opa straightened his hair, coughed once, then again, and looked over to his pipe under the eave.

"I don't mind if he...just talks to you, honey." Mom was Mom. "Really I don't." KC looked then to her husband, smiled mildly, and then turned back to Louis.

Opa removed both his pipe and pouch from their places. Then, affectionately to his grandson, Anton said softly, "I'll take over now, *mein Liebster.*"

"Are we doing errands today, Dad?" Charley suddenly asked. He had just about had enough of this business of standing around and waiting, and was eager to move on outside and play some hoops out in the driveway, before it got too hot. "So, whaddaya want to do, Dad?"

"Be quiet, Charley." Mom raised her brows and quickly nodded her head. "That's what *Mom* wants you to do."

Anton smiled lovingly at the boys and their mother. He looked like a man who still waited for something. But he looked almost real. Louis plainly saw that. Then, he slowly appeared to everyone.

Dad froze. As he looked his grandma's grandpa in the eyes, his mouth went wide open. Papers fell from his hands and mostly onto his lap.

The ghost spoke for all to hear. "I am Anton, the third child of Philipp and Maria Anna Dietrich. In life I beheld many things, much of which I have shared with your young Louis. In war I witnessed both my adopted country's worst defeats and its greatest victories. Since my body died in 1867, I have been here at the Bornheim House, a place where I exist in ghostly form between Heaven and Earth, awaiting my final orders to go home...to the Light of the Almighty. In life I was here at this house when I was

saved from certain death by acts of extreme kindness and true compassion." He pointed to the distant rafter where the elegant "A" was
carved deep in the wood, trapped in the branches of a great tree.

"I was taken to this very house to heal, in 1862, and right at
that very spot was my cot, my bed, one among many." He paused
to reflect. "There I convalesced while many others slipped into eter-
nal rest through weeks and months of pain. In 1863, I finally left
this place among the living and returned here only in death."

His audience—and he knew them all—was riveted in silence
and awe.

"Three things must come to pass before I can take leave of this
earthly purgatory and move on into the Light."

CHAPTER
28

*A*stonished. Stunned. Stupefied. Awestruck. Paralyzed. Mortified.

Still silence.

All her beliefs and all her years of Catholic teachings had not prepared KC for this. Here she stood face-to-face with a ghost. *Purgatory? The Light? Really!* Catholic school. The nuns. Nothing. Front and center stood a man who looked like Wilford Brimley with a German accent and a thick mop of hair that had to be the envy of a balding man like her husband. He looked like a cowboy without a hat, with old worn boots—square toes and small heels—that carried the dust and sediment of a century and a half.

Careful not to be overcome. Stay in control of your senses, she thought. *What you see is real.*

Yes, he was real all right. His hands—old man's hands with wrinkly, thin skin loose over his bones and uneven knuckles. *Ravaged by time.* He held his pipe in his left hand. There were deep lines in his face and crow's-feet flanking his deep gray and loving eyes.

She struggled not to be overcome by this preternatural presence. She must keep a lid on any chaos or mayhem that might ensue, although it was more clear to her that chaos and mayhem were within her own body and therefore within her power to control. Everyone else seemed okay. Louis, Thankful, and Zup were completely at ease—Thankful talked incessantly and babbled up most of her hundred-word vocabulary in a perfect storm. She rose from her blanket when Anton appeared, and began to walk, with fits and starts, all about the attic. *Keep an eye on that stairway!*

Her husband had done his math and suddenly broke the silence. "Hey, that'd make you only forty-three! You were born in 1824, weren't you, Anton?" *Book and movie rights to the Hereafter!* he mused.

"No. It was 1823. Using a Plain Time calendar, I had forty-three years and eight months in life, and the rest...here." He cast his eyes downward and slowly descended back onto the old trunk. Slightly fragrant, cool air gently moved about the ghost.

"That's younger than me," Dad observed with a somewhat confused smile.

"How'd you get here the first time, Opa?" Louis' wide inquiring eyes were magnetic. "You were sick, weren't you?"

"What about the three things?" KC chimed.

"Wait a minute, honey," he said to his wife. He had settled his own excitement down some and calmly added for all to hear, "Let Anton—Opa—please start from the beginning." He then looked at the "old man" whose soft image was that of a life bleached away by hard times and years gone by. "We know you came from Germany—"

Anton slowly rose again and started to pace around the garret. All eyes were on him. Opa wasted little time with his reply. "I started my new life in New York City in the year of Our Lord eighteen hundred and forty-nine. It was a lovely springtime." His words flowed, but for this time his mouth did not move.

Who noticed that? KC thought. *Was it just me?*

"There was great sadness in my body and soul. And here I was, in a new world; the calamities in revolutionary Europe were behind me, with tens of thousands of Germans, Bavarians as well, immigrants who like me wanted a new start. We shared a common language and customs, though those Bavarians are a bit peculiar, and we shared a love for America, our new homeland that would, with God's infinite grace, provide for a better life. Some were Swabians, like me. But I was still alone. I was without my families: both the family I knew through my years in my beloved Ertingen, and my young family—my wife and my son—those who I loved so much for so little time, and whose deaths cheated me of ever really knowing them.

"I found work as a paper stainer in Manhattan. A year later I met my future wife, Mary, the great-great-great grandmother to these beautiful children." He smiled and looked first at Louis, then to Charley, and finally to the little toddler, Thankful. "I moved from job to job in the coloring business, and it was not an easy life in New York. After a short courtship, we married in 1850 and were eager to start a family. We thought of moving west to Ohio. Our city tenement was so small even without children. We dreamed of the farmland and open spaces we knew in Europe, but once we had our son, it was not so easy to set off on such a long journey. Nicolaus, named after the uncle I never met, was sick with dyspepsia in his earliest years. Our living space grew smaller, and there the three of us lived for over a decade. Maria, and by this time she was Mary, sewed for others, and I worked outside the house, and occasionally as a cartwright—a trade I'd learned in the old country. When 1861 arrived—with it the War—it made even less sense for us to uproot the family. But trapped in the overcrowded tenements of New York City, the appeal of the old country—with its many pastures, and the sweet, cool air of its alpine meadows—invaded my thoughts, as did fear and uncertainty for our future.

"But everything changed when the War came. I was thirty-seven. My son, Nicolaus, was almost ten and was healthy as a stallion by that time. Our second child, our daughter Eva, your great grandmother," as he nodded to Dad, "was in her mother's womb, although we did not know it at the time." He stood for the moment in the rays of the morning sun that passed with some difficulty through his form.

"Our dreams of a large family drifted away years earlier. We Germans by that time had a thriving community of immigrants in many New York City neighborhoods. We were new and ardent Americans. We spoke German and most of us struggled to understand the language of our adopted country. How we believed in the promise of America, and we émigrés were almost all fervent Abolitionists. We detested slavery. We believed in freedom and dignity for all." He smiled and looked at everyone. Then he turned to face the southerly windows and filled his pipe.

"I shall never forget the day when, with my best friend Johan Hoffmann, or 'Hansy' as everyone knew him," Opa winked at Louis as if to say *Yes, mein Liebster, another Hansy*, "we swore we were sober, and signed up with the 29th New York Volunteer Infantry Regiment. Company A. We were paid well to join and promised even more money for later. And how our families were in need of that money! Mostly all German immigrants, we were now mustered for duty down South, barely three weeks since Fort Sumter was attacked. They called us the Astor Rifles—Astor Place was near enough—though at the time we had only been handed old muskets. Twenty-year-old muskets! It did not matter so much, since no one expected the rebellion to last for more than a few weeks. We believed we would be back home by Christmas.

"Patriotic passions took hold of New York City, and the first regiments were raised to quell the rebellion. Our regiment was mustered over only two days in early June, the fourth and the sixth. We were all eager to reach Virginia." Then, with a pause and a slight smile, he added, "Except for the fellas who deserted before we finally left."

Fellas? KC noted the southern flare to Opa's speech and wondered how he was heard by the others. For her anyway, he sounded quite local at that moment.

"The City gave us a grand sendoff on Friday, June twenty-first. There were bands that played and candies for the children who were all about us. There were flowers and great banners, and expectations for a quick victory over the traitors in Charleston and the others who joined them. Eleven slave-states had seceded.

"My wife, my beautiful wife, was drowning in sadness though, as she watched me that day at Elm Park on the northern part of Manhattan. We drilled while others were still enlisting. Our officers were strutting about like peacocks; all were proud veterans of European conflicts or the Mexican War. Our colonel, Baron Adolph von Steinwehr, was there with his company commander." Anton paused with these words. Then for the boys, he gestured over to their dad and quipped, "The colonel had a hairline not unlike your own, *mein Herr*." Then he cocked his eyebrow, smiled a warm smile, and finally winked.

"Finally at one o'clock in the afternoon, we paraded down Broadway and reached the City Hall. Proclamations were read while thousands of people stood under a warm rain. We were promised new shoes and new guns just as soon as we got to Virginia. Then we continued on to the docks, where we boarded the ferry that would take us to the trains for Washington. In the deep crowd I saw Mary weeping. As I raised my arm to wave good-bye, I noticed my son standing tall beside her, as if at attention. Then he proudly saluted his father. I will never forget that moment, a moment of time that is riveted to my mind." Opa took a breath and a sudden look of sadness came over him. He cocked an eyebrow and looked to Louis as if for permission to continue. None was needed. "And for all these years, *mein Liebster*, I have longed for my son.

"The love. The pride. The sadness of leaving my family. We journeyed south by train to answer the President's call for troops to defend Washington. As we passed through Philadelphia and then Baltimore, many more German units joined us. We were the volunteers. The Irish came in similar numbers to our own, and so many of us shared the passion of grand liberal ideals that were brought over from Europe. Values we embraced even more freely now, and more strongly, here in our New World of America.

"And together, as Americans, we finally arrived in the nation's capital. There we stayed in the U.S. Capitol building itself, the great seat of our government, its Great Dome not yet completed, and spent our first night there on the floor of the Senate chambers. We Germans sang and sang: 'Das Morgenrot,' 'Soldatenmut,' songs especially dear to my former homeland of Wuerttemberg. We drank our beer that night under the great unfinished dome of the people, the Rotunda.

"We soldiers, the Congress, and the general public all believed at the time that the war would be short. But for most of the rebellion, almost four years, that Capitol building was used as a military barracks as well as a hospital and even a bakery.

"And what a night it was. The next day, we moved on and occupied Camp Dorsheimer. There we helped finish with its construction. Newly arrived troops from all over the North were filling the camps that faced in all directions from Washington. We were especially concerned with which way Maryland would go with the string of secessions. A mob attacked our troops in Baltimore. Others cut rail and telegraph lines to the North.

"A few weeks later, our regiment moved on to Arlington Heights, an area where the earliest fortifications had been thrown up. With no regard for property or possessions, owners or occupants, trenches were cut through the earth, forests were taken down, and encampments set up. All the bridges and junctions had to be protected. Fort Albany, where my fate would be sealed four years later, guarded the rear of Fort Runyon, located at the important crossroads of Alexandria and Columbia turnpikes.

"The inexperienced Irwin McDowell was given command of Union forces south of the Potomac River, and the Army of the Potomac, as it became known to history, had as its heart our Army of Northeastern Virginia." Opa looked proud and almost relieved to share his story.

"Weeks passed and my bounties were unpaid; my young son was home supporting his mother. Nicolaus, too, was a color mixer of paints, as I had been, and was also a possemantier of fringes who, together with his mother, sewed and sold articles. Together they were able to survive. But Mary was now frail with common illnesses and pregnancy, and the happiness we shared, that Mary was with child after so many years, was truly overshadowed by the fear that our new baby could kill her.

"And down South, there was no action for months. There was boredom, watery beer, and drills. We traded coffee and tobacco. We played card games and checkers and dominos. We slept in relative comfort, compared to the days that would come in the small tents. As I said, our men and officers were almost all Germans. A few were not. And we existed as one. Then, things began to heat up." He puffed on his pipe for a long moment, in reflection. He smiled and moved in the direction of the old bentwood, which was tucked away with the boxes and clutter of the last century.

"By the middle of June, we were ready to fight the Rebels. There was a great camaraderie among us, and morale was high. In spite of shortages of clothing and shoes, these were good, happy times. The coffee was strong and the bacon was tasty. Still, most of us were sad to be without our families, and no one had been properly paid.

"Then suddenly we found ourselves in the midst of savage fighting. Most of us had never been shot at before. And except for the Prussian von Steinwehr, and our officers, all the rest of us were unseasoned soldiers.

"In those days, Manassas Junction was where the Manassas Gap and the Orange and Alexandria railroads met. It was near a not-so-easily-fordable creek called Bull Run." He sounded like a Southerner for the moment, though his lips did not move. "At the time it was called the Great Skedaddle. After forced marches, heat prostration, and the like, our Union Army—the Federals—having finally been given the chance to fight and vanquish the enemy, experienced instead great confusion on the battlefield."

Opa looked at no one really as he continued to slowly pace around the attic space. Charley, prodded by his father, walked to the rocker, where he set about to remove and position it for the ghost to sit. Opa politely signaled that he was fine, and remained standing.

"No one planned to fight there on Henry House Hill. And unlike our own regiment, with terms of enlistment for two years, many of the Federals were only ninety-day volunteers, with even less training than we had, and whose enlistments were just about up.

"The Virginia worm fences snaked their ways and marked off the surrounding fields. Birds chirped and nature simply went about its business. Berries ripened. Luscious smells of greenery smothered the senses. Hawks glided over the farm fields. They swooped and made tasty meals of the small rodents they caught. There were oak groves off to the sides of the hollows, fragrant pines and saplings in all shades of green, and sweet, sweet cornfields. This beautiful pastureland of Prince William County, common in these parts of Virginia, was so reminiscent of the rich Swabian meadows of my past, and picked by chance that day to serve as an open-ground battlefield of death.

"There had been smaller skirmishes before then, but the First Bull Run was the first big battle of the War. By 9:30 the sun had already been up for hours. Both sides took the offensive, trying to outflank each other. And in the stifling heat, muskets were lowered and fired. With no standard provision for a bayonet, our smooth-bores were still deemed excellent for both 'close work' and long ranges, and were more accurate than pistols, or rifle-muskets, and even many carbines. Yes, we were well armed, though we had little instruction beyond how to load and fire.

"By midday it looked like the Federals were going to win it and that the rebellion would be over. The Rebels had ragtag equipment. They were outnumbered and outgunned. But the air and the smoke were thick with the smells of gunpowder and sweat that Sunday morning. Mounted warfare raged around us, and everywhere there were bodies of strange troops. One artillery battery changed hands five times that afternoon. With a glimpse of a flag you would know where to volley. Training in drill had been minimal. 'Whose men are these?' you would hear in both German and English.

"It ended at dusk. Many soldiers threw down their weapons and scattered. Most did not. Some collected abandoned gear as souvenirs, or to replace their own stuff. There was panic among teamsters and spirited civilians, mostly from Washington, who had taken up to picnic at Centerville. There were nine hundred men killed and three thousand wounded that Sunday, that bloody Sunday: July 21, 1861. Our nightmares described what words could not.

"Finally our brigade stood between the Rebels and our nation's capital; the 29th Infantry protected the flanks and guarded the main road that carried our defeated army forty miles west, back to Washington. It took two days for us to get to Bull Run, and only one day in reverse the very next day. Some of our troops used the same narrow country roads to return from the battlefield as they did to get there, when they picked berries along the roadsides, drew easy water from wells and from springs, and marched leisurely into the fight. The Rebels might have succeeded in capturing Washington, had they continued to push, but they themselves were disorganized, and in the end we stood our ground. We skirmished with their cavalry. Blood was spilled.

"Our regiment lost forty-six men to guns and desertion, mostly desertion. Combat did not suit many men. And though this was without a doubt a great defeat for the Union, our men steadfastly defended the Warrenton Turnpike, and in doing so we allowed our troops to stream into the city for days. There the saloons filled up with skylarkers and many men who had gone AWOL. Southern sympathizers celebrated. Thousands of our men stumbled into the nation's capital, hungry and demoralized." His audience hung on every word, every expression. KC felt it was almost hypnotic.

"Once everyone sobered up, General McDowell was replaced and the Union had a new commander, 'Little Mac' McClellan, a term not always used with endearment. The twenty-ninth returned to duty in the defense of Washington, and Little Mac—this 'Young Napoleon' was only thirty-five years old at the time—assumed the tasks of organizing and retraining the Union Army. Calm returned. At Arlington Heights, outposts and new works were added to connect all the western defenses, from Key Bridge down to Fort Albany. Yes, George B. McClellan's arrival dramatically changed the framework of our army."

Anton stretched for a moment, then reached into a pocket and removed his heavenly scented tobacco. "From our vantage point those days we could see Rebel guns nearby on Munson's Hill, along with a giant Confederate flag waving over them in the breeze. It was two months before we found out that those cannons were nothing more than 'Quaker Guns'—wooden logs painted black at the muzzle to look like real artillery pieces." Anton smiled to himself, and then continued. "A few were mounted on real gun carriages. The ruse delayed Union assaults on those positions and probably prolonged the War.

"By now both North and South realized the War would be a long one anyway. And while our government gave us grand reviews to boost morale—we were told by our new general there were 10,000 new volunteers—we knew what we knew and the mood had changed. Bull Run was an awful reminder of what was to be; men had by that time even bought the area as a tourist attraction.

"The Rebels and even a lot of northern folks didn't think much of us foreigner soldiers when the War was young, but in time they learned to respect us. And for all who lived and died there on the battlefields of Virginia, a bloody code of honor was shared amongst both sides.

"Army life for my best friend Hansy and me was Company A. Ten companies of a hundred men made up a regiment. The 29th Infantry, minus those we had already lost, was about eight hundred men at the time. The regiments made the brigades that made the divisions that made the corps. Our shared experience brought us closer than ever as comrades and fellow privates. We were told when to eat, when to drink, bathe, and wash our feet. We were told when to sleep. For all of us, Colonel von Steinwehr was like a stern but fair father. He helped us through. We were blind men without him.

"We were assigned to the 1st Brigade—Blenker's Brigade—named after its commanding brigadier general. Louis Blenker was a commander of the Bavarian Legion back in Germany, and was a member of the Revolutionary Government of 1848. He came to America after being exiled, first from Germany and then from Switzerland." Anton looked down to young Louis with a warm smile and then turned to KC. "Our regiment fell under the divisional command of the famous Fighting Joe Hooker from your own home state of Massachusetts.

"Now, do you all want to hear all this?" The man paused for an answer. He looked for some reassurance.

There was a resounding "Yes" by the males, which collectively drowned out KC's own intended vote. So, with a deferential nod to KC, Opa continued.

"Hansy and I had been friends since meeting years earlier on the Lower East Side of the City. He was a Bavarian, and lived nearby with his young wife. We vowed that if we should survive the War, we'd do our best to bring our children together in marriage. A strong bond emerged between our families, and survived for generations. Both my son Nicolaus and my daughter Eva married children of Hansy and Ilse." Then, looking down in the direction of Charley and Louis, Anton smiled sweetly and added, "Eva and John Hoffmann are your forebears."

There was an assortment of *oohs* and *aahs* from Opa's small audience.

"Months passed. Christmas. Boredom was cruel at times but would be no match for the cruelty that lay ahead. In March and April '62, well into the New Year and with the fighting season again upon us, the 29th Regiment, now part of the 2nd Brigade of Blenker's Division, was organized under the 2nd Corps of the Army of the Potomac, the main fighting force in the Eastern Theatre of what we struggled to concede was a civil war.

"The twenty-ninth remained with the Defenses of Washington until April 1862. That was when the Shenandoah Valley Campaign began in Virginia, and Blenker's Division pursued Stonewall Jackson's men like bulldogs. Those days were some of the worst ever. We carried everything on our backs through the mud, and lived in 'dog tents' when we sheltered. Those tents, named so, could comfortably accommodate one dog, and a small one at that.

"Now the army camps were for us an even worse enemy than the Rebels. Malady, disease, and filth caused more than half the wartime deaths. The camps were littered with human refuse, manure, slops and offal, and other rubbish. Young soldiers who had never been exposed to common contagion were the most vulnerable and fell in great numbers.

"In June '62 at Cross Keys, our division—Blenker's Division—tried to surround the Rebel General Ewell's men. We were within easy musket range before we were driven back. We suffered eight men wounded or missing. They were all men I knew. By nightfall we put it all behind us and played checkers at the campfire. Our tents were dry. Our bedrolls were warm. And these things provided great comfort.

"The next day, near Port Republic, the twenty-ninth lost ten more men, dead or missing. We fought with clubs and bayonets that day, as well as with our muskets. Skirmishes continued and we crossed the Shenandoah.

"Two weeks later we became part of the 1st Corps of the new Army of Virginia, under General Franz Sigel, a graduate of the German Military Academy, a northern German who also fought in our German Revolution of 1848. When the war started, Sigel was a community leader and a director of schools over in Missouri, a border state. Sigel's commander was John Pope, the general that President Lincoln personally selected to lead the Federals, and the man now chosen to face the deadly combination of Robert E. Lee's strategy and Stonewall Jackson's tactics."

"That was Abraham Lincoln, right, Opa?" offered Charley.

"Yes, *mein Liebster.*" Anton took a breath, not an especially deep one, but a long one. He took an equally long puff on his pipe, and as he did he repeated the name of John Pope. "May God rest his soul," he said, "but that man...really pissed off the troops, as people would say today." He smiled as if he were proud to have spoken such slang. Then, still smiling for his speechless audience, he continued. "He said he would lead us from the saddle, and he made a grand speech for us to hear. He boasted of his time in the

West, where he said he always had seen the backside of his ene-
mies. This general vowed to look before us and not behind. Men
later said that John Pope's hindquarters were where his headquar-
ters should have been. Our company commander translated the
whole speech for us, and all in all it—the speech—was quite good:
forcefully delivered by a fine and soldierly horseman. But a man
who made us pine for General McClellan.

"With the reorganization of the units, General Blenker lost his
command and clashed with McClellan. Our regiment's commander, von Steinwehr, was promoted and assumed divisional command under General Sigel.

"Our short-lived Army of Virginia was then soundly defeated at
the Second Bull Run. Pope's actions were solid at first, but his talk of
'success and glory' rang hollow. There were impossible orders, and
the failures to obey them. Some spoke of conspiracy and intrigue. For
whatever reason, Pope lost complete control of the situation, and the
Second Bull Run ended on August thirtieth, 1862. The bulk of our
troops were able to retreat across that Bull Run stream and Stone
Bridge, famed from the last battle, and by way of some neighboring
fords. It was another defeat for the North and for our Union. Robert
E. Lee succeeded in driving our forces back to the defenses of Washington, though, fortunately, tactical failures on the parts of Jackson
and that 'Old War Horse,' Pete Longstreet, deprived him of the
opportunity to destroy the Federal Army.

"My regiment, the twenty-ninth, took over 150 casualties, with
twenty-six dead and many others wounded, including Colonel Soest,
the man who replaced von Steinwehr. How awful it was. With neither
food nor rest, our regiment endured steady action for over five hours,
and exchanged fire till we managed to regroup and finally rejoin our
brigade. Our little encounter at the unfinished railroad on a line
between the Manassas-Sudley and Groveton-Sudley roads was one of
the fiercest little skirmishes of the War.

"Friends of mine were dead and maimed. Rough slats of
uneven wood marked the graves. Surgeons worked in barns and in
houses like this—churches too—to save the wounded, most often
by amputation. I recall one man, a northern Rhinelander, was
amputated twice. His fortitude was remarkable.

"The next day, the thirtieth, Pope tried again to breach the
Confederate lines, and we were gradually overwhelmed by their

counterattack. Our brigade fought a delaying action while other elements of our army fell back. We tried to blunt their advance, and after our brigade commander was killed, we fell back toward the Warrenton Turnpike.

"Nearly everyone believed General Pope suffered for us a decisive defeat. He was relieved on September the second. The Army of Virginia was merged into General McClellan's Army of the Potomac, and General Sigel's divisions from its 1st Corps now formed the 11th Corps. Once again, McClellan was in charge and heading up our army, and that included our 29th Regiment of the 1st Brigade, 2nd Division. Folks knew us as 'The German Corps' because of our high number of German-speaking units; some derisively labeled us 'Flying Dutchmen.' We knew ourselves, throughout our service with the Army of the Potomac, as the 'hard luck outfit.'"

"Wow," said Mom as all kinds of images danced around her brain. From the moment she saw him, and once they got past the initial introductions—he the kindly "old man" and she the mom of Louis the young boy—she found him exceedingly warm and familiar.

"But what about the three things?" asked KC. The men were all caught up with the war stories that followed his earliest remarks. Or were they just stories? For the first time KC noticed images alive on the old mirror, like old vintage film, and to these old images her family was fixed. Anton's stories and imagery alternated from spoken word to telepathy while pictures danced around on the mirror. Opa's narratives were taking the flavor of a private home theatre.

The family sat enthralled with the tales of Anton Dietrich's regiment and the battles of Bull Run. KC for one was thoroughly connected to the man. She felt his tenderness and his honest manner. *Disarming environment.* KC loved him like a father she never knew, and as *the* father she had never known. There, finally seated in the bentwood rocker, he used his graceful motions and soft words to describe a life that was lived 150 years ago. And she wondered half aloud, "What are those three things, Anton?"

Though it should have seemed remarkable to her, KC knew now that after this, there was nothing that would ever surprise her again. As she watched her sons and husband affixed on Anton and on the mirror, she asked once again, and this time a little louder, though not so loud as to be impolite, "What are the three things...that keep you here?"

It seemed he had not heard her.

"We lost a number of officers and men over the following months. By September our regiment was less than three hundred remaining for field duty. In addition to casualties, we lacked reinforcements and supplies, and our pay. One month later, and as was the case with so many other soldiers of this era, I fell victim, not to the enemy's bullet, but to sickness and disease. Many comrades succumbed to cholera, typhoid fever, or pneumonia. For me it was consumption, a lung infection of which we knew practically nothing in those days. You know it today as tuberculosis, or just TB, as your modern world seems to be so fond of abbreviations, right?" Everyone nodded blankly. "And after sixteen months in service to my country, my company's muster roll reported me sick from October thirteenth, 1862."

"That's my half birthday," Louis exclaimed.

Opa nodded. "We, the afflicted, were kept apart from people and encouraged to rest and get lots of sunshine and fresh air. We were packed together in this very attic space, weak with fever. Some were emaciated and all of us were closer to God, with plenty of sunshine, heat, and stale air. We were brought outside at times of day and night that would not mingle us with those whose lungs were clean. There were no medications for TB back then. Opium, morphine, and quinine were used by camp doctors and nurses to deal with a wide variety of different medical conditions, but these drugs often brought on problems of their own." After a long pause, Opa added, "I understand that these days there are much better treatments for TB." As if for effect, though everyone knew it wasn't, Opa let pass a slight cough.

And with those words, KC could see that Anton was laboring to continue, as if he were both emotionally and physically drained. His intensity had begun to fade.

"It's getting late. We should be going," she offered.

"It's not late, Mom," said Louis.

"It's getting late," insisted Mom. There was plenty of love and respect, intrigue and sadness, and warmth, and a slight chill when the tired ghost slowly disappeared.

CHAPTER

29

*A*ll that time in the attic and it seemed the clock had hardly moved. It was still early morning! So that was how Louis had managed these encounters so easily, thought Mom. "And how he could learn so much stuff from Opa," she murmured to no one in particular, though Oona came to mind for an instant, followed by Dad and the kids, who were not very far away.

Within moments Thankful was in her father's arms, and the routines of normal life for a family of five took hold of the household.

Indeed, time stopped for Anton. KC needed now just to chill—to go sit in her favorite chair and watch a little TV for a while. *As if Heaven puts time on pause to let the poor soul speak with us.*

Time passed easily in the family room. It remained touched with sunlight when she awoke from an unplanned and very pleasant nap. The birds sang outside. And the reason why she was so calm and relaxed at this moment had more to do with Louis' mental health and well-being than her own. Her dear son was vindicated and somehow served as a channel to a dead relative—her own connection through marriage of course—and another world so fantastic that anyone outside her intimate circle would think them all crazy. How could she ever tell her mother such a thing? How could she tell her friends—her best friend, Vicki—or any one of them? Anaïs? *Well, maybe Anaïs could be told.* Maybe Anaïs would believe her. She was, after all, into Tarot cards and that sort of thing.

113

Yes, she'd believe. But the others? No way! The friends back home already thought she was crazy to have left Westbridge in such a hurry. Now, how could she tell them about a lovable ghost in their new attic?

For the here and now, KC stood up on the cool hardwood and walked out into the hallway. The place was quieter than usual it seemed, as if everyone had gone on in their own directions. *And how about the people I used to work with?*

First to emerge was her husband.

Would those people ever believe her?

"Honey, time seemed so...regular up there, didn't it?" she asked. "Let's be sure to check our watches and cell phones the next time we're upstairs with the old guy."

"You got it." He looked like he just woke up. "Hey, uh. What about lunch? I'm pretty hungry," he said.

"I suppose everyone will be thinking about lunch pretty soon. But did you notice that the clocks had barely moved after we left Anton?"

"I didn't notice but with all the shit that was going on, you've gotta figure that far stranger stuff has happened." The couple entered the kitchen and noticed Charley was sprawled out nearby on the white wicker couch that sat out on the porch. Thankful napped beside him.

And where was Louis? "If the clock moved fifteen minutes, I'd be surprised," KC said as she started to prepare some sandwiches on the granite counters she so loved. "Didn't we go up around 7:30?" Lunchtime always produced an eclectic assortment for various moods and tastes. "You know there's a lot of unfinished business up there," she continued.

There was no argument there. No argument. None at all. Her husband was deep in thought.

"I mean, God! It's still morning. It's only 11:30!" KC's hazel eyes invited her husband to say something. Anything.

"You know, we can't just let this guy rule over us," he finally said.

"What?" KC looked at her husband, expressionless, with her full face and bleached hair in sharp contrast to the maple wood cabinet behind her.

"I mean, we're so busy," he said with forced purpose.

"So busy?" KC was surprised with where this conversation seemed to be headed.

He shrugged like a tired old man. "It's kind of weird."

"Huh." She stopped as if to carefully plot her next words. Then she sternly announced, "He's your relative!"

"I'll bet those witches on your side of the family had something to do with this...with Louis. You can't deny that." He looked tired and serious.

"Stick it," she shot back. *Twenty-three in all, but only one by marriage.* "We've got to help him. We've got to."

"Look. Don't get me wrong. I love the old guy."

"He's younger than you are, you jerk. What's wrong with you?" KC was ready to call a time-out for lunch. She wiped her hands on a nearby towel. *All set for lunch.*

"I just don't need this problem. There's too much: work, the kids, you..." He sounded overwhelmed.

"Me?"

"I don't need another problem, hon. This whole thing is crazy and people are gonna think *we're* crazy. I'm supposed to be at my new job, and I'm spending more and more time tracing my freaky ancestor. People are gonna think I'm fucking off."

"Well then, consider yourself lucky that you are a federal worker. Fucking off is institutionalized there. Isn't that what you used to say," she paused, "before you became one of...them?" The last word was dramatically emphasized.

"That, at least, is not the same as the kind of fucking your former bank bosses do to people. Oh, no."

It was really time to call everyone for lunch. With a steady voice, KC said, "Look, calm down. Let's call the kids."

"I am calm. I just see a whole lot of work on this stuff, and I don't even know what it's gonna be. I just know it, though. There's gonna be a lot of time on this. And a lot of bullshit." Dad looked in despair. "Hey, do you think he hears us?"

"So what if he could." KC looked to her husband with honest eyes, and could see he was torn. "He's on our side. I can tell, and so can you."

The two then seriously discussed their morning encounter. They agreed to return to the attic after church the next morning, not to be consumed with the affair and, for as much and as long as possible, conduct business as usual, both at home and at work. They speculated that putting too much attention on this paranormal phenomenon could traumatize their boys. And especially with Louis, they'd gently discourage solo trips in favor of regular, scheduled family encounters with Opa. They hoped all this would work, and that this event would be no different than handling other family challenges. Yes, the parents would attempt to manage visits and assist the ghost with whatever it was that needed to be done in order to free him. And for now at least the last few weekends of their summer would have to do.

Once the boys were at the lunch table, promises were made to follow rules, help Opa, and enjoy the rest of the summer like kids are supposed to do. For KC, normalcy in the house, with a plan to help Anton, met her needs. The boys seemed most interested for Anton to just continue with his story, and promised not to share the adventure with the babysitter. Collectively everyone insisted they'd return to the attic the very next day. Even Zupper barked her approval.

CHAPTER
CHAPTER
30

"I love you to death, Anton, but where's the beef?" She loved him and wanted to grab him and insist he reveal why this was all happening. Sounding exasperated, KC asked, "What's the point of it all, Opa?"

There was no telling how long they had been there. Her cell phone displayed time when she wanted it to as an analog clock, and time trudged along so slowly that the second hand moved barely faster than a normal minute hand. Time seemed to fly when with him, but it really crawled. *A barely noticeable movement of time.* She really adored the old guy—the "old guy" who, when he died, was actually younger than her own husband. She just wanted to cut through some of his babble in order to arrive at what was needed, and to plan accordingly. She *had* to plan for things. Chances were that helping Anton would disrupt some of the family's routines, especially as they prepared for kindergarten and school only a few weeks away.

Again, it seemed as if he had not heard.

"In ways I was one of the lucky ones. With commencing tuberculosis, contracted since my recruitment, and stricken with other afflictions, including hemorrhoids that were quite severe in those times, I was treated first at the Fairfax Seminary Hospital in Fairfax. In those days, Fairfax lay about twenty miles west of Washington. There I remained until January '63, when I was sent here to this very house to convalesce. The hands of kindness weighed heavily on my soul, and I pulled through. When I died, I returned here. For the penitent, it became my purgatory."

Finally? she hoped.

A stifled chuckle from Charley was quickly followed with a thick and sudden silence. Opa winked for all to see and cocked his right eyebrow. Then, with a slight crinkle of his ghostly nose, he continued. As the conversation advanced, his form grew brighter and more distinct, better all around.

"The point is," as he turned to KC, "I convalesced here, in this place...in this attic, a long, long time ago. I was very sick and my life was saved at this house. I was transferred to a station camp in January and a convalescent camp the next month. In Fairfax Seminary, I was finally discharged for disability on February seventh, '63, and finally shipped back to New York City. There were over one quarter million men honorably discharged for physical disabilities arising from wounds, accidents, or disease. I'd finally be home with my family after months here and in Washington and Arlington.

"Contraband camps—where former slaves were kept—dotted the area at the time I left for New York. And while I would be most happy to see my family, it was still with mixed emotions to leave my comrades who now, by the power of President Lincoln's famous proclamation from January first of that year, were the armed liberators of those poor, emancipated souls. Our soldiers were thus given small placards with Lincoln's words inscribed in miniature right on them. I didn't read much English in my life, but I knew what those words meant: that Black folk were free at last, and that our men were the ones who were letting them go.

"How it sparked life into my weary body when I saw, for the very first time in my life, my beautiful daughter Eva. She was already a year old. After I returned home, I eventually healed and regained my strength. There I was officially mustered out of the service alongside my former comrades, months later, on June 20, 1863.

"On that day, the 29th Regiment was honorably discharged and mustered out under Colonel Louis Hartmann He led my company at the outset of the war, rose through the ranks, from captain to major, and on to lieutenant colonel, having taken command of the whole regiment at the Second Bull Run. His success suggests my company performed well in its military duties." He smiled contentedly and drew on his pipe. The fragrance was rich and inviting.

With plenty of color and detail, and background befitting a Disneyesque rendition, Anton related through his lips and his mind and projected depictions onto the old mirror. As he described the expiry of his two-year term and the gumption of comrades, Charley alertly arranged the old mirror on its side for a wide-screen viewing effect. Mom lifted her eyebrows slightly, as if to object, and while she managed to mildly glare at her older son, she was privately happy with his initiative.

"Sssh," whispered Dad, to keep the noise at an absolute minimum. "Let Opa continue."

"As with other war veterans who returned to civilian life while the rebellion continued unabated, we remained comrades and shared in the hard memories of Virginia. We endured more than our share of army hardships, and for now, the War went on without us.

"Then the Battle of Gettysburg began on July first. There were talks and rumors. Things were unsettled. On July thirteenth, draft riots broke out across the City, and the immigrant communities were no exception. These lasted for four days until troops returning from Gettysburg put down the riots, which, I'm still sad to say, reminded me of my last days in Munich.

"Mary was always a gentle mother to Eva and to Nicolaus, who was age twelve by then, but at this time my wife was quite frail. Eva was only eighteen months in August of '63, and right around the age of your little one." Anton smiled slightly and waved his briarwood pipe in the direction of little Thankful. "And we were poor, very poor."

Charley studied the man as he winked at his little sister. "How cool is all this?" he whispered. *The kids back home would never believe it. Sitting around, with the family ghost telling me about his life and the Civil War. This is just too cool.* "Get to the good part, Opa," he said. His hazel eyes, just like his mom's, sparkled.

"The killing stuff?" Louis asked, as if he directed the question to Opa.

"Louis!" admonished his mother.

The boys, Louis and Charley, laughed as if they shared a private joke.

Seemingly oblivious to his chatty audience, Opa continued in a steady voice. "On October third, 1863, President Lincoln declared the fourth Thursday in November as Thanksgiving Day, a national holiday. I heard that the Rebels held their fire while our soldiers feasted. We Americans needed something from Mr. Lincoln, and this surely helped our country's morale. A few weeks later my family, the four of us, celebrated Christmastime as best as we could, in the German traditions of the time, with smells of German cooking that wafted through the air where we made our home at 306 East 13th Street, Manhattan.

"I managed to recover my health, as I said. My consumption subsided earlier that year, and I started a candy business, where I remained Anton the Confectioner for nine months." He smiled and winked at Thankful, who walked now to the comfort of her portable car seat. "Fortunately, and for me as well as my customers, the tuberculosis had healed."

"She has your eyes, your deep-set eyes," KC said, then smiled with a wink of her own. "But Thankful's are blue."

Opa looked slowly to everyone and, smiling down again to Thankful, he said, "I'm told her water blue eyes will one day be a deep and beautiful gray." He knew it was a peculiar remark, but no one seemed to mind it.

"With the Conscription Act still menacing men age eighteen to forty-five, and after only a year of civilian life, with young children and a sick wife at home, I decided to reenlist rather than risk being drafted."

"What's drafted mean?" inquired Louis. "What's re-en—?"

"Forced to serve…in the Army, Louis," chimed his dad.

"*Ja wohl!*" chimed Opa.

"A military draft," resumed Dad. "Hey, Anton, how could they draft you? You had already served."

"After almost fifteen years in America, I am sorry to say I did not fully understand the ways of my new country or our rulers. Confusion and rumors had hung over our 'Little Germany' neighborhoods and households since that summer. Our communities simply did not know much about our country's laws and, for that matter, the rules of our state or our city. How could we? The War only made things worse.

"I tried, unsuccessfully at first, to get my best friend Hansy to

120

come with me. The bounties and the promises of money bonuses that were paid for volunteers, which were quite generous for my family, but not generous enough to take Hansy from his wife and baby son, a young boy who in time grew to manhood and married my Eva. But over the time of a few days and more than a few beers, he relented. He gave way to my cajoling and I have never forgiven myself for it." He drew a breath, it seemed, and looked at his audience. "On the ninth day of February, 1864, at forty years old and mostly jobless—the candy business could no longer support my family—and together with Hansy, I reenlisted, this time with the 15th New York Heavy Artillery Regiment.

"After a year at home with so little pay, I signed on for a promised bonus and three months of advance pay. My wife and baby needed me, no doubt, but the family would be much better off with money in such a handsome amount. It would have taken far longer to earn such pay in New York, even in the best of times. Gettysburg was months behind us, and we hoped that the War's end was near. Our president's visit there still inspired us, and though at the time I did not fully understand his words—with the language and all—I do know now that his Gettysburg Address stands unequalled in its simple elegance and class.

"My reenlistment term began for three years, one day before my baby Eva's second birthday. No one knew exactly when the War would end, and so began the final chapter of my life.

"The fifteenth comprised men from all over New York and Philadelphia. There were only a few Germans in our Company, Company L. As you may know, those of our nationality were well-regarded artillerists. I was fated to drive an ammunition train, laden with missiles and projectiles of all shape and size, which would be used to vanquish the Rebels. By the end of February 1864, my regiment headed south.

"Hansy joined the regiment as a gunner and shortly thereafter blew himself to bits while moving a crate of heavy projectiles. The explosion killed a number of other men, and nothing was left of any of them, really." With another puff of his pipe, he added, "The accident occurred before Hansy poured even a single volley into the enemy." Extreme sadness filled the face of the ghost.

Silence.

121

"From what I received in her letters, Mary said our children were well. The money helped and Nicolaus worked steady in the factory. Eva grew and was a beautiful sight, I was told. And of that I had no doubt. Mary promised a picture. It was hard, going down South again, barely three years from when I first joined the infantry. But my country still needed me, and the money surely provided for my family.

"As it was, I saw things through. I was at Appomattox Court-house, where the War's final engagement ended in April '65. I died two years later, hundreds of miles from here and almost 140 years ago."

CHAPTER
31

Over the next few days, the attic resembled more of a family room, with the trappings, toys, and comforts of the kids strewn about, and punctuated with several chew toys and rawhide bones for the dog. What began with the family's first encounter quickly evolved into regular visits. While her husband worked, KC and Louis—whose attendance was believed to be necessary for Anton, who was never visible unless Louis was there—and usually Charley and Thankful, when her daughter wasn't busy napping or terrorizing the house, were all in the attic at least once a day and sometimes more. And regardless of who was there, Opa's presence was felt at all times.

Opa was fixed in the attic, at least for the time being, and his tale continued. KC noticed that Anton was telling his saga in a number of ways: first through Louis hearing and then repeating his words; then when stated directly and at times spoken telepathically; and at other times as graphic depictions on the old mirror. It seemed pretty clear that Anton was approaching the end of his story, and she accepted this and remained determined to get the reasons for his story as soon as possible. It was August already and usually quite hot outside by late morning. The attic was sunny and also hot, though when Anton was present, a slight coolness swirled in the air about him.

By Friday the whole family was ready once again to make the ascent. The whole week saw quite a lot of traffic to and from the attic space. Now, following dinner, the family, one by one, with Dad carrying Thankful across his chest, made their way and took their seats upstairs. The hanging yellow light bulb, switched on to flood the entire attic space, mimicked the daytime, except for the dark black rectangles that filled the windows there.

KC knew that Anton was ready, and he solemnly began to speak.

"As my soul is saved here now, I must achieve Three Great Thresholds before I can move on to the Light and toward my ultimate redemption. My First Threshold was achieved when I gained the unconditional love of my little man." He gestured over to Louis and winked. "I knew this was so when he first noticed me and trusted me." The smile filled Opa's face with expression. "He loved me without pause and, in fact, gave me the power to appear in his presence."

There were smiles all around, none who beamed more broadly than the ghost. He paused and then with his mouth drew deeply on his pipe. He slowly exhaled the sweetly scented smoke.

"The Second Threshold requires earthly redemption for a young and distant cousin of yours. Frank Lowry is a fourth great grandson to me, and now a war veteran sleeping rough in Boston."

"Homeless?" asked KC.

"Yes, and in danger, even as we speak." There was no smile on Opa's lips.

The words hung in the air. *He waits here for his redemption,* KC thought. *Oona had said all that.* "So helping this cousin helps you. Is that right, Opa?" she asked. She was certain of his answer. Things crazily all began to make sense to KC, but it was still so unbelievable. So remarkable. Opa would leave his purgatory here and go on into the Light. "And why do you need redemption?" she asked softly and clearly. "What happened?"

"My third and final Threshold is met once my earthly remains are removed to hallowed ground. Ultimate redemption requires this."

KC's brow was furrowed in thought. Her eyes twinkled. "And that caused you, our ghostly ancestor, to require redemption?" she asked.

"The unmarked grave, and what begot it, and what would lead to this all, yes."

"And what about the homeless man?" she asked. KC was desperate to stay on track and on focus. She looked lawyerly. Her manners were crisp, yet loving.

"Tell us about the War, Opa, and beating the Rebels." Charley was highly animated, and his eyes gleamed. Dad and Louis stridently concurred. Mom took a deep breath and settled back as if to relax in her chair for a moment. Charley wondered what this area looked like during the War. He wanted to climb to the roof and have a look. He'd never been up there. He wondered if Louis had been. *My little brother.*

"Charley!" admonished his mother.

Anton smiled to all and continued. "I was a teamster for an ammo train. I drove a horse-drawn wagon full of ammunition. It was lighter on my feet than the infantry, though we were often referred to as 'Foot Artillery,' and I was half deaf by that time anyway. So there we went, off again to Virginia with the new regiment. I never was the best soldier, but there were many far worse than I. And now, aside from the officers who led us, drivers like me were the ones Johnny Rebel shot at the most." In pause, he took a long puff on his pipe. The aroma was heavenly. "Of course the horses that pulled each gun also made inviting targets. Dead and wounded horses made our guns immovable.

"My English was still not so good, and as a second language, that hurt me from time to time. Unlike the twenty-ninth, the fifteenth was much more an 'American' unit. I missed the twenty-ninth more than I liked the fifteenth. I missed my old commanders, the use of our mother tongue, and the old customs. The twenty-ninth was like a German family of Catholics and Jews, and Evangelists, of Hessians, and Sauerlanders and Prussians."

"Anton. Let me ask you: What is going on here now?" KC looked and motioned around the attic space. "We can get back to Boston and the homeless man too, but what's going on in this attic?" Her face was kind in expression. Her words were firm.

"To make this all possible, I have had the help of the Scribes. In time I was able to influence some events, but doing so requires great strength. I am warm to the touch, yet coolness surrounds me, as when I wave my arms or move away. I can fade and be enriched by your love. But, as with millions of other poor souls, I could not pass into the Light when I died. For a variety of reasons, and as is

125

often the case, dead people sometimes enter an in-between place. Where one spends one's purgatory depends on one's transgressions or unfinished earthly business. For me, purgatory returned me to this house, where I slowly convalesced from consumption and the War's other wounds.

"My petition to pass into the Light has been 'in progress' for over a century. There are so many appeals in queue: lost or forgotten souls, victims and sufferers. This time has been an enormously long time for me to reflect, and to hope and pray for my petition to be heard."

"How long does it feel like?" Louis asked innocently.

"God's clock is quite different from humanity's, *mein Liebster*. It has, however, been a good time to practice my English." He winked.

KC noticed that Anton spoke telepathically. How remarkable this whole summer had been, she thought.

"So,"—his warm accent always made this word sound like "Zo"—"finally, Heavenly Scribes appeared to me, and working in threes—those fellas always work in trinities—they assisted me and helped my patience and my hope. Some Scribes were—are—heavenly messengers and doers of good things. Their deeds are done in Heaven and on Earth and," he looked around his attic prison, "in places in between. They support a heavenly bureaucracy from what they've told me, and their abilities are far greater than we can imagine. Scribes do so much more than write. The Scribes give all those like me hope and stamina. And for us to have joined together now, it's the Scribes who lent their 'assists,' which were specific to and critical for your relocation and transplantation here."

"Multi-taskers to the nth degree, I suppose," KC softly stated.

"Their first assist came when a hiring clerk at the National Archives noticed your husband's résumé and subsequently offered him his 'dream job' in Washington."

"Anton, you speak of 'assists' as if it were a basketball game," commented KC.

"Bas-ket-ball?" Anton slowly repeated.

"Never mind. What you're saying, I think, is that this whole thing—us moving down here and meeting you—was arranged through these Scribes."

"Yes, their assistance was necessary." Anton looked down slowly and paused; the air was sweet with fragrance from his tobacco. "There were three assists." Then, Opa looked to Louis, and the boy reached toward his ancestor and offered his opened bottled water. The ghost lifted it to his lips for a long moment and returned the bottle. Louis' blank-faced father looked on in disbelief.

"The second was when the previous owner of the Bornheim House suddenly decided to put this lovely, historic antebellum residence on the market. The third assist was in casting a small spell upon you, KC, to see the good in this old house over the more practical considerations, such as lack of closet space and the abundance of horsehair plaster." He coughed slightly and smiled. "And that, *meine Frau*, was by far the hardest of all for the Scribes to achieve." He gestured toward the heavens. "Or so I'm told."

Dad rose as if he had just had an epiphany, and he clearly announced, "It *was* as if this house just fell into our laps! The place was too good to be true! It had a ton of space and was just what the family needed."

CHAPTER
32

*S*tunned was the word. "Should we feel used or privileged?" KC asked her husband. Torn emotionally now, KC was also worn down physically. She felt offended that there was a lack of control over her own affairs, as if she were just a pawn in God's plan—His game. Then again, she thought, maybe she and her family should feel fortunate to be so close to such an awesome reality. But having always felt so sure of her adult self, KC wondered how, after these revelations, she could claim to be the master of her own destiny. *Just get past it and help the old guy get on with his own destiny,* she resolved. *It's the right thing to do. See it through.*

Her husband sipped his coffee. It was Saturday morning, and somehow the kids were all still in bed. He stared at his lovely wife but could offer her nothing. No words could describe his sense that he had led his family on a blind adventure, tearing them from their roots in New England. He felt despair and failure.

KC struggled to keep focused on the big picture: the whys and the wherefores. But how could she compete with the boys' love for their ancestor's history? *Here we are in late summer already, and there's still so much to know and to learn.* Meanwhile the stories continued.

"With the financial benefits of rejoining the Army, sufficient money was left with my family, who sorely needed it, and additional installments were promised. Money was hard to come by, whether one was inside or outside the military, and paydays were scarce in those days. Still, I bemoaned my reenlistment. It was not that the cause was less noble in 1864 than it was in 1861, but that this particular choice led to the dark events that caused my early demise.

"The ongoing cycle of war brought the seasonal winter lull to a close with the start of the spring that was suddenly upon us. The final campaigns of the Civil War followed. Vicious fighting in Virginia, Georgia, and Tennessee provided the backdrop for the reelection of President Lincoln in November. I was by this time a full United States' citizen and, by the gift of derivative citizenship, so was my wife.

"Though under arms, it was both a privilege and an obligation for every American to vote. And we did. It seemed everyone in our company voted for Lincoln, though General McClellan had earlier been our commander. Election Day was surely an uplifting event, but 'a flash in the pan,' in sharp contrast to the continuing horrors of death.

"Two thousand men a week—the dead, the wounded, and the maimed—were coming to Washington. And let me add here that far more men died in the War than what you'll read in the history books. I know. The Scribes keep count. They told me. Many dead were buried at General Lee's ancestral home in Arlington.

"The War was perhaps most vicious as our Army of the Potomac marched in cadence toward its eventual and inevitable end. From the defenses of Washington, our regiment found its feet in May, with the Fifth Army Corp and its campaign to the Rapidan and James rivers. Barely catching our breath, and proudly wearing the symbol of our Corps—the Maltese Cross badge that was conspicuously fastened on our caps—we moved to and from some of the most infamous battlefields of our time: the Wilderness, Spottsylvania, and Totopotomy in May alone! June started at Cold Harbor—cold death. And less than three weeks later, we arrived, part of the 3rd Brigade, 2nd Division of the 5th Corps, at the fringe of Petersburg, Virginia. The Siege of Petersburg began.

"Petersburg was crucial to the supply of the Rebel army and the Rebel capital, Richmond. The 'Siege' was more a series of battles around Petersburg. After repeated and unsuccessful assaults on the city, our forces engaged in trench warfare that eventually extended for over thirty miles, from Richmond to Petersburg. Commanded by none other than Ulysses S. Grant, the Rebels under Lee were eventually defeated, setting into motion its final retreat and surrender at Appomattox.

"And though death remained at our door for over nine months, occasional rest brought some comfort. Putting our guns in position to fire was always a daunting task. Open rail lines that supplied both Petersburg and Richmond were captured in June, and my outfit aided the raids on the Weldon Railroad and the destruction of many miles of track that led to North Carolina and the Rebels' only remaining open port."

The stories, the history lessons, needed to be told. KC couldn't explain it, but if the reason were to tell his story to cleanse his soul or his conscience, or to simply "clear the air" or just be heard, she knew she needed to listen. But guns and battles had always brought her study of history to a grinding halt. Years later, when her husband remarked that history—being everything and anything that ever occurred anywhere—held the key to managing our present day and our future, it hadn't helped. Now the truth of those words helped her sit patiently, and she listened and learned. The kids glowed as the family ghost, who sat now in close proximity to them and beside the old and action-filled mirror, looked every bit the proud and seasoned artilleryman. She hoped and believed this was all part of a process that would soon play out.

"On the thirtieth day of July, the greatest explosion I ever witnessed occurred when thousands of pounds of gunpowder, buried deep underneath the Confederate line by Union engineers, caused tons of earth and debris, bodies and armaments, to rain down on us. I thought for one long moment, 'This is the end of the world.' It was not, though it was the beginning of the end of the War. The plan, had it succeeded, would have allowed our army to move through the gap area of the 'Crater' and advance to the enemy's rear. Instead, our men were slaughtered—as hundreds of Rebels had been slaughtered by the explosion—when they moved down into the abyss with no means of exit. The sad affair ended when the Rebels reclaimed the area of carnage. Thousands fell. *To what depths of butchery will we descend before it ends?* I asked myself. I cried as I did when I last left my family.

"The Siege continued. July became August, and conflicts continued at the Weldon Railroad, Poplar Springs, and other locales. Once we advanced on Peeble's Farm in late September, a new line was drawn from the Weldon Railroad to a place called Pegram's Farm.

"General Grant ordered a hundred gun volleys when he heard Sherman's Federal Army marched into Atlanta on September second. The event was by any account a serious blow to the Confederacy, and was for those of us in Virginia an immense morale boost. Then again, after hearing the news of Phil Sheridan's victory at Cedar Creek on October the nineteenth, Grant ordered us to fire another hundred gun volleys. That victory was no less sweet, as it effectively ended southern threats on Washington, less than sixty miles east, and any talk of invasion through the Shenandoah Valley. And without a doubt, Cedar Creek helped with Mr. Lincoln's reelection a few weeks later. Everyone knew the War was lost for the South. It was just a question of when. The nest of traitors in Richmond lay only twenty miles from us, and we knew they could hear our cannons. Even Jamestown, the birthplace of Virginia, was full of our men and our supply ships.

"With some rest and comfort, 5th Corps divisions withdrew from the Petersburg lines and moved west with 30,000 Federals toward the Boydton Plank Road and a nearby railroad. It was near the end of October, and the road was a prized objective for Union planners. Our gains were quickly reversed with counterattacks, however, that left the Rebels in control of the area for the rest of the fall and through the winter.

"Until that time winter had been a period of relative peace and quiet for the armies of North and South. But with the belief that our Union's inevitable victory was on the horizon, the winter of 1864-65 offered neither peace nor quiet. Though war weary, elements of our 5th Corps finally crossed Hatcher's Run in February, and while our advance was stopped in spite of the arrival of many thousands of reinforcements, we did manage to extend our siege works.

"And the killing continued for two more bloody months."

Worries were on KC's mind: worries about school and tasks, and stress and fights, and separation. Anxiety. Still, she managed to listen as she looked around the garret. The mirror was simply

131

unbelievable, as was the thought of a talking ghost a few feet away. As was the sight of her family: her husband and boys, who listened attentively, and her daughter! Her baby, the hellion who just sat there, enthralled by words, most of which she could not possibly understand. *Or could she?* She'd continue to sit and be patient for this story of one man's life to end.

"Finally the War ended in the front parlor of a house that belonged to a man named Wilmer McLean. Now do any of you recall talk of the McLean family?" There were multiple sideways head motions that indicated no one had except for Dad, who politely nodded for Anton to continue. And after a moment, and a puff on his ever-present old briarwood pipe, he said, "Well, the McLean family moved to the small town of Appomattox Court House after fleeing their home in Manassas, Virginia, about a hundred miles away, near Bull Run, where the War began in their front yard." Anton paused for reactions, then rose and paced a few feet into the sun's rays, which magnified his translucence.

"Both General Lee and Ulysses Grant were good and honorable men. Every soldier, North and South, knew that. And the two leaders sat down and made peace that day, on the ninth of April 1865. I was lying outside on a patch of cool grass when I heard the news. Those like me, sprawled out on the ground somewhere in the vicinity of that house, rose up and cheered. The Southerners remained mostly silent. They weren't far away. When the generals and their aides exited the house, both sides took to attention. Blue and Gray saluted, and so ended the War's final engagement.

"Some raucousness followed, and some of our men even emptied the house of all its contents. Tables. Beds. Everything. Every stick of furniture was carried away as a souvenir. Fistfuls of northern money were handed to Mister McLean. 'There will be no looting,' the officers had said. And then, with the long fight having finally ended, I expected my life in the army would come to an end as well.

"Our regiment signed on for three years, and we were just one year into our term. Still, we all expected to go home soon. The Rebels headed home that day, and sad as they were, they were headed home. We marched back toward Washington."

So the point of the story, Anton? No, she thought. It was time to remain silent and to be respectful.

"Days later our beloved President Lincoln was shot and later died by an assassin's bullet. It was Good Friday when he was shot at the theatre. Supreme sadness settled over our bloodied nation, just as the euphoria of victory had taken hold of the air. How the men in uniform cried when the news of the treacherous act was received."

"Opa, did you go to Abraham Lincoln's funeral?" asked Charley.

"No, *Liebster*. But my wife and children saw his coach when it processed through the streets of New York. There was an official mourning procession, from Washington to New York, Philadelphia and other cities, before it finished its journey in his home state of Illinois.

"In New York, Mary and so many ordinary citizens marched in Lincoln's huge funeral procession, as his Death Train coursed for four hours through the city's crowded streets. Her letters mourned the loss of him and all those who had died in the War. She told me that scalpers sold the 'best' window seats for four dollars! Imagine. That was nearly two weeks' pay!

"So, by the Grace of God, the hostilities of war had finally ceased, but peace was not yet at hand. Now, with Lincoln's passing, constant word of conspiracy and traitors lurking in the shadows threatened to make real peace nearly impossible. Back in Washington, we thought the War's end was at hand when Lee signed the surrender.

"Finally, on May tenth, President Johnson declared the War was 'virtually at an end.' For many of us the end would not come anytime soon. Plans began for a 'Grand Review' of the victorious armies, and great fanfare followed. Some called it our Victory Parade, and for two days Union armies paraded down Pennsylvania Avenue. William Sherman's Army of Georgia, and my own Army of the Potomac, under George Meade, camped on either side of the Potomac.

"We marched on the first day, as the defenders of Washington, and ours was a sunny and pleasant day. We started on Capitol Hill and paraded down Pennsylvania Avenue, and I believed at the time the entire population of our nation's capital was cheering us on and singing our songs. At the reviewing stand, in front of the White House, were President Johnson and Mr. Grant, general-in-chief of the Army. There were others as well, including General Meade, who joined them once the procession was under way. The proudest moment of my life came when my horse-drawn wagon slowly passed for review, and I caught the eye of the President. Briefly, but I did. Hundreds of artillery pieces passed in the same manner. There were miles of cavalrymen, and infantrymen marched twelve men across. On and on we marched: Massachusetts, New York, Ohio, one state after another, regiment after regiment, and in the presence of our new President, as Lincoln, of course, was gone."

"Gee," the boys sounded in unison. KC noticed Louis' position was odd in relation to the old mirror.

"Don't stress your neck, honey," she said.

"Don't worry, Mom," said the boy. "I'm only stressing my scalp."

Anton smiled and drew on his pipe; the smoke spread thinly in the warm air. He moved toward the rocker.

"And once we were done there on the parade route and later in the barrooms of the city, my regiment returned to Fort Albany, and we remained in Washington. Orders were orders, they told us. And we stayed and stayed. At this time, over one million men were Union soldiers, under arms well after the War had ended. Many like those in my regiment had signed on for three years. My paid and unpaid bounties for joining up were tallied to that three-year term, and one dollar of my regular monthly pay was held until the expiration of that term as well. When I should have been paid twelve dollars a month—two of which were 'additional pay' for reenlisting, pay dates fell further and further in arrears. Things got very difficult for us once the joy of the Grand Review of the Armies faded into history."

"Not exactly a Rambo ending," said Dad.

"What's that?" asked Louis.

"You know Rambo. He's the shoot-'em-up guy who wears the bandana." He looked down for a long moment at his son, who looked up but said nothing.

"Is he an Indian?" asked Louis.

"No. Tough guy. Big chest?" Dad smiled down at his son. "He sweats a lot."

"The guy with the twelve-pack?" asked Louis. There was sudden laughter from Mom and from Charley. Neither could be sure exactly who Louis had in mind.

"It's called a six-pack, Louis," Charley said before his dad could respond.

"But why do they call him Rainbow?" asked Louis insistently.

"What? What are you talking about?" a clearly puzzled father responded.

"Rainbow. Why do they call him Rainbow if he's a tough guy?"

"I do not know of a man named Rainbow," interjected Anton.

"The man's named is Rambo—R-A-M-B-O—a fictional character, that's all." Then, with a look of mild annoyance directed at his younger son, and then with honest eyes for his ancestor, he politely said, "Please continue, Opa."

Anton now sat back in the bentwood rocker that would not move regardless of his, the ghost's, actions. "Even after returning to postwar Washington, so cold and so wet for so many days and weeks, the muster rolls recorded monies due time and again for bonus installments and back pay. Of my promised $300 bonus for volunteering the year before, only $180 of it had been paid by June '65—fully two months after the War had ended. Payday came with alarming irregularity. For me and for most of the other volunteers, the issue of pay delays got quite severe and especially distressing for those of us who barely spoke English. Thousands of men deserted to return home to care for their wives and children.

"After all this time—well over a year—pay and monies were still due. Then, making matters far, far worse, my pay was stopped altogether, officially because of a lost bayonet, one that I left in the side of a Rebel soldier at Petersburg. With the bonus installments still due, I found myself at great risk of losing every dollar that was owed." The ghost was rich with color now and confident in his speaking voice, though he sounded quite sad.

It was clear to KC that Opa would follow his own script, would choose what to tell and when to tell it, and would do so at his own pace. The boys looked delighted. Her husband looked as if he were waiting for more. "Anton," she calmly and politely said. "Please tell us about that homeless man in Boston." With a slight emphasis on the word "please" and with a smile showing hints of her perfect teeth, KC was direct and ready to engage. "The kids are starting school in a few weeks, Opa. What can we do now to help this man?" And as she waited for a reply, KC thought of the plight

135

of Boston's homeless. KC remembered her own childhood days with her mother in those sad women's shelters of Dorchester, and drew the unavoidable comparisons of her own experiences and those of this unknown man named Frank.

Anton was silent. He seemed to be deep in thought.

"What about the Scribes, Opa? Can they help us find Frank?" KC leaned in toward Anton, eyes wide with expectation. She silently implored him to speak.

Still he said nothing.

KC looked ready to lunge at the ghost when she unmistakably heard him say,

"No, there are three assists only. The Heavenly hierarchy is quite strict with this generous endowment. The regulations are quite clear. Amity and casual communication are permitted far more generously, and everything known beyond the confines of these four walls has been brought to my attention through the Heavenly Scribes. All the news I have received through these 140 years has been through the Scribes. It helps to lessen the purgatory of profound boredom that often descends upon me here. Afterlife and earthly news have been shared modestly, though I have even extended pleasantries with many of those who have gone into the Light before me, and especially with those of my own generation. Small talk is favored over the substantial."

CHAPTER
33

The family clearly felt enriched by the presence of a "real ancestor," and especially one with such a colorful history. This morning KC planned to lead the family back upstairs and gather around old Opa for a story or two before leaving for church. She needed to understand Frank Lowry and his particular situation so she could begin to plot out the rest of the summer. In a few short weeks school would start, and she needed a game plan.

Casualness and warmth enveloped the whole family as they took their places around the old trunk in the attic. Anton was dressed in what appeared to be the faded blue of an aging uniform, and he looked as if he had been waiting for them to arrive. Everyone exchanged morning pleasantries, and at that time, KC felt as if Anton were just another member of the house, and literally so, since he was locked here in place.

"Do you—have you ever left this attic, Anton?" KC asked.

"No. My place is here. Only here." Anton seemed rested and eager to start.

"What do you do, Opa, when you're not with us...or with the Scribes?" she continued.

"You might say I have a lot of dead time to do whatever I wish, and far more time not to do what I want. I never eat. I have read only what has been left here over the years." He gestured around the attic space. He showed a faint smile.

"Anton. Tell us about Frank." Her voice was gentle and alluring. "Frank Lowry."

"Frank is a distant cousin, a fourth cousin, once removed, to your children, and heretofore unknown to you all." He looked at KC and added telepathically, "Your connection is through marriage only, of course." Then he winked at her and returned to his speaking voice. "Both Frank and his wife, Cathy, were born and raised in Peoria, Illinois. Frank is a descendant of my son, Nicolaus, and his wife, Trude, Hansy's daughter. Trude was named Edeltrude, but no one ever called her that. And as Hansy and I hoped for, when we spoke of it during some of the darkest days of the War, our dreams came true—indeed, they were more than realized—as my son and my daughter united with Hansy's daughter and his son."

"Opa, how do you know these things?" asked Louis.

"Years after I died the Scribes appeared and provided a brief postscript to my life. I learned my wife died barely three years after I passed, leaving Nicolaus and Eva without parents. Fortunately, Ilse, Hansy's widow, was at that time living in Brooklyn, and took the pair in with her own family. The next year Nicolaus married Trude. He was twenty years old at the time. Remember, please, Ilse and her family never held me responsible for Hansy's demise, as I did. And may he always rest in peace. Our families fortunately remained close for generations.

"Nicolaus and his wife traveled west with Hansy's oldest son and his family in 1879. Charles was a young man with an English name who the old-timers preferred to call Karl. This was one year after my daughter Eva married 'Little John' Hoffmann. They remained in New York and raised a family from which you are descended." He looked at the children and then to their father. "Frank Lowry is a descendant of Nicolaus and his wife, who settled in Peoria in '79."

Opa paused with a slight cough, as if to clear his throat. No one spoke. Then Opa lifted his eyes and finally continued. His deep gray eyes were dark with what seemed to be tears.

"Six generations later, Frank Lowry is in Boston, the only child of an only child from Peoria, Illinois, and who, like you, is of my blood, a grandchild." Radiant warmth suddenly streamed from the ghost. With the heat in the attic, this sensation was strangely pleasing. It flowed and gushed for all to feel. His visage was greatly enriched.

"Frank Lowry was eager and ready to leave Peoria once he finished school. His parents were both dead by then, and he lived with an aunt. One special night he and his sweetheart got in an automobile and drove east, where they eventually landed in a sleepy hill town in western Massachusetts. They were married there and Frank eventually found work as a union carpenter. Once the work was steady, the couple had a son, who they named Andrew.

"When America was attacked on September eleventh, in 2001, Frank joined the Army and was posted in Texas. His wife and son joined him a few months later, and a career in the military was contemplated. One year later he was sent to the country of Iraq, where he struggled through multiple deployments and a variety of injuries and illnesses. He returned last year and was honorably discharged, only to lose his way. Frank searched Texas and then Illinois before returning to Massachusetts to find that his wife and young son had left him. He lives now as a jobless and homeless veteran, one of 7,000 such veterans who exist around Boston. He sleeps usually on the streets, without hope and in great sadness."

"How do you know about September eleventh, Opa?" asked Charley, innocently enough.

"Everyone knows about September eleventh," he said.

Nine eleven flashed on the "magic mirror," as the boys called it, followed by projected images of the young man Frank, first as a soldier and then as a vagabond. Louis unsuccessfully tried to snap a few pictures of Frank (and of Anton) with his new digital camera, but had no luck with capturing any images. Charley searched for paper.

"Frank is in great danger of harming himself. He is in dire need of his cousins' help," the ghost announced with some measure of emotion.

"Gee." Charley yawned as he began to sketch and write on the back of a folded page he pulled from a pocket. Around him, his family was deeply engaged and obviously eager to assist Frank in any way they could.

His father then pressed Opa for more of his own story. "Thanks for this information, Anton, but can you tell me about what happened to you once you got to New York?" Then, almost giddy, Dad quickly added, "And do you think you can help me on a family tree issue? I've been struggling for years to figure out who married—"

"Wait a minute! Anton, please go on," KC insisted. "What about Frank? What needs to happen?" KC placed an icy stare on her husband. Her mouth and locked jaw looked poised to grind teeth.

"Of course," said Anton. He nodded to KC and then turned to her husband. "Another time, *mein Herr*. I will share much more of my own life and…hopefully be able to answer some of your other questions."

"Bravo! For now then, our family must plot a course to Boston," KC proclaimed.

Dad imagined dozens of questions about the family tree, questions he'd had for years about people and places and dates that he needed answered. He thought of adding new names and unknown families from Anton's era. He thought of subjects other than Frank Lowry, and did not relish the thought of returning to Boston when he hadn't even settled down in Fairfax yet. Yes, he thought of relaxing and working on his computer with his beloved family tree software, with Anton at his side, or nearby, rich in anecdotes about people who had barely even been names on a page till now.

Perhaps I will tell you more than you care to know.

Before Dad could react to that unmistakable voice in his head, he saw that Anton nodded in agreement with KC.

"Yes, to Boston you must go." His lips moved. "Frank's needs are in the present." He spoke softly. "And those needs must be addressed in Boston."

KC could plainly see stories of two veterans, 140 years apart; two men who gave much to their country and whose lives were forever changed by their service to it. Many questions remained, but Anton's short life after the army drew the inevitable parallels with the current plight of the man named Frank Lowry.

It was almost time for church.

CHAPTER
34

*K*C thought long and hard as she paced around the house. *Is this the "new normal"?* She found it strange that regular life seemed to continue unabated, though occasionally punctuated by the ghost of Opa. As of right now, she had taken control of the schedule, and she wanted to keep it that way, just as she'd controlled car pools and schedules in the past. Just as she'd controlled budgets and play dates, for that matter.

How remarkable it was that the ghost's appearance changed with his words and moods. And there was never a swagger. There was never anything even close to that from this honest and humble ghost.

Where to begin? KC knew psychologists keep "visit counts" of residents in behavioral health clinics and at the homeless shelters. But trying to get an accurate number of homeless people in Boston would be like searching for a needle in a haystack. And the people working at those places were not so much concerned with tracking down new individuals as they were with providing for those who were already there. This undertaking was shaping up to be one mammoth task.

It was Tuesday evening, and he had just returned from work. *What a day!* He drove to the Archives that morning, only to realize—when he was already halfway home on the train—that he had in fact left his *car* in D.C. Truth told, he was a bit scatterbrained all week, as a mission back to Boston now seemed inevitable. Vacation time or time off still needed to be arranged, though it'd be nothing to negotiate some extra time away. As busy as it had been there for him, his newfound status as a federal employee permitted it. And thanks to Anton, he mused, he just had to take time off if he were to save Frank. *Yes, what a day, and week, it had been.*

Everyone was ready for dinner as Dad approached the dining room. It wasn't too late for the family to sit together that evening. "What a frickin' day it was," he said as he sat down for a meat and spaghetti dinner with garlic bread. "I've been thinking about Boston, or rather about this Frank thing."

"So have I," KC responded. The kids offered a variety of background noise and activity as the couple recounted the last few days and surmised what lay ahead.

"I think the boys and I should drive north and find Frank, and that you should stay here with Thankful."

"I agree."

"What? Why are you agreeing with me?" He was genuinely surprised by his wife's reply.

"I just think it's the way to go. I'm not ready to go back home."

"You mean to Westbridge?"

"Well, yeah. How could we go up there and not see my mom, our relatives? I think it'd be way too much of a distraction."

"Yeah," he agreed.

"Yes, I say you go there and bring Frank home, wherever that is, or wherever he wants to go, I guess. Well, no. I don't know about that part yet: where Frank will go. But anyway, you and Charley know Boston. Go. If anyone can find this guy, I'm sure you guys can. There's so much going on right now in addition to this Frank business. I should stay home. I've got bills to pay and gardening to do. I have days' worth of laundry and some school shopping I can get done without the kids. And I also have to sign Charley up for his after-school stuff. There's a lot...I *can* do."

A profound sense of foreboding briefly took hold of her. She dreaded to break up the family, yet her rational senses persuaded her they were doing the right things.

"I'm glad you agree," her husband said. This was *exactly* what he had been thinking, given their knowledge of Boston from both work and sports: They'd get in, find him, and get out. Done. *KC and Thankful can stay at the house with Anton.* Now he didn't need to worry about how to tell his wife she shouldn't come. What a relief! Yes, this was clearly something for the boys to do, he felt, and the whole family should *not* be going. It would make far better sense for KC to stay home with the baby and with Zupper.

"Yeah, it makes sense," he continued. *But what about Louis?* Dad and Charley, though only nine, could track anyone down in Boston. They'd managed to catch many a Major League athlete at Boston hotels, and found many an obscure address around its many winding streets. If Frank could be found there, then they would be the ones to do it, he thought. *Should Louis stay or go?*

She nodded.

"You can call shelters and confer with Anton when necessary," he continued. "Get some guidance, you know, when we need it. We'll stay in touch through our BlackBerrys."

He was a man about to embark on an important mission and counted on a good measure of support from his sidelined wife. "I'm sure of that." How he missed Boston, though. He wondered how he'd react and if he could stay focused on finding Frank. Comforted by the realization now that he and his wife were in sync, he was mostly content. A little bit anxious, but mostly content. "There'll be no distractions. We'll just find Frank and get out of town."

"We need to figure out...with Anton...what to do with Louis," KC said blandly. How in the world would she ever let him go? He was such a special little boy, with such a special bond between the two of them. *And such a tender age.*

It was decided that after dinner, and after Thankful was put to bed, the four of them would ascend the attic, sit with Anton, and begin to lay out their plans. Her husband promised to tear Charley away from his usual after-dinner video gaming. Louis' TV time would be preempted.

CHAPTER
35

*T*he last couple of days were a jumble of activities, as KC scrambled to keep the kids occupied and stay on target for school. She bought the boys both new school shoes and backpacks and some new clothes. They both seemed to have grown a few inches since Memorial Day.

Now, before her, Anton sat dressed in bland civilian garb from a long-ago past. He looked serious and sometimes solemn as the last nuggets of information on what was known about Frank were shared. Anton looked very concerned. They spoke freely of possible whereabouts for the man, but these things really meant nothing to someone who had never set foot in that city and was 140 years from the Boston she knew.

The boys and their father would depart shortly. These long-lost cousins were totally unknown to Frank. He surely had no idea who they were or, for that matter, anything of what had been going on with Anton down South. As for Louis, he had to go. Anton made that clear the moment they had asked. He'd indicated Louis' presence was necessary. "*Mein Liebster*, you must go with your father," he had said. *Dear boy. Go.*

"Opa... Are we gonna save Frank?" Louis asked with his honest eyes that showed the deepest blue, in what had become a Sunday morning attic ritual for the whole family. It was August thirteenth and, while still early, everyone was warm already.

Looking to Louis, Opa responded, "My beloved progeny, it is you, *mein Liebster*, who makes this possible." He waved his arms to

144

indicate he meant the paranormal events of the whole summer. "You know, seers are not uncommon. Good ones like you are very much appreciated by souls like me. Though many families have one, and while these sorts of things—you know, with ghostly relatives, imaginary friends, and other creations—go on all the time, seers are often completely overlooked. A few doubt their abilities; others are ridiculed."

"Wow." Louis left his mouth hanging for a short moment.

"You may not fully appreciate how important you have been for this, honey," Mom said. Then, turning to Opa, she asked, "Why now, Opa? You've been here all this time, and you probably have hundreds of descendants by now, some of whom must have been or still are seers like Louis. Why him?" She drew her breath. "Why us?"

"I have asked these same things of myself," he said. "Everything finally aligned with you and yours. The boy of course is...very special." He looked over to Louis. "Your husband, with his skills and education, is very valuable." He looked at her husband, who stood by an open window. "You, with your remarkable resolve: a capable mother who could rally her family to a cause, any cause, and make things happen. The time is critical and you must move now if you are to move at all." He took his pipe into his mouth and puffed a few times to bring its bowl back to life. "It is God's plan. Frank Lowry is in imminent danger. And my unholy grave will be covered with roadway...imminently."

"Can you guide us to Frank once we get into town?" asked Dad.

"I cannot. I can only influence small events in my immediate surroundings."

"Like what?"

"Well, I can cause you to stand, for instance," he said to Charley, "although doing so requires great strength."

"C'mon. Do it, Opa. Do it," implored Charley.

"Settle down, Charley." Mom was steady in her voice. *I'll bet he helps Louis with that ladder.*

"Do a little trick then," Louis offered in a compromising spirit. "One that doesn't require your great strength."

Ignoring the boy's comment, Mom leaned forward in her opened beach chair and quickly interjected, "Before leaving on their journey, planned for early next Saturday morning, as you know, we," she gestured in the direction of her husband, who still stood by the open window, "want to be reasonably certain we have all we need, well, all we can get from you. I assume you'll be incommunicado once they leave."

"That is correct, *meine Frau*. It is only through the eyes of Ludwig—Louis—that any of you can see me. And only through your boy will Frank believe the love and truth of the mission. The boy's powers are great, but mostly untested beyond this realm." Again the ghost waved his arms around his surroundings. "But the black-haired witch may help you where I cannot."

Dad approached his ancestor and pressed him about his own past. "Look, Anton. I'm getting a little bit overloaded on this Frank business and with events that are yet to unfold. Can you continue with your own story?"

"Not before you tell us about the third and final Threshold!" KC was irritated with her husband, and it showed in her eyes and her clenched fists. "Tell me, and tell my impaired husband. Please."

As the family looked on sympathetically and alternately to Anton and the old mirror, it was telepathically understood by all that what they aimed to do for Frank would in itself not free Opa for the Light. That only by attaining the Third Threshold—moving Anton's remains to hallowed ground—would they finally free this man for ultimate redemption.

"And if we fail?" asked her husband.

"I fear...oblivion" was his reply. He took a deep puff on his pipe and asked Dad if he was ready for the rest of his story. Dad nodded and moved close in to the others who were gathered about the ghost. Opa then looked for approval from each remaining member of his audience. Approval was easily granted.

"Back in New York news was not so good. My son, at fourteen, struggled to support his mother and sister. Eva was still a toddler, as you say. Nicolaus worked odd jobs and still worked in the factory, and he was even a possemantier for his mother. Remember?" he asked. There were blank faces. In response to their puzzled looks, he added, "A possemantier is a fringe maker, and he did so for some of the items sewn by Mary. And while Mary still sewed for a living, she could not survive on that profession. Mary was fair in health at that time, but seldom with happiness. Hansy's widow fared even worse, with the sudden loss of one of her five children that summer. All this time, I remained in Washington, standing guard for an ever-receding threat from the past. The men, my friends and even some officers, began to question why we continued to be bivouacked months after Lee and Grant had signed their famous surrender.

"As July came around, Mary's letters told of very sad times. Both Eva and her mother fell ill, and the little man of the house, Nicolaus, continued to work wherever and whenever he could to bring money home. I was still at Fort Albany, built years before on the high ground just outside of Washington. My pay and money issues remained unresolved. Extreme boredom set in and was a daily routine more than ever, oddly mixed with giddy anticipation for, and a longing to return, home. A baseball match occasionally broke the monotony, when officers and men gathered on the parade grounds to play. And at those times there was no regard for rank or social status." His head pointed down in reflection, and as he looked back up he added, "You know, balls caught on one bounce were an out back then." He sighed. "We played by the New York baseball rules."

"Wow," said Charley.

"And I hear it is still played, though many rules have changed," said the ghost.

Dad and Charley, in awe, silently nodded. "Go Red Sox," Charley softly lamented.

"Payroll had not caught up to any troops. My pay was docked for the lost bayonet and otherwise resumed, though still far in arrears. Other monies owed me were still outstanding. Gambling remained the favorite pastime among the men, especially for those who could afford to lose the least. Then things changed—very quickly.

"One night I won over $80 at poker. This was over a half a year's pay! I cashed in my earnings when it was appropriate to do so, and no one objected. Oh, how I remember that night. My poker chips—certain grains of dark yellow corn—had served me so well that night. Oftentimes, for me anyway, it didn't matter so much whether I won or lost because so little changed hands. And whether I won or lost, I usually preferred faro to poker. But that night I left the game with a well-deserved smile on my face, and mostly well wishes from my comrades. I retired to the comfort of my bedroll and blanket.

"Later that night, with my comrades spread out around me, in deep sleeps and stupors, my group commander, Sergeant John Ewing, woke me and whispered in his breath so stale with the stench of alcohol for me to rise quietly and prepare to go home. Ewing was in debt and had lost big by the time I left the game. He was a man few men liked, and he was never a friend to the immigrant soldier or to my friends.

"As if in a dream state, I could not believe the words I had heard and was much inclined to shout my joy and assure myself at the same time that this was not a dream. But Ewing cautioned me to remain composed and collected and silent. At this ungodly hour of night, he told me that orders were received earlier the previous day to start releasing his men to their homes and families. I could hardly believe my ears, but my heart believed his words to be true. He said this had been known to the non-commissioned officers, like himself, since the day that had just passed, and that everyone was sworn to secrecy and a carefully laid plan, fearing a riot if good numbers of men were freed at once.

"'These must be your lucky times,' he said, his eyes dim in the darkness of the night. I could barely see the papers he waved at me that he said bore all the hallmarks of officialdom. He cautioned me that there was little time to pack, but if I hurried along, I could board the day's first train for New York City and my tenement home and family in Manhattan. The sergeant's speech was thick with drink, yet my excitement to return home thoroughly obscured presentiment and natural suspicions concerning the veracity of his fantastical tale. And my English was not so good. It still isn't." He paused for his pipe.

To this comment his audience objected vigorously and in unison.

"I wish I could speak German as you speak English," offered Dad.

"Yeah," added Charley. Louis squeaked something as well. And then the youngest boy said, "Opa, I never don't know what you're saying."

"You know, when I have to, I say it without words." Anton smiled. He asked for a small amount of water, which was quickly handed to him by KC. "To refresh…myself." He took a long sip of the still cool bottled water and was then poised to continue his story.

For KC the scene was unforgettable. Anton was not quite solid, and he visibly gained in appearance with his worn hand and knuckles wrapped around what should have been a floating Perrier.

"So, I wanted to understand him fully, and I heard what I wanted to hear. The things I knew with no doubt were that I must depart without delay, and without good-byes to men I had fought alongside and lived with and bathed with for the last year and a half. And my sergeant insisted, lest 'all pandemonium should break out among the others,' he said, and he assured me that all back pay and monies owed would be made in short time, once our regiment mustered out."

For one long moment, KC could see the ghost's lips move in total sync with Louis. And there on the old mirror, Anton's talking head was also in full view behind her mild-mannered young boy. This was so strange and mildly narcotic to her. There was no fear. No concern. *Should there be?* No. It was like sitting down for Thanksgiving dinner, loved ones bathed with adoring eyes, while two cousins sang a favorite song in perfect unison.

"Barely had I arrived at the B&O Railway Depot when I was approached by several men who asked me for my name and purpose. I was dressed in civilian attire, not unlike the clothes I am wearing now. There was no greeting in response to mine. There were only those questions. I told them my 'orders' that Ewing had given, and I was immediately arrested as AWOL and taken away. In the near distance I could hear the train's whistle, the steam train's deep throbbing whistle, and I could see the gray-black smoke of its locomotive as it approached the station. I felt its vibrations and I knew it was not far away. The money in my pocket, almost $60, minus twenty that I gave in heartfelt gratitude to Ewing that fateful night, was confiscated, and I was thrown in jail.

"No one came to my defense. How could they? No one but Ewing and I knew the truth of what was said that night. In my small cell I recounted over and over again the sad affair. Only the night before, I gave Sergeant Ewing a good share of my winnings when I left the game, to help defray his losses and carry him further into the evening. He said that partly 'as a way to remedy for past difficulties,' but also in thanks for that money, he'd helped to arrange for me to be the first of his men for early discharge.

"Now, besides me, who could believe his horse manure? I had been so easily tricked by a man I never should have trusted. It was nothing more than a hateful yarn to land me in serious trouble. It was treachery." He rose from his place on the trunk and walked toward the west-side chimney. He turned and faced his listeners.

"Often in my life, as was this case to my most severe detriment, I wanted to believe a man's words. I always saw, or tried always to see, the good in people. And while the logic of it all was in such very short supply, the love of my family and the desire to be with them trumped the ridiculousness of his story." His words carried a slight echo. His mouth had for the moment not moved, but the sounds were clear enough.

"Sergeant Ewing, and may God have mercy on his soul, even showed me documents, as I said, documents which I know now were quite unreal—'orders' he said that stipulated only that the best men should be selected one by one, and for each to return home unaccompanied and void of companionship, to rejoin their families. Sergeant insisted I depart on foot and before dawn so as not to rouse the other troops and to assure that I reached the depot in time. In my haste I never asked for the 'orders.' And I still do not know, nor do I care now, what they said.

"Sitting alone in my cell, there was no comfort from anyone or anything. As one who could speak English far better than I could read it, though neither skill could I do well at all, there was still no one who would hear me speak. 'To spare disruption or cause for delay with the others,' he said. Germans in my company were few, and regardless of their number, none would help with my translation; no way could I adequately describe the details of my story in English. And as incredible as it was, no sane man would have believed me. For all they knew or surmised, I was just another soldier gone absent without proper leave, or, even worse, a hated deserter, one who had failed in his flight." The ghost seemed close to tears.

It was time to go.

CHAPTER
36

*A*s the weekend rapidly approached for her boys' departure to Boston, KC managed to focus as much time as she could on her sons: their doctor's appointments and shots, and back-to-school shopping. And while Thankful and Zup seemed especially needy for attention, Trixi assisted on that front quite capably, and even helped plan a family beach day to Lake Anna, and a couple of library visits. (How KC pined for New England's ocean beaches and the pool they so enjoyed back home in Massachusetts.) There was even an Open House for kindergarten that needed to be attended. Alone time was largely out of the question for KC, though she was able to get a few minutes of aerobics in each hectic day. And when everyone was not consumed with these things, it was perhaps KC's greatest challenge to keep Louis out of the attic as much as possible, though in seeing no harm or threat from the ghost, she admitted to herself that matter was really an issue of control rather than one of safety or concern.

While these days provided no time for Opa, each evening KC, her husband, and the boys ascended to the attic to collect the remnants of Anton's troubled past, and to cobble together the strategy for his redemption. And time was carefully budgeted against all other necessary tasks. How do you manage the presence of a ghost? the wife and full-time mother asked herself. Then there was the new old house itself, which had plenty of work for Dad, when he wasn't working outside the home, and for herself.

By Wednesday night—somehow, some way—tasks had fallen into line, and right after dinner, KC and her following ascended the attic and took their usual places around Opa. Predictably, KC's priorities did not quite align with the boys'—including Anton—and the niceties that were usually exchanged between all gave way rather quickly to the continued sadness of his storytelling.

"Thirteen long days went by, and I languished in misery in my cell. Dreams, when I dreamt, were no longer of home, but of my former homeland and the bank of the blue River Danube, where I fished as a child. I wished I had never come to America, and I even questioned why I served such an honorable and necessary cause. It was August the seventh when my jailers came under cover of night, and I was unceremoniously returned to Company L of the 15th Heavy Artillery. I was in complete despair over all that had happened, and though happy to be free, I noticed that over the last two weeks I evidently forgot much of the English I had learned over the last fifteen years. Even worse, after years of war and, of late, the artillery batteries I serviced, I was more than a little hard of hearing, and in general was a shadow of my former self. Friends and comrades avoided me like the Black Death. Not a one came forward in my defense. Ewing scorned me as a lowly deserter, and men with whom I had risked my life in battle even spat at me, scorned me, and laughed in my face. I learned to stay quiet and to keep my eyes to the ground until my time came to defend myself to my superiors. I was cautioned by a few, including Ewing no less, and assured that penalties would be far worse—beatings and even death—were I to profess my innocence offhandedly and prior to the appropriate setting.

"That Ewing could even look me in the eye after what he had caused! The cold eyes of a filthy soul that was as black as a moonless night. For two weeks I existed in a world that was even worse than my days in jail had been."

No one moved, not even Thankful. And even she was silent.

"Accusations of desertion were authorized against me. Those charges were far more serious than AWOL, a simple absence without leave, which even in wartime was a fairly common and often harmless occurrence. I remained in a fog, and even more unsure of my fate. My faith in God and country was greatly shaken in these days, and it seemed that my only hope now rested with a military court of justice. How I wanted to believe that American justice would save me. I hoped for what you call 'my day in court.'

"That day never arrived. I was hauled before my regimental commander and several other officers one day and told I would be dishonorably discharged and that I would forfeit all back pay and allowances that would otherwise have been due. 'Leniency,' they called it, in recognition of my past service. The alternative, they said, was to go before a military judge and make my case. If found guilty, I would await sentencing of a general court martial, after a presiding officer ran proceedings that would, quite possibly, hand down a death sentence. This of course was all explained to me in English, and a kindly Major Dieckmann helped me understand the seriousness of it all. And as kind as he was, and also a German, he dismissed any notion of my innocence.

"I hadn't been properly paid since June, and hundreds of dollars in bounties were still owed. All would be forfeited. I was not willing to risk my life for this money, and my honor meant as little to me then as it did to my superiors. So just as quickly as the whole affair had started, it ended, with no sentencing and no further punishment. I would soon be on my way, they said.

"My tenure as Private Anton Dietrich ended a few days later, when our regiment, including me, was finally mustered out of the service on August twenty-second, 1865. Spared one indignity—that of being excluded from the last roll call—my nightmare did not end with this. Later that day, wearing only my faded blue forage cap and my belt buckle—my cherished belt plate, as testimony to my service, with all army insignia removed from my person, and carrying only a blanket full of personal belongings, I left Fort Albany on an eerie afternoon, in silence, with not a penny in my pocket.

"I was not allowed to board the trains alongside my former comrades. Doing so, I was told, would besmirch their honor. I headed north by foot. I walked by the stars, and when the moon rose, I walked by it. When I could rest, I built only small fires, so as not to attract attention. I begged, stole, and even fought my way north. I beat a man senseless just for his shoes; I left him bleeding and dying in a gutter. This desperate journey also took me back to those dark times, years earlier, when I made my way to Bremen in search of a new life here in America.

"Three weeks later I arrived home, which was now East 12th Street. Within minutes I was mobbed by an adoring crowd of friends and family who welcomed me back, along with other well-wishers, their names and faces unknown to me. Men had been returning from the War for months, and still the exuberance remained for those still trickling back. There were the very sick, of course, and the invalids. There were also men like me. No buttons, no ribbons or pins adorned my chest, and behind my smiles and words of thanks, I was very much tortured and broken inside.

"With the jubilation of those late summer days still thick in the air, few people discerned men like me from the greater numbers that had already returned. Some men had, after all, just taken their time to return home. Others were adverse to the trains. Still others were mad with 'Soldier's Heart'—shell-shocked from combat and no longer right in the head. PTSD as you call it nowadays. And Lord knows what that means."

"Post—" offered Charley before he was abruptly silenced by his father

The man continued, as if there had been no sudden drama.

"But with welcoming arms, the people of New York City embraced those of us who straggled back. We were home now, and that, they supposed, was all that really mattered.

"My wife was frail and looked much older than her age. Her hair was already thin and gray and had replaced the blond braids I left less than two years earlier. My letters said only that I would be coming home 'soon.' So, as weeks and then months passed, that promise meant really nothing to her. But now, finally I was home. At fourteen, Nicolaus looked the fine young man, and my Eva, only four, had grown in both physical beauty and soundness of mind. Alone with Mary, I expressed my great shame as I returned penniless to my wife and my family. I confided to her that I lost all my money—our money—and was elusive as to the reason. And as if my life had not already been rendered so at odds with a good Christian man, I had, in addition to all else, become a liar. I told her, finally, I was robbed and swindled along the way home.

"Mary was at a huge loss already, yet her love for me was affirmed in all its ways, and we resumed a life together. I never spoke of the War and she never asked. Everyone knew I was deeply troubled by it. They believed the War had changed me; how little they really knew how much it had. To say I was not the man they knew and loved when I left is an understatement. I worked one odd job after another to try to support my wife and children. I tried to be a loving and caring father, but took to drink and petty thievery to meet emotional and material needs, and quickly became an object of scorn to many of those who knew me. Dreaded by most and hated by some, the last years of my life were disgraceful. I lost my health and my character, took to fighting, and many a neighbor was relieved when I died of a broken heart in the summer of 1867."

Louis was quietly sobbing with his mother. Charley and his dad were open-mouthed and Charley was fidgety. All waited for Opa to continue, which he did after taking a long puff of his pipe. "At this time my life went black, and I descended into nothingness. Later, many years later, the Scribes disclosed that Mary and my dear son, not yet sixteen at the time of my demise, arranged for my burial at the new veterans' cemetery in nearby Brooklyn: the Union Grounds, it was called, on the Old Field. Today this place is part of the expansive Cypress Hills Cemetery." At these words Anton paused to gain his composure.

KC saw the great pain it caused the ghost to relate this part of his story. Her children remained fixed on Opa, as was her husband, and everyone patiently waited for him to continue.

"I was mute and blind to the events around me. My senses were nothing and surely nothing in comparison to the shock and despair when my son was told that the burial request was denied. No one knew the truth about my months of service. Even on my deathbed I never confided my story to anyone. Not to Mary, not Ilse, and surely not to Nicolaus. And still after this final insult, the whole truth was never known. Rumors and stories inevitably surfaced about my discharge, from those who had served and from others who only gossiped, but no one told the tale that I have shared with you now. How could they? I took it to my grave.

"The grave keepers could only disclose the disgrace of my dishonorable discharge. No details were known to them, and the rules were quite clear: There would be no burials here for those who besmirched both flag and countrymen. That night, Nicolaus secretly entombed me in an unmarked grave, near to the revered, fallen veterans, in what was wasted land just outside the cemetery's edge. He then tried unsuccessfully to keep the deed from his mother."

Leaning forward, Anton turned to Dad. "Once you tend to Frank Lowry and make your way back south from Massachusetts, you *must* make sure to find my bones in Brooklyn. If you save Frank and move my remains to hallowed ground, my Three Great Thresholds will finally be met." The ghost fought to stifle a cough, and added, "I have been waiting almost 140 years for this time to come." Then Anton coughed a good loud one and seemed to clear his throat.

"Do you want something for that cough, Opa?" asked KC. "Can you take some medicine perhaps, or would you like some water?"

Opa offered only a slight shrug of his shoulders, and then proclaimed, "This (the coughing, he meant) will all go away once I pass through to the Light. Waiting a few more weeks, or even months, is nothing."

"Well, we do need to wrap this up in time for school, Anton." She looked to her boys and then back to the ghost, who nodded in agreement, followed by the rattled noise of another cough.

"We all smoked in those days," he said. "There were no *Warnungs*."

"Huh?" said Charley.

In a not-so-quiet whisper, KC offered, "I think Opa means to say 'warnings.' You know, honey, like you see in cigarette ads?"

"What are cigarette ads?" her sons cried in unison. Louis' five-year-old brow was furrowed with youthful curiosity.

"No big deal, guys. Let Opa finish up. It's getting late." As she looked back to Opa, she could see the tiredness in his sad, gray eyes.

Anton took his cue from the lovely woman and proceeded to provide Dad with a number of important clues to assist with locating his remains. The old mirror disclosed the stark landscape of modern Brooklyn. Construction areas loomed ominously nearby. Louis and Dad scribbled notes onto a pad and notebook respectively. Charley, without his own, grabbed a number of loose papers off the floor and, as the best artist in the house, dutifully and excitedly sketched detailed images of Frank.

"The Scribes have assured me that my remains remain undisturbed. That is, for now."

"Is there anything else you can tell us, Opa?" KC was eager to stay on point. "Did the Scribes reveal anything more to you that can help us now?" KC's look suddenly turned a bit flustered, as if she had read through a good story and was left with an ending that wasn't.

"I heard through the Scribes that, years later, in 1882, a friend of Eva's family inquired to find that my military records showed no evidence of charges or of a trial. The acquaintance, a New York attorney, told Eva, who was at the time only twenty and was by that time aware of the family's shame and committed to finding the truth about me, that he knew of additional records which would clear me of this shame. He wanted money of course, and sadly, before Eva could raise anything close to what he said was needed, the man died unexpectedly, before he could do anything more for me on Earth. My daughter would pass into the Light as did the others, without ever knowing the truth."

Dad loudly and suddenly vowed to do everything he could to help his family, and promised, "I will work till my dying day to get you exonerated, Opa." Then, with a wry smile, Dad timidly added, *"Du gift nehmen."* ("You can bet your life on it.") Everyone nodded in agreement. Everyone understood, and all were of one mind as they parted ways for the evening.

Anton smiled as he began to fade away. To Louis and his brother, both of whom stood closely beside the specter, he said, "Go, Godspeed to you, Ludwig and Charley."

Louis professed his love, and as Anton faded to nothingness, he left a faint and fragrant humidity hanging in the air.

"We're on our own now, Louis," said KC, as she, her sons, and husband returned to the fold-down staircase. After pulling on the string to extinguish the light bulb that hung near the entryway, the four descended into Louis' room.

KC was very concerned that Anton's assistance would no longer be accessible once the boys left on their journey.

CHAPTER
37

*T*he next morning began as just about every other weekday had that summer. Over breakfast, KC engaged her husband in all matters of home and family. The couple quickly turned to priorities, and set about operationalizing their plan for the journey north.

"I'll be alone," said KC. "Well, not exactly. There's Thankful and Zupper." Though a bit tired—it was still only 6 AM—KC had her usual color and character firmly in place for the day ahead. She was already dressed as if it were she who was going to work that morning.

"Maybe Louis *should* stay here?" offered Dad. "That way, we can keep Anton engaged, right? Otherwise, he's out of the picture."

"No, Anton said Louis *must* go…for the success of the mission. Don't worry. We'll be all right. Leave in the morning as planned: the three of you. Anton's told his tale, and after hearing his story, you know what we have to do. I'll be in touch regularly: I'll make the calls, get the leads. I'll find more time now that we've wrapped up things here on the home front. Don't worry."

He looked at her and knew then why, after over fifteen years of marriage, he was still in love. "I'm not worried," he said with a smile. "I love you."

Just then the doorbell rang. It was Trixi's parents, who arrived as planned to chat with KC and her husband before Dad departed for work. Even after nearly three months as neighbors, the two men had never met. KC's own bland introductions and subsequent friendship with the babysitter's family was, unfortunately, shallow at best.

"What the hell do they feed you people over there?" joked KC's husband as he held out his right hand in friendship. Loek, a broad-shouldered and bald man in his forties, smiled and deferred to his wife Jeannette, whose Dutch was far better than her English. She smiled and said mostly nothing as the four adults faced one another in the hallway.

"Come on," joked Dad again. "Dutch sounds like a German speaker with a pain in his throat."

Loek politely shot back, "You know, to Europeans who are accustomed to hearing the King's English, Americans sound mostly like killer cowboys."

"Aw, like Bush you mean?" Dad was animated and visibly enjoying his time with Loek and his wife. "No way."

Once those barbs were flung, the two men hit it off quite nicely. Jeannette smiled some more. Loek assured Dad that KC and Thankful would be safe and secure with his daughter. He knew nothing of Anton or of Dad's mission, but his honest eyes and muscular build were reassuring.

"Where is Trix? Still sleeping?" asked KC.

"Ja," offered Jeannette.

The chimes and the ornate Roman numerals on the face of the giant case clock told Dad it was time to leave for work.

PART III

CHAPTER
38

*L*ess than twenty-four hours later, the same grandfather clock told Dad it was time to leave again. Saturday morning, 4 AM. With luck the ride to Westbridge would take about ten hours, with minimal traffic tie-ups. He recalled it was about 500 miles. The boys could sleep for a few more minutes, thought Dad, and he prepared an extra pot of coffee to fill a rather large thermos for the road. With mixed emotions he greeted the approaching day.

"Been there, done that," he muttered as he went over his final lists of things to do and things to bring on their long, long journey north. The kids were generally good on road trips, with minimal pit stops, and this time would be no exception. He simply would not tolerate any whining or crying either. They knew that. But he truly believed the boys were pumped for this journey that would first take them past D.C. and then through that godforsaken tunnel under Baltimore. From there they would see the sights and more than a few pretty places before having to decide whether to take the Turnpike in New Jersey or its less offensive cousin, the Garden State Parkway. And once they'd gotten past that grimy George Washington Bridge, they'd stop for lunch somewhere in Connecticut, New England, at last, before finishing up on the final leg home. "Home?" he asked himself softly. "Why is it still 'home' for me?"

Dad had it all figured out. *Gassed up. Packed up. Ready to go.* He believed they'd arrive with plenty of sunlight to spare. Two o'clock

162

he reckoned for an ETA at the old homestead, their still-unsold suburban home in Westbridge, about thirty miles south of his beloved Boston. There the three would set up quarters—camp out—in their empty old home that was sure to flood them with sad and wonderful memories. Yes, Westbridge would be their base of operations. It made sense. It would cost nothing and the electricity was still running there, per the instructions of their realtor, Todd Grundy. "Stick to your price," he advised. "This place is an awesome investment," he said. "You'll get what you're asking. Just be patient." *Four months and no takers.*

Yes, it made sense. There'd be the inevitable chitchat with the old neighbors, but more importantly, there was electricity—a working stove and even the fridge, which was left in place when they left. Using his BlackBerry, the boys would stay in touch with KC, coordinate strategies, and make calls to find that guy Frank. They'd scour the homeless shelters in Boston while KC did the bulk of the research and fed them with hit-lists, along with as much background information as she could find on programs and outreach. "Yup, it sounds like a plan," he said half aloud, and he exited the kitchen, on his way upstairs to wake the kids. He hoped it'd all be over in a few days.

CHAPTER
39

*A*s she moved about their stately manse, KC wondered how the boys were doing. It had been a few hours since they'd arrived back home. "Back at the house," she corrected herself. By now they were probably sleeping: camped out in the old living room, perhaps. Her thoughts jumped to the homeless, to the shelters, to her own dark experiences surrounded by those battered women of Dorchester, and having lived what seemed half her youth—stolen—hijacked to those unsavory places. Great sympathy she felt for Frank Lowry and those like him.

KC continued her wanderings about the old Virginia house. Charley's room was adorned with all his Boston sports posters. Louis' walls were still all blank, testimony to all his other endeavors this summer, she supposed. Even some boxes of his were still unpacked. She'd set up her boy's room for him, she thought. Then she thought again. "Not now," she whispered.

There in the corner of the master bedroom sat one of many telephones scattered throughout the house. It beckoned for her to pick up and call someone. KC moved in its direction, in the darkness, then sat nearby on a small cushiony love seat. *I wonder if she's returned yet.* Thankful and Zupper slept nearby. *Pick up the phone and dial.* Her mind raced. Should she or shouldn't she? They hadn't spoken in well over a month, but Oona had promised to call when she returned. How she'd love to update her dear friend on everything. Then again, KC felt strangely odd about doing so while her

164

husband was engaged in their rescue mission. "But odd about what?" she wondered. She rose and picked up the phone.

She tried and failed to make sense of her feelings and imaginings at such a late hour. With stirred emotions, and feeling vulnerable, she decided to place the phone down and wait. She thought again to call Oona, but her thoughts moved on, to her husband's eventual return. She was confused—confused and anxious. And suddenly very horny.

She could not explain the giddy frisson of what had enveloped her. She was so alone, now that her husband had left with the boys. She felt *so* alone. It was way too late to call her husband. He'd think for sure that something bad had happened. She knew she could call Oona at any hour. *Incommunicado*, she had been told. She'd just have to wait. She could leave a message. No, she'd wait to hear from her friend.

It was the first time she'd been really alone all summer. She walked back into the hallway, and then to Thankful's bedroom. Thankful was thankfully asleep in her lovely room. All was quiet but KC's mind continued to race. The house was quite beautiful and coming along nicely, she thought. The family had reached some sort of a crescendo, and now it was torn mildly apart. The boys were in Westbridge no doubt, a half hour from that Dorchester neighborhood where freckly-faced Kathryn Cliona Callahan once lived in a triple-decker on Adams Street. How everyone hated that middle name of hers. That is to say, everyone but she and her father, the person who gave it to her. And the one thing he could never take from her. Still no one ever used that name, and everyone eventually settled on KC, only the remnants of a name people grudgingly acknowledged.

KC wondered where, if at all, they'd find Frank Lowry. For a small city, Boston was huge. There were a ton of places Frank could be. He could even be dead. Who knew, really? God, what an unusual summer it had been: a summer complete with strange, and sometimes wonderful, happenings.

She retired back to the comfort of her bedroom and sank onto her king-size Posturepedic bed. *Saturday night.* Lips parted. She thought long and hard about the summer's events. She wondered if Anton could see her, and convinced herself that he could not. She thought to hide in the clothes closet, so no one could find her, where, as a little girl she hid from the fights, from Mom and her stepfather. Sometimes fights with horrible screams. It was time to stop now and think of more pleasant things or she'd never get to sleep. By now, Zup was most likely lying down back in front of the baby's door. No, no one could see her now. Alone for a change, she pulled up her usual fantasies and slowly moved her right hand down past her belly. *Pleasurable things to come.* She thought first of her husband. Pleasing pleasure. Want more. *That cute cop, what was his name?* Officer Lee. Yes, Officer Lee. Arrest me! Please. Again, her lips parted. *Please...arrest me.* She'd be done rather quickly. She stretched her body for one long moment. Then, a fleeting image of Oona. *Flawless skin.* Thoughts of a phone call that was never made. She felt the irrepressible brightness of her glow. *And the boys had never been away from their mom for such a long outing.*

It was a lovely morning, and Oona sat alone in her guest villa overlooking the beautiful beaches of Rovinj. She surmised that Anton's affairs had by now been fully vetted, and she considered to what extent her services might now be required. *Unfinished business.* "Of this I am sure," she whispered. It seemed they had not talked in ages. Six hours behind. Istria had seen to that, yet all the lovely distractions had not tempered her desires and interests back home in Virginia. Holidays were strong remedies for many things, and her time away had generally been good. How she needed to push her reset button at least once a year. She had been doing so ever since she was a teenager.

Now, while her so-far-incredible life had by no means been dominated by one sliver of a Venn diagram that represented KC and her family, she—they—were seldom far from her thoughts. She took her green tea to her mouth, careful not to mess her lips. *Distractions? Yes!* It would no doubt be a lovely day.

CHAPTER
40

"*H*e has glasses and a moustache, Dad. He must be a general." Louis smiled and pointed as his father's Buick Century passed the Humvee and what else he could see of the National Guard convoy.

It was early Sunday morning. The small procession of military vehicles offered little competition for Dad as he raced up Route 24 North toward Boston. "No, honey," he said with a smile. *No stress this morning.* Though he had done a ton of driving only yesterday, for Dad, this morning seemed worlds away from the rush hour traffic of workdays. This morning's casual sprint even had a somewhat calming effect on him. And whether it was commuting here to Boston or there to D.C., either drive was rarely enjoyable. "This guy is more like Opa was. He's probably a private. Opa drove a wagon. This guy's driving a Humvee. That's all. Who knows? He may be hauling ammunition, just like Opa did with horses."

"Wow. May-be," said Louis with a long drawl.

It was barely 7 AM and the boys were well on their way to save Frank. Dad had already spoken with KC a couple of times, and the two had drawn up an itinerary for the day. This being Sunday, Dad and the boys would visit the soup kitchens of Dorchester and "Southie." Dad had a list that KC provided. They'd focus their day in the southern part of the city, check under the bridges and the overpasses as well, and just ask around. If they didn't find Frank today, they'd move west and hit the Fenway area and the fringes of

Longwood tomorrow. They would give it as long as it took. *Or until school started.* September sixth, he believed it was. *Weeks away. No sweat.* Then, a twinge of anxiety suddenly beset Dad's thoughts.

The Boston neighborhoods…the sidewalks. "It'll be like finding a needle in a fucking haystack," he said to himself. "The Commons and all its park benches. What about those?" They had to stay with the plan though, and not lose hope before they even began. The kids were pumped and positive, and that would help in a big way. And owing to their knowledge of Boston, from the Fenway and Back Bay, to Charlestown and the North End, and from Summer Street to Beacon Street, and all in between, they'd competently search and search, and trek through the city's blocks and shelters. Using the sketches of Frank that Charley had drawn up, the three would visit the hospitals and the health clinics, if necessary, along with the other facilities and the alleyways, and more likely than not, some real shit holes in Boston. *Checking under bridges and overpasses, with two little kids?* Was this really the way to go? he thought. *Stay with the plan. Stay with the fucking plan,* he insisted to himself. Anton's images of Frank were engrained in their heads, and any one of them would know Frank if he saw him.

Sunday ended mostly with frustration, and a full day of searching their designated quadrant had only succeeded in wearing everyone out. While the soup kitchens were more than willing to feed them, he and the boys came up empty as far as intelligence gathering went. They drove back to their mostly empty home, their heart-wrenching home, their home without furnishings. *But it was still home.*

Monday was even worse. He'd run his BlackBerry dead from speaking with KC. He'd need a better car charger or something—a better battery perhaps—to keep that critical means of communication open as much as possible. His former neighbor's network connection provided for spotty laptop connectivity, and the landlines were still the best way to regularly connect to exchange intelligence and profess everyone's love and support.

Tuesday dawned and Dad refused to go into town without first taking his sweet time. The boys slept late and Dad's laptop dependably offered a wireless connection to the outside, through

Mary, his nearby, former neighbor's source. For the short time they were gone, Dad filled in his former neighbors about his family's new life in Washington, and was sketchy at best in describing the nature of their current business. The kids were coy on that subject as well. Still, the neighbors offered the boys all the local amenities, and this included extended use of landline phones to speak with KC, home cooked meals from a variety of folks, laundry, and nighttime TV. Mary, from across the street, was especially kind.

A couple of small leads suggested a better day ahead. Still, Dad needed a ton of change and dollar bills to get anything out of these people. Just because they were homeless did not mean that many were not savvy business people. All seemed skilled survivors. A clean and casually dressed father-and-sons team was no less a threat to those who were suspicious of people asking questions, and a risk to those who wished for simple anonymity. Intelligence gathered was few and far between so far. He heard about a couple of vets who were hanging out in Downtown Crossing. He pegged the area's homeless shelters on his list and figured they'd start their day around U Mass and Columbia Street. There, under the bridge, a number of vets were also said to be camped. *Did they stick together?* "Find one and we could get lucky," he whispered with a smile.

Today, Tuesday, there would be no driving. They'd take the commuter train, the MBTA, into town from the Westbridge Station. They'd work their way up to Downtown Crossing via South Station and St. Anthony's Shrine. *Patron saint of lost articles.* Now that would be one stop really worth making, he thought. *Right on the way too.*

The boys encountered many rules at the different shelters, all with different rules on disclosures. Small donations were always appreciated, and Dad wrote more than one check on Tuesday. Louis' simple veracity to "find our cousin Frank" helped some. The cute kids were usually an asset as they went to the shelters with the renderings of Frank that Charley had drawn and the visions in their heads of who Anton had shown them to be Frank.

There were a couple of churches near the State House that were known to welcome all without reservation. These houses of worship fed folks out back—it didn't have to be Sunday for them to be kind to those in need. On the street it was a different story, and while people in Boston were always generous with their coins and dollar bills, making real connections with the homeless was quite rare. To many they were just panhandlers. To a few they were just "bums."

Dad and the boys trudged on into the early evening under a pale blue summer sky. They were ready to pack it in for the night when Dad spied a certain street person up against one of South Station's sand-colored granite walls. He held a sign in one hand that simply read, "Homeless." In the other hand he held a disposable plastic cup. He had the look, thought Dad, and though he knew this was not Frank, he approached the tall and burly man with a crisp new dollar bill.

"Hey, would you know a homeless man named Frank Lowry?" he asked. Behind him Charley waved the sketch he had of Frank.

"You'll have to do better than that," the man said and nodded toward the dollar bill.

Dad shook his head in brief but apparent disbelief. It had been a long day, and the next train home was leaving shortly. He reached for his wallet. All he had was a twenty. He shook his head again as the homeless man watched. "Do you know him?" he asked again.

The homeless man smiled at Dad, and in doing so showed what appeared to be good, well-kept teeth. He reached with his cup for the twenty as Dad slowly removed it from his wallet. The boys were nearby, mostly watching the people fly in and out of South Station in all directions.

"What's his street name?"

"Frank Lowry, I said. That's his name." Dad suddenly felt like he had missed a major element in tracking down his long-lost cousin. *Fucking street names!*

"No self-respecting street person would use his own name. He's gotta have a street name. Like yours can be 'Asshole.'"

"Look, pal," Dad shot back with a sudden sneer.

"That's not my name," the homeless man stated flatly.

"You people wonder why you're the way you are." He reached back for his twenty, but his speed was no match for the homeless guy.

"My name's Steamroller. Used to drive one. Now I am one. Quick though." He looked at Dad sternly now. "And don't ever call me 'you people.'"

"Look, just give me my twenty back."

"Sorry. All contributions are non-refundable."

Dad reached again in the direction of the man's cup.

"Watch it, Asshole." Steamroller danced like a boxer in the ring. Passersby deftly navigated around the two men. "Come on, Asshole. I'll kick your sorry ass...in front of your grandchildren."

My grandchildren? Steamroller waved his battered old cup, with the twenty inside it, at Dad. "Dirtbag!" said Dad.

"There *is* a man named Dirtbag who may be the man you're looking for." With those words, Steamroller sounded like a Harvard graduate.

He was right though. The bum was right, thought Dad. He'd need a street name to find Frank. This mission was more like *Mission Impossible*, but he had to keep trying. He needed Frank's street name.

"Hey, Dad. The train's gonna leave," called Charley. He and Louis were standing at the main entryway into South Station. And he was right. If the train was going to leave on time, he had only a minute left to try to get his twenty dollars' worth from Steamroller.

"Come on, Steamroller. We need to find a guy named Frank. He's a vet—homeless and destitute." His eyes were honest and tired. "Please. Help us."

"There's a guy they call Roy Boy. He's out of his mind, from the war in Eye-rack. Then his wife disappeared on him. She left with his kids too. Yes, she did."

"Where is he?" *This is too good to be true,* thought Dad. *This "Roy Boy" could be Frank. He only has one kid, but hey, close enough.*

"I haven't seen Roy Boy in weeks. I only saw him once, as a matter of fact, over near Salem Street. He could be dead for all I know."

"Dad!" called the boys in unison.

"Don't say that, man." It was a real possibility: that Frank was already gone. They could check the morgues as a last resort.

"Well, there's another guy named Smokehouse. He's *real* crazy. I think he might have killed *his* wife. I see him all the time. He lives over in Chinatown."

"Dad! Come on, Dad," the boys yelled, eager to do something other than stand and watch.

"Okay, thanks." Dad backed away gingerly in the direction of his boys, turned, and darted away. For the first time in three days, Dad felt that he had a little something.

CHAPTER

41

*H*e couldn't wait to call KC and fill her in on the latest developments. His boys were tired but eager as well to give their mother the latest. But back in Virginia, things had not gone so well. On Tuesday Zupper fell ill, and, as KC spoke with her husband, she noticed that Thankful was quite restless. Her baby had been inconsolable earlier in the day, and it looked like sick baby time was upon her.

"She started bleeding from her nose," KC said to her husband. "What?"

"And I had to bring her in to the vet." KC enunciated each word for her husband to hear without question.

"Oh. Thank God. I thought you meant Thankful."

"I know." Back in Virginia, she rolled her eyes in disbelief. It had been a very long day for her too. "But I am afraid Thankful is coming down with something. I've been changing diapers since early this afternoon, and watching her temp go up and up."

"What about Zup?"

"Well, the vet said that he can't be sure without some tests. They took some blood, but I'm not okay with an MRI. Do you believe it? An MRI? We'll wait and see, I think. She's lying by Thankful's room, but I have to tell you, she took forever to get up the stairs, and—"

"What?"

"Her tail. She hasn't wagged it at all today. It's like she's not happy anymore. I'm sure she misses you."

173

"Well, with the nose bleed and all. That *is* traumatic. So I guess we'll see." Dad was clearly reminded of his family life hundreds of miles away, and his aging dog. "Did you find anything? On Frank, I mean."

"Oh yeah. In my spare time." KC rolled her eyes again. "Actually I did get some stuff done." She took a deep breath. "As best as I can determine, your cousin is not in a Boston hospital, nor does he seem to be in jail. Or have a record—at least not under his real name." She paused. "Does Frank have an alias, maybe a street name? The cops were asking."

"Don't start with the fucking street names."

"What?"

"I said the kids miss you. It's been a very long day for me, for us, too. I'm sorry." He waited for a response and when he didn't hear one, he continued. "Listen, honey. I think we might be inching closer to finding Frank."

"You really think so? Do you realize how many calls I have made? How many places? The police said to go hire a private investigator. There are many hundreds of shelters, they said. Clinics and homeless services. The Public Health Commission and soup kitchens, as you know. There are thousands of places if you add in all the inns and local dives, and even the beer joints and beaches this time of year." KC was exasperated. "And then you have Greater Boston."

"But let's focus on vets." Thinking of Zup, he quickly added, "Veterans. I think Frank will be among them. I just think they stick together." He went on to tell her about the day's events and especially of their last few minutes in Boston with Steamroller.

"Well, yeah. You know there are vets' homes. Some are open twenty-four/seven. Maybe I'll make a call or two tonight."

"I don't know that you should. Take care of Thankful and Zup. Give them a big kiss from Dad."

"Hey, you know what day this is, right?"

"Should I?" he said. He was totally spent for the day.

"It's August twenty-second. Remember? It's the day Opa left the Army for good. In 1865."

"BFD," he said. "I wanna go to bed."

"Okay. I'll make the calls in the morning and see what I get for vet-friendly places. Directories and community listings. You know. We'll see. You guys sleep late tomorrow."

"Don't worry 'bout that. Louis and Charley are exhausted already. Louis' legs are so young. Not as bad for Charley, but even with the T, it's a lot of walking. I think that tomorrow we'll just stay in town. Some cheap lodging somewhere. I know a rescue mission house in the Fens."

"Jerk. It is smart though to stay put for a day. You have nothing to go back to...there."

"It's still home, honey. Empty...but home."

She listened to every word, every inflection.

"Hey, the lawn looks good. Nicky is doing a great job keeping it nice. I wish the pool was open. We could pay him for that too." He was only half serious, but it had been a hot one in town that day. "And at least now, with us, and the old Buick parked in the driveway, it doesn't look like an abandoned property."

"Stop talking before I start crying," she said.

"And be on the lookout for Roy Boy and Smokehouse, especially Roy Boy. Two vets. Two street names for you."

"Go to bed."

And he did. He couldn't tell her how tired they really were.

CHAPTER
42

*N*ot far from its harbor and castles, its beaches, and its naturist camps, she knew why she came here to Istria year after year. But inevitably, as always, Oona needed to make her journey back to reality, to return from Europe. Depending on her mood, and the famed Orient Express, she would find her way to Paris and ultimately make her way to America from there. *A little early to decide for sure.*

The pine and olive trees mingled as freely there as the visitors. *There are so many Germans this year.* She thought of the ghost and of KC. Her impact on the family was certain. Her impact on KC was not. Could she ever escape that woman's allure? Oona's polished fingertips nearly crushed the wineglass she held in her hand. Great distances are like time; both lessen the intensity of lustful desires. Perhaps that young and innocent beach goddess could assuage her passion today, though making love on these gravelly beaches was not at all recommended. She could wait till evening, she supposed. Perhaps some scissoring in the steam room. Or perhaps Josef could work for her tonight. Either would do just fine. While Serbo-Croatian was no problem for her, especially when mixed with the language of love, and after nearly ten years summering in Istria, it came as no surprise that she could always get what she wanted or needed here. And anytime along the way, she could use her Italian or German in this part of the Balkans. *Yes, the local fare was quite fine…and diverse.*

Those thoughts predictably stirred her typically unquenchable sexual appetite. Yet time here was rapidly coming to a close. Her veil of silence would soon be discarded. Her inaccessibility to the outside would soon end; the curtain of mystery was about to be lifted.

How she wanted to help them, and how she was determined not to bring disaster to the beautiful family she so much wanted to assist.

CHAPTER
43

*M*orning came early for Charley and Louis. Both were excited for the day ahead. It was Wednesday and Dad promised them a nice lunch, a good dinner, and a night at the Hyatt. The pool there would be awesome.

It was noontime before the boys arrived at Downtown Crossing. Their day would start there, near the State House, and from Downtown Crossing they would travel to Chinatown and, time permitting, the Financial District. It would be one hell of a day, as the next day would be as well.

"We have been chasing our tails," he said to his wife at the close of yet another day. Over the last five days, the trio had crisscrossed Boston. Generally pleased with the level of cooperation at the shelters and soup kitchens, and wherever else they'd gone, they were finding that street people were in many ways a cloistered society. They were exhausted now, and Dad already felt defeated.

KC was caring for a sick baby Thankful. She'd gone through a ton of diapers, and it looked like a rotavirus. To make things even worse, Zupper's nose was still bleeding and her final days seemed certain. All week KC had been back and forth to both vet and pediatrician.

"Oona should be returning anytime now. She'll help us. I'm sure she'll help," she said.

"It's Thursday night!" He was stuck on this being Thursday already. In almost a week they had managed to wear themselves out along with their shoes, and with practically nothing to show for it except sore feet and broken hearts. "Fuck!"

"Cursing won't help. Maybe you want to come home...to me...and us, down here in Virginia. But listen: We've got to see this through. Frank is in imminent danger, and I think we have to keep trying till Oona gets back. Look! I've supported you from home, and I'd be there if I could. You know that. Please try again. Tomorrow. I've got a couple of promising new leads: one in Chinatown and one in the North End."

"We've been all over both."

"Really." She wasn't sure about that. "Well, I spoke to a guy this morning at a place called the Holly House. He said that a guy fitting Frank's particulars had been around since about the time we knew him to be in Boston. He recently moved on, he said, with another man, another veteran, somewhere. He said they may have been caught up in the Sweep. Their names were not Roy Boy and the other guy."

"Smokehouse?"

"Yeah, not Smokehouse either."

"What about their names then?"

"He wasn't sure. Listen: First, go to Saint Anthony's. The Holly House was about spiritual development as much as soup. Boston and Downtown crossings. You know. It might be a start."

"A start, yeah." Dad was worn down. He never really thought too long or hard about the scope of this mission. He was down and practically gone.

"And what about Louis?"

"He's been good. The bums love him. Sorry. The transient community loves your son."

"Watch it, jerk. And he's *our* son."

"Yeah. You know, he has those honest eyes. Those big blue eyes. His presence adds a steady dose of love and truth to our mission." He was slightly sarcastic in his tone. "And the other one—Charley's a real charmer too—has no shortage of conversation with all these people. I'm going through a hundred bucks a day, even more, in 'non-refundable contributions.'"

"Is Louis *feeling* anything?"

"I don't know. I thought he was a 'seer of ghosts and spirits' and not some kind of clairvoyant."

"Well, it doesn't hurt to encourage his...development."
"Yeah."
"Who knows?"
"Oona," he jabbed back. "Oona knows."

CHAPTER
44

O ne man who evaded the big sweep was Tea Time, a Black
man with a British accent.

Tea Time had lived all over Boston for years, he said. He left
his former life down in the Caribbean, and appropriately enough,
he knew the Waterfront. Tea Time was dressed in camouflage pants,
worn sandals, and a T-shirt that proclaimed, "Armed with a Mind."

"Is your Roy Boy Black?" he asked earnestly.

"No," said Dad. "He's my cousin. A vet. Veteran. We showed
you the sketch."

"Oh yeah," he said softly.

"He needs us. Look: Don't worry so much about the name.
We're not so sure that's him anyway."

"There were a good number of men who got picked up by the
police."

"Yeah, we know."

"And others are always moving around." Tea Time looked like
he had something on his mind.

Dad reached into his pocket. Statements like that were always
cues to ante up. Today's tips—and there were many tips he gave to
get tips—and KC's help had given him a renewed sense that he was
closing in on something. Occasional advice from some wizened
street sage led to multiple leads from other people, a steady stream
of which pointed to the North End and the Garden, the Boston
Garden. And assuming they didn't find Frank today, they'd stay at

the Hyatt again and get right back on the trail Saturday morning after breakfast.

And where is that beautiful bitch Oona? he wondered.

He gave Tea Time a couple of bucks and then a couple more.

"You know, the cops tell you that the 'bums' sleep and grub all over town," said Tea Time. "And while that may technically be true for some subset of people as a whole, it is not true for all individual persons."

"Okay, I think I get all that, but where do you think my man is hanging out?"

"There are a good number of gentlemen near the Garden. It's the home of the Bruins and Celtics, you know, and their seasons are soon to be. Check the Beverly Street Extension."

He nodded to Tea Time. Turning to his son, Dad asked, "Hey, Charley. Do you recall Opa saying anything about Frank and sports?"

"I don't think so, Dad."

"No, Dad," offered Louis. His four-foot frame stood nearer to his dad than did Charley.

"But wait," interrupted Tea Time. "No self-respecting street person would shun Boston's rich sports culture. And if that were to happen, gentlemen, I'm afraid your man could very well be lost. He could be dead."

For Dad this statement seemed eerily prophetic. *A down-and-out guy, the last straw being the failure of his team or teams—the Bruins, the Red Sox, the Celtics.*

"The Red Sox! He's had it! Six nothing was the score last night! First his family! No. First it was Iraq. Probably PTSD! Then his family. No money. Jesus! Then the Sox! No!" *It's definitely not their year!* Dad grew even more upset.

"Yes, he's probably had it. You know your man may also be sick."

Tea Time's remark reminded him that Anton had not appeared since their departure. KC told him his presence was simply not felt; the enchantment seemed gone. And he also recalled the words "imminent danger," and that meant that this guy Frank could go at any moment. Any spark could do it.

"There's one guy who left one of the halfway houses for fear of contracting tuberculosis. Maybe your man is in hospital."

"Nah. We checked there. Well, really, my wife did. She checked all over: BMC and Tufts. You name it. The General and the Brigham. She was asking for Frank Lowry of course. You can't use street names in a hospital search." Then, sarcastically Dad added, "No. Nooo way."

Respectfully, the homeless man responded, "Aliases though may be used."

"Yeah, of course. I suppose so. And you know what? Connecting to the right guy anywhere in Boston is proving to be Mission Impossible."

"Don't lose faith. I think you can find your man."

"Okay." Dad was losing faith.

"Start in North Station early tomorrow morning. The men sleep late there and over by Beverly Street. Salem Street has places too: nooks where they find sleep. If you find no one there, check near Saint Anthony's." Tea Time offered a small smile.

"Been there." *Anton is the German version of Anthony.* "Done that."

"A number of veterans' shelters are listed therein. Commonwealth Progress House is one such place, but start your search at North Station. The Orange Line has the best places for men to find peaceful rest." Tea Time added, "Good Luck," and turned away.

CHAPTER
45

*T*he trail was already warm at 7:15 in the morning. As Tea Time had suggested, he and the boys first scoured the Orange Line at North Station. The complex that included the TD Banknorth Garden was massively large, newly named, and very imposing. For Dad this location was still the hallowed ground of his beloved, now-razed Boston Garden. Having completed their sweep of North Station—its platforms and commuter rail and subway lines—and deeply disappointed that so few homeless men were found there, they were ready now to go outside.

Charley was clearly distracted by his surroundings and by the few pedestrians who were already milling about. The vegetable market spread out in the near distance. Little parks and some stands were waking up to the morning as the trio emerged onto Legends Highway, with its mix of redbrick and blue stone walkways. It looked to Charley like it was going to be a nice day.

Dad followed the mesh of metal and aluminum that spanned the Causeway Street overpass. The run of light metal poles, in a variety of shapes and sizes, guarded the already busy highway—thirty feet or so beneath the Causeway—which led to the strikingly modern, gray concrete though still beautiful Zakim Bridge. He recalled how for years he'd followed that road to New Hampshire and other points north. And though he felt he had no time, he reminisced how he loved New England.

Fancy Jersey barriers crowned the overpass with a granite step, one of several, that led to a ledge which could easily accommodate a grown man if one could just meander his way through the small—only about ten inches—gap between the wire mesh supports and the spaced bars on the inner side of the ledge. All the bars were about four feet high and about eight inches apart. Half were fixed to the outer side of the ledge that overlooked the Expressway below. Even with the early hour, brisk traffic steadily hummed along.

A kid could easily pass through those bars—
"Louis?"
And fall to certain death!
"Louis!" he called in panic just as he noticed his son pass through the space—a gaping hole for a five-year-old kid—and onto the ledge. His heart plunged as he screamed to bring his boy back from the edge of oblivion.

His boy did not turn back. Seconds later his father arrived at the mouth of the open space, his arms extended. Louis looked straight ahead, frozen in place and serene. Charley was at his dad's side and both saw that beyond Louis was a shadowy human being of a man. A man wearing a long overcoat—in this August heat—with military-style boots, still with thick soles, a full beard, and long, dark hair that covered much of his face.

Dad looked back to Louis, still frozen and just beyond his reach. Then he looked out to the man again, wedged between supports and whose presence apparently went unnoticed by the vehicles that passed underneath. No one was pulling over—yet. If he could just pass through the space and grab his boy, he'd be done with it. But no. He could not pass through, no matter how he tried.

"Louis. Come here, honey. Come on," Dad called out. He was careful not to shout but was loud enough to talk above the noise of the traffic.

"Are you my cousin?" Louis blurted out. He was still looking straight ahead. Then, for no apparent reason he added, "Boston Cream Pie." With those words, he appeared almost relaxed and pleasant. The man looked as if he had not heard the boy at all.

"Louis. Come on," said Dad. "Don't worry about your cousin. Just come to me."

"I think it's him, Dad."

"Jesus Christ, Louis!" he said madly. Then with a shout Dad thundered, "Are you Frank Lowry?" After a brief pause, Dad said to his son, "Come on, honey." Charley was holding onto his father. Inexplicably, it seemed all this activity went unnoticed. There was no answer from the man on the ledge. *Not sure he heard.*

"Frank?" Dad repeated unconvincingly. His mind was void of every possible street name he had associated with his cousin. His concern was wholly for Louis, beyond the safe hands of his father, and probably within reach of the mental case, whatever his name was, who stood on the ledge over the overpass. And if he chose to, the man could push, pull, or carry his son away.

"Who are you, asshole?" the man suddenly yelled.

"Dad, call the cops. Where's your BlackBerry? I'll call 9-1-1." Charley was eager to help.

"Not now! Relax" was all Dad could advise. The morning sun silently reflected off Louis' dark hair. The North End market would be booming within minutes. Focusing on the man again, Dad said as calmly as he could, "I'm your cousin, man. And so are these guys, my sons. We've come to take you home. Frank?" Dad could not discern whether this man could be their cousin. All his basic statistics—the renderings they gathered from Opa—were thoroughly obscured from view.

"Assholes," he finally heard from the man.

"Look!" he responded. "Do you people call everyone assholes?"

"Only assholes...like you." He looked anxious. It looked like he was ready to do something rash. "And don't call me 'you people.'"

He could climb over the bars. He could grab Louis. God, please! Please, God. No.

"I'm sorry. Come in. Come on back, man. Be careful. My son's right there. Please...come back."

"You better pray I don't come back there. I'll kick your ass...asshole." The man was anxious still. "And get this kid of yours away from me."

"Dad, it's him," Louis said. "I think." He was barely audible.

"Are you Roy Boy?" asked Dad.

The man's face changed, but it was still hard to see his features.

"Roy Boy?" Dad repeated to the man. He could see the man's brow furrow and his eyes tighten.

The man said nothing, but his look suggested, "Maybe."
But Roy Boy? He struggled with it. *Don't get the connection.*
The man looked lost. Despaired.
Maybe all the good names were taken.
"I have no one," the man suddenly said.

"Sure you do…Frank? You have good people who care about you. You have no idea, I guess, but you do. You really do. We're gonna help you now and we'll tell you all about it." Acutely aware of the incessant din of the background noise—four people spread out over the highway—with the world still passing by as if they were invisible.

"Opa told us all about you," chimed Louis.

"Who's Opa?" The man locked eyes with the young boy, and Dad could see his eyes *could* be green—that'd be a match for Frank. His height looked about right too.

The man fixed his stare on the boy who stood stiffly only a few feet away. His look and his manner, oddly enough, flooded him with something good. He could not be sure why, but he felt something for that boy. *Is it love?* he thought. He always liked kids. He had one, a boy, about the same age as the kid who now stood practically next to him. The kid even resembled his own little guy.

"He's—" Louis started to say.

Interrupting his son, Dad repeated, "Just come on back. Please, come in." Then, as calmly as he could muster, he said, "The Expressway's a real bitch this time of day."

Despair was crushing the man now. "Who the hell is Opa?" he asked again. "Tell me, asshole, who's Opa?" The man started to reposition himself on the overhang, inching a bit closer to those pleading with him to climb down from the precipice.

"He's a relative of yours, if you're Frank Lowry. A relative of ours. All of us." Dad waved his arms to show the man who he meant. Slowly, he was finding his nerve. "Infantry, like you, right, man?" No matter how hard he tried, he just could not slip through the space to grab his boy.

"Field artillery," answered the man.

"He was that too." *Too much sweat. Too much stress.* "He's…retired now but he did both. He was in the…the 15th Regiment. Heavy artillery. Before that he was in the infantry. He really was."

"You're full of shit, asshole." The man's tone had not changed.

"Dad, tell him."

"No. Really, Opa was an old artillery guy, like you. Right, Frank? Weren't you in the 120th Field Artillery over there…in Iraq, Frank? Weren't you? Opa told us that." He still struggled to make his way out onto the ledge.

"When?"

"Uh, it was the…sixties." He suddenly felt as though they had turned some corner with the man.

"Nam?"

"No. State-side. Opa's really a guy named Anton. Opa's his street name. His nickname. He really cares about you, man, and about what happens to you…and your family. He is family. Our family, right…Frank? You gotta believe me, man. Come back. You have a wife, Cathy. And a kid, Andrew. Right? Please. Frank?" He wasn't sure if he should have mentioned the wife and kid. He could go at any moment. He could snap.

"I don't know any guy named Opa," the man said after a long pause. He knew he could never go lights-out in front of the kid.

Dad felt relieved since the guy's wife's name hadn't caused him to jump. "Fuck, man," he muttered. He didn't know what else to say.

"Dad, don't use bad words," said Louis. "I hate it when you use bad words." Louis looked straight ahead toward the bridge.

"Don't say 'hate,'" his father shot back.

Christ. Please, Christ. Dad noticed the slight movement of his boy—still staring straight ahead—but he moved slightly toward his father. Then the man he believed to be Frank Lowry moved similarly. Louis was still beyond reach, and froze again in his place. The busy highway was only getting busier. The moments passed like hours, and scattered horn blasts suggested suddenly that they *were* noticed.

"He's down in Virginia now, and you—we—" He heard the ring of his BlackBerry, which was tucked into one of many pockets in his khaki cargo shorts. Four rings and it'd go to voice mail.

"This guy Opa is key, man. Come on in and we'll tell you all about him." The long beep of a car horn suddenly sounded underneath. And Dad knew that the distant wail of a police cruiser was meant for them. Traffic started to stop. People started to gather.

"Come on, man. The Expressway's a real bitch." It was only a matter of time, he thought, before the whole city focused on this drama. "Listen to me!" he continued. "We gotta get you down before the cops come. They'll take you away, man, and we can't let that happen. Right? Frank?" His truthful eyes were firmly locked onto the dark green eyes of Frank. "We can get off this ledge and disappear into the North End. No sweat."

Louis slowly turned his head up to the man who now looked down on him. His father's pleas continued and were muffled in the din of the morning. His father's eyes were no match for his own honest eyes. This man was his blood cousin Frank. He just knew it to be so.

"Let's get out of here now, and talk," Dad pleaded. His eyes noted Louis was a few inches closer. Then, finally, he grabbed hold of his son's short sleeve. With a gasp he added, "We can get some coffee." He yanked his son toward him and took a deep, long breath. Louis was unfrozen, fresh. "Espresso if you prefer."

The BlackBerry rang again, and Charley frantically searched his father's pockets. His dad was oblivious to the world beside him as he pulled Louis firmly into his embrace. He cried in absolute joy and great relief.

The man briefly froze and then followed the boy off the ledge and on to the granite step. Frank Lowry, once the gregarious and successful entrepreneur, proud father and husband, brave soldier and patriot, a man who was only a few moments ago down and out and hopeless in Boston, now felt something—or more likely someone—had reached deep into his soul and given him hope. And as he took Dad's outstretched hand in the universal sign of peace, Frank said, "Now that you saved me, what are you gonna do now?" The men embraced in a quick, silent motion and were just as quickly joined with a group hug from Louis and Charley.

"We've gotta get out of here," said Dad. "That's what we gotta do." The sirens, now more than one, were growing louder. "Walk, don't run, guys. Let's cross the road and get over to Hanover Street. Now." His voice was smooth yet forceful enough to command obedience.

They would have little time to melt into the crowd before the cops arrived. The group of four walked briskly in the direction of the open-air market, and just beyond it was Hanover Street. "Thank you," Dad offered repeatedly as pedestrians made space. They'd have to lose Frank's overcoat and buy a T-shirt or something somewhere, in order to freshen up the man's homeless-suicidal appearance. Dad's eyes were dark with tears and his heart was full of contentment. Somehow, some way, they had actually done it.

CHAPTER
46

*S*hould she call the house? Email perhaps? She was still thousands of miles away and perhaps a week or more. From the ancient palazzo in Venice, with its marble floors and restored murals, the last leg of her summer holiday was staring her right in the face. There'd be a brief stay in Milano, then along the Mediterranean coast to the land of her forebears, before she journeyed on to Geneva, and from there, finally, Paris.

Ready as she was to return to the States, Oona felt right at home in this lovely part of the world. Her father's father was an Italian, and her name, Neeci, was derived from that heritage. In fact her grandfather's family had settled in Nice long ago, and some said that connection lent to the origin of her surname, though she was not sure of that.

Right there on the Cote d'Azur, and only a stone's throw from sunny and beautiful Neptune Beach, her father left his family's villa at La Colle-sur-Loup when he entered the foreign service. And far from the luxuries to which he was accustomed, Paul Neeci was eventually assigned to France's Haiti mission. But there in the Caribbean he found his first true love and future wife, Oona's gorgeous French-Haitian mother, Julette. The couple relocated to Jamaica when Paul was posted there on assignment, shortly before the birth of their only child, who came into the world on January first, 1982.

When she was only one year old, Oona and her family, now including her Mamie, again relocated on assignment—this time to

New Orleans—where her diplomat father finally assumed the station post of his dreams, in the United States of America, a position for which he had long aspired.

Languages always flowed easily for Oona, who grew up with French and Haitian-Creole in the house. She quickly leaned Italian, and English followed thanks in great part to *Sesame Street*. Her childhood vanished at the finest boarding schools in Europe before she returned to America in the year 1999, at the dawn of the new millennium. Not yet eighteen, Oona, with her distinct features and exquisite mix of ethnicities, entered Harvard in the fall of that year to begin her higher education.

Now, in a few short days she'd fly to New York, as she generally did—but not always—at the close of her annual summer pilgrimage. *Wait till you're in the States*, she thought. How she'd been drawn to her from the time she'd first entered her office. *To enjoy her touch.* Emotional and physical lust. The struggle within was about to begin all over again. *To taste her fruit.* Her determination to keep at bay what remained for her an unquenchable sexual appetite made the conflict within no easier to bear. *Unrequited lust.*

And all she could think about was placing a call to KC.

CHAPTER
47

*T*he place was filled with Italians, and the kids were remarkably relaxed. Frank sat opposite his older cousin at the tiny, round table. The boys ate their cannoli and bantered about as their father sipped his espresso. Frank drank his black coffee. While he seemed fully aware of his surroundings—he was lucid and even personable at times—the depth of his mental despair was evident. His health was questionable but he had no obvious sores or open wounds on the visible parts of his body. He had washed up in the bathroom and tied his hair back away from his face. He donned an old Donny and Marie Osmond concert T-shirt—only two dollars— that they bought on the fly while evading the law. In his own way, Frank Lowry had taken care of himself, with regular trips to the Roxbury VA for his meds and check-ups. He said he was being treated for anxiety and depression that were associated with, but not exclusive to, his PTSD.

"I have the meds to prove it," he said. There was no smile, but his rugged good looks lay just under the surface. Tenderly, he stroked Louis' back, leaned back in his chair, and crossed one leg over the other.

"Let's get over there while it's still morning," said Dad. "We can get you checked out, refill your meds, and drive down to West-bridge to figure out what to do next. You see, Frank, now that we've got you, we need to drive to New York to help Opa."

"I thought you said he's in Virginia."

"He's a ghost," Louis said quite casually. Frank and Dad chuckled, and their eyes stayed on each other.

"It's a long story, man," said Dad. "Look, we can try the family introductions, but for now let me just say we have common ancestors who, a long time ago, split up. I can say my great grandmother stayed in New York, and her brother, your…third…great grandfather, I believe it was, moved to Peoria, Illinois."

Such talk of ancestors meant nothing to Frank. A half hour ago he was ready to call it quits. Now he was sitting in the company of Middle America, snatched from the brink of disaster, and listening to a guy talking a mile a minute as if he really was his long-lost cousin, which of course he told him he was. *Yeah, let's all get in the car and drive down to suburbia.* "Well, what are we waiting for?" he finally said.

"The cops to clear the area," said Dad. His voice rose slightly as he ended the sentence. "Let's give it a little more time, another coffee perhaps, before we walk back out into public." Dad was direct. "Whaddaya say, Frank?"

"Sure." He'd need his meds pretty soon, and he was getting all teary eyed now, thinking about Andrew, his kid, and even his wife, that bitch! "And thank you. Thank you all."

Dad couldn't wait to call KC.

CHAPTER
48

$\mathcal{T}$he night was special. It was "Mission Accomplished" in Boston. Now KC and her husband needed to figure out the next, even more intimidating phase of their mission.

"I think you should bring Frank with you to New York. He's an extra body and can help you tremendously...with the digging." She hoped for a light-hearted acknowledgment, and when she didn't hear one, she continued on a more serious note.

"Honey, I wish I could be there with you. You know I do. If Thankful wasn't sick, and Zupper too! God, I don't know what's going to happen with her."

"I know, hon. I feel so relieved, but I'm scared shitless for New York. How are we gonna pull this off?"

"I'll do the heavy lifting in D.C. I can go any day with Jean-nette...or Loek. Trix can take care of Thankful. She's doing okay— still getting over her virus symptoms. I'll get the ball rolling with the egg heads, the bureaucrats there and in New York. I'm certain there are many we'll need to deal with."

She heard her husband's long, deep breath and the kids yelling in their echoey house and former home. "Yeah, let's see," she continued. "We need Anton's discharge to be reversed, and his unmarked grave located, and his remains removed for a proper burial. In between these simple tasks, we can make the case that he was screwed out of the Army while we confirm, through expedited DNA testing, I suppose, that the bag of bones we find somewhere in Brooklyn will in fact be…Anton's." She smiled. Her baby was held tight in her left arm while she sprang up and down on the balls of her feet. For now anyway, Thankful seemed okay.

"This New York escapade is scarier by the moment," he said.

"Oh yeah, and we have to wrap everything up before the kids start school. Right?"

"I think so. Anton's redemption can probably wait a little longer. Don't you think so?"

"I'm not so sure." She seemed thoughtful and resigned. "He didn't say exactly when this stuff had to be completed. Frank was different. We know that. He was suicidal and would have died for sure had you not done what you did. Now, Opa's dead already, but I think he's in imminent danger too. Remember, his grave's about to be covered with asphalt. And then, what're we gonna do?"

"Yeah, I guess we'll 'push on' as the Brits say." He smiled. "Honey, I'm so happy we found Frank. And if we can do that, we can do anything."

"You know, Opa's presence is nowhere to be felt in this house. I'll never forget it. I was sitting on the sofa. It was still the morning that you left. It was cool and sweet, sweet like his tobacco. It passed over me and through the house. The faintest smell of his pipe tobacco upstairs in the attic is all that remains. He's gone, honey, and I think he may be in some kind of…waiting room of sorts, somewhere in limbo, let's say, waiting there for the outcome of this…story." KC drew her breath and then planted a soft kiss on her baby's forehead. "I think we need to see it through as soon as we can."

Celebrations in an empty house with a newly recovering alcoholic and two children were muted for Dad and the boys. The outside fire pit was still functional, and there was no shortage of pine wood to burn. Otherwise there was no party, and the kids didn't seem to mind. Tomorrow they'd go to church, though not to their old parish. There'd be too many people there; too many questions. Then on to the mall, where they'd fix Frank up with some decent clothes and shoes. While doing so, Dad would casually broach the subject of looking for an unmarked grave in New York City. He had, earlier, sworn the kids to secrecy. He didn't want to shock or terrify Frank with more mention of ghosts. *Not now.* If anything, it

196

should have been Frank doing the terrorizing, he thought. From the mall, they'd stay in Westbridge till they collected supplies for their journey to New York City. Things like food and drink were needed. But shovels? Digging? He wasn't so sure about that.

Amazingly, Frank was happy to go along for the ride. In one short day, after a shower and a full round of new medications— compliments of the Veterans Administration—he was looking and sounding pretty normal. And if he thought that a clandestine mission to Brooklyn to "dig up" an old ancestor's grave was weird, Frank didn't show it. Instead Frank had a fresh new look; he loved to talk sports and quickly caught Charley up on the Boston scene. Stats flew inside and outside the house that Sunday. The boys heard that even in the darkest of times, and occasionally because of it, Frank was a diehard Red Sox fan. He seemed like family to them, like the cousin you rarely saw, but who was always cordial and friendly, and fun, when you did.

The plan was to beat rush hour traffic and leave Westbridge at 3 AM Monday, the twenty-eighth of August.

CHAPTER
49

*K*C was tired. Exhausted. It was a good thing that young Trixi was around to help with things. The week had, so far, been awful. Thankful came down with an ear infection. Zup went back to the vet. The weather was terrible as well, especially with multiple Washington excursions. And all the phone time at home was no better.

KC sat on the sofa and looked over at the beautiful young girl with the steel-blue eyes and all that hair. *Tons of it.* Pulled back, only with some success, in one large ponytail behind her ears. *All legs and hair.* "And somehow we still managed a beach day," she said with a smile. Over the last few days, KC had drawn on Trixi for all the usual things. And while KC did not speak of ghosts or angels, or Anton's century-old intrigue, she told her newly anointed confidante more than enough for the girl to appreciate the general contours of her family's undertakings.

The girl smiled. Her blond hair was the color of the sun, long even for someone her age. Her deep-set eyes crinkled a bit around the corners. "Thankful has been very kind to us, KC." Trixi called her KC. Everyone did. Trix was situated opposite her boss, seated comfortably in a big leather wing chair. "It could be much worse."

"You know, it's looking more and more like a desperate situation." KC's remarks seemed to come out of nowhere.

"Don't feel that way, KC. You never do." Her English was nearly perfect, complete with the occasional colloquialisms. A European girl. A British flavor to her speech.

198

"Oh, Trixi, thank you. It's just that we have such an abundance of useless bureaucrats in both Washington and New York. I swear these people work from ten till two, with a three-hour break in between."

They laughed.

"I fear I am beside myself with…failure." KC couldn't recall ever having said those words before.

The young girl listened sympathetically and said nothing. She smiled softly. While she understood every word KC said, she struggled at times to understand the context of what was being said, though her words sounded like the way grown-ups talked about the government back in Holland. *Rantings about politicians.*

"I guess I need a little encouragement from time to time. Honestly, it's my husband that I'm worried about…more than myself I mean. They've been wandering around for the last couple of days, which have been blazing hot, and he has no clue what to do next. And neither do I.

"We have managed, I think, to narrow the search to a busy intersection in Brooklyn that kind of matches a description we have. And we did that all by ourselves. We've learned we won't be getting any assistance from the City or from the Feds." KC shifted her position on the sofa and took in the airy comfort of their family room. "That's the federal government, sweetheart. The Archives won't get involved at this point, and the veterans—the VA—who are actually handling New York's affairs in Philadelphia, well, they're useless too. There's nobody in any official capacity that is going to help us find an unmarked grave in New York."

Trixi nodded politely. It was really such an interesting story, but she didn't get the stress of it all. Why was this all so urgent? Boston, then New York. Why now? The girl wished there was something more she could do for this woman. But for now all she could do was listen.

"Luckily, with my husband's connections, his people are checking on Anton's military and discharge records, and those of other men in his regiment, to see what official records said and to build a bigger picture, maybe find some pattern of misconduct. But these people—they're all really nice, but not one among them has any clue what it's like to work in the real world. They all love my husband, but they're in by ten, out by two!"

They laughed again.

"And that was an understatement when I was there on Tuesday. No, it was only yesterday. I had time with an assistant deputy researcher, a guy named Steve who was supposed to meet me at the branch at nine. It was almost ten before he got there. Then he had a family emergency right after lunch."

Trixi smiled. She could hear Thankful starting to stir in her beloved car seat. She'd be awake in a minute and probably crying, the poor baby. Her expression changed slowly. School started next Wednesday. *What then?* How would KC manage without her?

"Well, Steve delegated to his assistants, and I have no doubt they are working on it. This stuff is their passion, if they can be passionate about anything." She drew her breath. "And there I go. I'm sounding like my husband. He can be so sarcastic."

"I know." Trixi smiled some more. "My father is the same way."

Loek. How lucky we are to have Trixi and her family, she thought. Yes, KC admittedly felt better with those Dutchmen around. But she thought, *When the hell is Oona getting back to the States?*

He never should have gone into the cemetery and never should have asked questions there. The gravediggers were okay at first, but when he went to their supervisor, the guy looked at him like he was some kind of terrorist. *Paranoid*, he thought. *But why?* He could see the kids. Couldn't he?

So, they succeeded in raising suspicions the very first day. Afterward, they drove out to Long Island to pick up the stuff they really needed: shovels and flashlights and lanterns. The next night they went back for a metal detector and a big brown tarpaulin to cloak them under cover of night. He added a large Tupperware container on impulse, something in which to throw Anton's bones if they ever found them.

After three days on the streets of Brooklyn, they had also succeeded in sampling all the neighborhood had to offer: its people, and especially its greasy spoon diners and food joints.

Now late Thursday, they were getting quite desperate and would have to start digging somewhere. "Come on, Louis," said his father. "Get your brain rolling over there. Please."

"I'm trying, Dad." In truth the boy *had* been trying. Trying very hard to feel something.

Charley and Frank were somewhere else. No doubt they were talking sports and taking a break from the walk-arounds. And that was okay. They'd be available as soon as they were needed, when the real work began. At a time when they'd finally pull the duffle bags out of the old Buick and start digging.

He thought back to the "magic mirror" and the construction cranes and signs. No street signs though, he didn't see any, but this was the place. *And from when were those images?* Charley's sketches and some notes and scribbles were all they had. He hoped that Anton wasn't buried under a paved road already. *It had to be the place.*

And what the hell had he been thinking? That the proud people of Brooklyn would just drop whatever they were doing to help him dig up their neighborhood? Yeah, the locals were friendly enough. Only a few were weird or cold, and that was to be expected. In general they had all been welcomed with open arms, and the story about a great-great grandfather buried nearby was truly a hit. But he didn't say where it was, and with all the cemeteries in the area—hundreds of acres staring out right in front of him in Cypress Hills—it was certainly believable that its location would need to be searched. But the actual location? He needed to tread very lightly on that subject. Locals would logically assume they'd be scouring the cemeteries for listings and locations for their loved one. But the clues they had collected from Anton pointed to what was probably one of the busiest places in the whole city, that part of Jamaica Avenue where Highland Place and Force Tube Avenue converged. There'd be bystanders wondering why, after three days, his group was still sampling street food, or wandering around with a metal detector, or taking pictures of what could only be boring buildings and scanty city commons.

"Yeah, we gotta be sure, Louis," his dad said with a smile and a wink reminiscent of Opa. He drew closer to his son. "That's when we start digging. When we know it's the right place."

"Why don't the dead talk, Dad?" Big eyes. Rich lips.

"I'm not so sure that they don't. I'm not sure about anything, anymore, hon." He feared their ruse was wearing thin.

"Why don't they tell me something? They're all across the street, and they're not saying anything to me, Dad. Nothing." His eyes were adorable.

His father stared at his boy. He didn't move. His mouth slightly opened.

"Do you think we can dig tonight?" Louis continued.

His father rose out of his stupor. "Where?" he asked. "We can't just pitch a tent and start digging anywhere. We'll piss people off, or look like crazies. Probably get arrested."

Louis looked up at his father while off in the distance his brother Charley and cousin Frank sat in the pale shade of a struggling and twisted old tree.

"If we can be sure, or reasonably so, well, then we'd at least have something to show for our trouble...and people's curiosity." Dad's eyes were tired and he was so hot and sweaty. A headache ached and his feet were sore. "Whaddaya think, Louis?"

CHAPTER
50

ew York City and the Statue of Liberty were in full view. Shortly the jet would be landing at JFK. Once she had navigated through Customs, she'd find that locker where she stowed her cell phone and laptop, two things so critical to her modern American lifestyle; two things which she deposited for safekeeping at a time that seemed centuries earlier. She had a few hours before she'd be on another plane, headed home to D.C.

She couldn't wait to call KC.

"*Ma chère.* How are you? It's Oona."

"I know it's you and it's so wonderful to hear your voice."

"And for me as well. How is everyone?"

"Oona, there is so much to tell you. Where are you? When will you be here—home?"

"I'm in New York, waiting for my plane. I cannot wait to see you." *Seduce you. Rape you.*

"Oona, the boys are in New York right now."

Cast a spell on you.

"They're looking for Anton."

"His...earthly remains?" she asked. As she had always suspected: His was a detached soul. An unfree soul. "Anton's is a tortured soul, *ma chère.* His soul, in Virginia, is his subtle body, distant and distinct from his physical body, which comprises his remains."

"Yes. It's a long story, but we did make contact with Anton. He's a great-great grandfather to my husband, and he told us his story and why he's there—you know, where we live. He's in the attic. I mean he *was* in the attic until the boys left. Either way, he's stuck until we can free him for Heaven. He calls it the Light. And there are three things, well, two really—"

"*Ma chère.* Perhaps I can assist them with their search?" *It's the right thing to do.*

"Yes. I know you can. That'd be fabulous. They're with Frank Lowry from Boston. That's where they found him. He was ready to jump off that Bunker Hill bridge; that white cable-stayed Zakim Bridge! Do you believe that? He's a cousin of theirs who was in a lot of trouble. Now he's okay, I guess, and they're all in New York, mainly in Brooklyn near the Cypress Hills Cemetery, looking for Anton. They've been there all week."

"Well, I can certainly help in that regard. We will take care of that business. I promise you. Anton is likely in an unholy place."

"Yes, that's exactly right. Opa's trapped there. That's Anton."

"Yes, *ma chère.*" She felt almost drunk, hanging on every word of KC's luscious deep voice. It had been nearly two months since she'd seen her.

"He needs to be found and moved to hallowed ground," KC added.

"Of course. And from there he can pass into the Light. We will find him." Oona paused to think of earlier events in Fairfax. "So the little man, Louis, how is he?"

"He's good. Real good. Everyone there is good." A pause, then, "Well, I'm not sure about Frank. I mean, I never met the man, but they say he's nice and, it seems, he's back from the edge."

"I'll reach them by cell phone. I'll just need the number and I'll take a cab straightaway."

"Yes, that would be great. But what about your flight? Your baggage?"

"This will not be a problem. I have not checked in for my connection. I can cancel my flight and leave my bags here until I return." She paused and then quipped, "I may just catch a broom back."

"You're funny." KC sensed a smile on Oona's face. "You know Thankful's been sick. Both she and Zupper have been sick. I'd love to be there, but I'm also cracking the whip on those apparatchiks in Washington. Things are moving on several fronts." There was a short pause, then, "Hey, why not travel home with the boys, once you guys take care of all your business?" Her thoughts lingered for a moment, and then she said, "My dear, you'd make for one interesting car ride."

"For sure." Oona wondered if that reply surprised KC. Her thoughts moved to the man named Frank Lowry, and with that she added, "Of that I am sure."

"I never imagined it would take this long."

"For me?" Oona asked.

"Well, of course, but I was speaking mostly of the boys and their odyssey. It's September first already." KC provided Dad's cell phone number and what she knew of their current whereabouts. She felt relieved and confident, not only that Oona was willing to assist with their search, but for the fact that she was back in the States and seemed ready to pick up their friendship exactly where they left off, months earlier.

"I feel like you never left," KC continued.

Oona listened closely. She said nothing.

"I feel like we're so...connected."

Oona waited for the slightest indication of something other than face value.

"I feel like we can talk about anything."

"Be careful of what you wish for, *ma chère*." After a brief pause Oona added, "I will see you soon."

CHAPTER
51

The second he saw the rhinestone flip-flops, he knew it was her. There was no way to describe his relief on seeing her magnificent feet emerge from the side door of that yellow taxi, followed by her long, tanned legs. For four days they tried to discreetly locate Opa's bones for clandestine exhumation. Time spent in brutal heat, though time not completely wasted. They mapped a good number of small patches of turf which were about to feel the impact of the Cypress Hills Local Development Corporation, and which he thought could include the spot they were looking for. *A crap-shoot, really.* So it seemed to him. That is, until now.

Oona was as he recalled her, completely stunning. Her hair was artfully mussed, and her matching jet-black eyes were framed with brilliant sky-blue shadow. *Long, thick lashes.* Those eyes complemented her hair, while her precise nose complemented her full, full mouth. Full, too, were her breasts and, like KC's, perfectly shaped though larger. Her torso was encased with a tight red cottony top that revealed the outline of her glorious attributes just enough. *Perfect.* Perfect, period.

As she approached them, he saw her painted toes mirrored her fingers. There were ten strong shades of utterly mismatched neon colors.

She smiled her smile.

Frank smiled. The kids and their father smiled.

"So the City did not find Anton for you?" she said, still smiling.

"We almost blew it the first day with the cemetery officials," Dad replied. "I put my foot in my mouth more than once as I tried to describe our purpose. I think we almost got arrested. Only the construction crews can tear up the ground around here." He smiled. "Hey, you know the kids already. This guy here is my cousin Frank, from Boston."

She is so fine.

"How do you do, Frank? I am Oona Neeci." She reached to lightly kiss both of his sweaty cheeks, and then turned and did the same for Dad. A polite hand was extended to Charley, and what seemed like a telepathic greeting was exchanged with Louis.

"We have to find Anton's spot before the road work claims him, if it hasn't already. City bureaucrats won't do a thing unless there are public hearings and court orders. If we pursue it legally, it'll take years and probably millions of dollars to delay the development, to search for what? What do you think is left?" Dad wanted to show Oona that he welcomed her opinions and was on top of things. He took a sip of his bottled water and shyly offered her the same. He was, for sure, a little intimidated by the beauty that stood a few feet in front of him.

She said nothing. She looked around the area. Everyone's eyes were on her.

He took another sip. "I'm convinced we need to do this thing under cover of night, by ourselves and very discreetly. But where do we dig? We have lanterns and shovels and spades and all kinds of shit, Oona, but we don't know where to go. We *think* it's in this area, but that's by no means certain."

"How's the boy?" she asked.

"Louis said he saw dead people across the street."

"Yes. I see them as well."

"He said they don't talk."

"They speak at midnight." She slowly scanned her surroundings.

Dad nodded earnestly, and while he did he noticed that Frank was staring at her as if he had never seen a woman before. He realized then that from here on in, Charley would have to compete for Frank's attention. *Let's see now: sports or the most striking, most intense and sexy creature on the planet?*

"Midnight is the time we will return to this place." She rotated her view again, slowly and deliberately. "Tonight we will see what…intelligence we can collect. Evening activities in this place will *not* work to our favor, and we shall deal with that as well." Turning to Dad, she said, "You said you have a tarp, a cover of some kind?"

"I don't think I said it, but we do…have a tarp. It's a big one. Well, big enough. Lanterns, shovels, you name it, lady. We've got it."

Mildly annoyed but skilled not to show it, she continued. "We may need the tarp."

"You got it," said Dad and Frank in unison.

She regarded the two men standing before her. The first, KC's husband, was a handsome man, a hard worker, a good father, and an interesting character in many ways. *KC only sees the good in you, my good man. You are very lucky to have her love.* Then to Frank she turned. Now here was an irresistible man, with rugged good looks and perfectly shaped green eyes. *Dark like those of my father.* This man was well built, and well endowed, and handsome, with full lips and mouth as is preferred. *He is manly and articulate, when he wants to be. My gentle hands and quiet words will calm you.*

After a time-consuming detour to JFK to retrieve Oona's luggage—and fortunately the Buick's trunk was large enough to accept everything of hers in addition to what they already had—the five returned to Brooklyn, to the base of operations that was a no-frills chain motel, and the second such establishment the group had used since Monday. It had not been discussed but was clear on arrival that Oona and Frank would be sharing a room and that it was time for Charley to move in with his father and brother.

"Let's regroup here," Oona said. She hadn't made love since Paris, and to describe the intensity of her carnal requirements in terms of others' desires was to understate those cravings. Frank and Oona were left to their own devices, and regroup they did. And the thin walls that were shared by the two adjoining rooms were testimony to a not-so-intimate celebration.

"Man, don't you have a wife?" he mumbled. He sat up, wide awake in bed while his cousin and the bitch got it on next door. *That hot bitch!* He listened to the wailing and swooning and, while there were two queen-size beds in their room, for now both his boys were crashed on either side of him. He had to get some sleep too. *Don't torture yourself.* He clenched his jaw and reached for the phone to call his wife.

What a day, KC thought. What a wonderful day Friday had been. Things were finally coming together. First Oona arrived back in America. Then both Steve at the Archives and a guy at a veterans' group called, both with major progress to report.

Steve said a "disproportionate number" of men in Anton's regiment had faced similar disciplinary actions. All forfeited pay and monies due, in return for "leniency." None had any records of courts-martial. And in the months after the War's end, three other men in Anton's company quietly fell victim in this same way. All were under Ewing, though he was never implicated in anything. Those occurrences seemed sporadic enough and well beneath anybody's radar screen, until now.

The story got even better, she said. Beside herself with enthusiasm, KC could not wait to tell her husband. The truth was apparently confirmed in 1880, when the U.S. Census cobbled together strikingly similar stories from a number of immigrant soldiers who, a good fifteen years after the War's end, with many in failing health, and some with failed families and marriages, started to speak. Monies owed in bounties and unpaid sign-up bonuses seemed an unfair and disproportionate hardship for those for whom English was a second or even a third language.

With a million men under Union arms at the close of the Civil War, the government was presented with a number of transitional choices. Most of those men who chose to remain in the service were sent west or remained for occupation duties down South. Immigrant soldiers, many of whom were eager to collect monies due and return to their adopted homes and families back north, were vulnerable to swindles and treachery in the months following the War. Quiet conspiracies cheated many men of what was promised them for fighting a war that was already won. Victims— those like Anton—with little or no evidence of charges or courts-martial against them; with no testimony, and no sign of Commissions of Inquiry established to examine their records of conduct or indiscretions, would never have warranted dishonorable discharges—extreme discipline—neither during America's prior wars nor those since, even when legitimate, documented offenses were recorded. And while Anton was long dead by 1880, a few survivors did manage to find some measure of justice in the years that followed. Sadly, with what had been gleaned from the Archives' vaults, history suggested that most men died unfulfilled, victims of apparent conspiracies for which no one was ever held accountable.

KC stopped to think of Anton's plight. The government apparatchiks had time and again corroborated his story to a tee. Likely there were many other ghosts like his out there, and probably other families, such as her own, that were called on one way or another to help. And poor souls cannot act without strength drawn from the living. *I can't wait to tell him.*

Her mind drifted once again. Though she hadn't yet heard from her husband, or her sons, she surmised that all had gone well now that Oona was there on the scene.

She breathed a sigh of relief, and then turned her attention back to her immediate surroundings: the baby had a double ear infection now. *Good Lord, when will Thankful's ailments end?* And Zupper—for over a week she was careful not to reveal the true seriousness of her condition, neither to her husband nor to her sons, for fear that, were they to know, their mission might be aborted. And how the kids were missing their mom, she thought. She could hear it in their voices and read it in their messaging. Even the smallest reason, the most minor of excuses, could change everything, and she knew in her heart, they were so close to the finish line. *So close.*

The phone rang. She knew it was them.

CHAPTER
52

*I*t was a few minutes before midnight. Everyone was up and ready. No one wore anything bright or white. The night was dull with humidity and still sharp with the noises of the weekend's start.

The Buick was parked a few minutes away from the main entrance to the small National Cemetery, which met Jamaica Avenue, and protected what was less than three acres of the Old Field, long known as the Union Grounds. The place, especially at night, was hard to separate from the veritable megalopolis of dozens of interconnected graveyards.

In contrast to what was dull and sharp was the skilled medium, the breathtaking witch who looked like a succubus to Dad, on her way to seduce the dead. The group approached the main gate with some trepidation.

"It's getting scary now, Dad," Louis said to his father, hands together as they walked a few paces behind Oona. They attracted no attention yet, and carried nothing except the folded-up tarpaulin, lugged by Frank. The tarp's medium brown color could not be discerned, thanks to the cloak of natural darkness and the canopy of the few high trees that remained in their immediate surroundings.

"What do you see, Louis," whispered his dad. He was scared of ghosts in normal times, but that was before he ever actually met one. Dad thought to times when he didn't know any Black people or Asian Americans either. How easy it was for misplaced fear or hatred to fill the voids of knowledge and familiarity.

"They're darker than today, but they're there, Dad."

"Don't worry, honey. One: we have Oona. Two: you know from Opa that ghosts can be good."

"You say there's good and bad with everything," the boy responded.

"Think 'good,' Louis. Think positive." Buoyed by his wife's latest revelations, and confident now that things were coming together at last, he finally saw the proverbial glass as half full.

"Like Mom?" asked Louis.

"Yeah," his dad whispered.

Louis was suddenly jolted by a small battery of wailing souls. They lined the gates, arms poked through with tortured faces squeezed against the wrought-iron fencing. He squeezed his father's hand, and his father reflexively squeezed his.

Oona turned to Louis and his father. "You face the ones on the left, boy," commanded Oona softly and firmly. "Stand behind your son," she instructed his father. "I will engage the rest." Then, in the direction of Frank and Charley, she said, "Open the shroud—the tarpaulin—and keep it behind me. Fold in the ends so as to be on my side of it."

With his father in tow and acutely unaware of the ghostly activity only a few feet away, Louis proceeded toward three figures—soldiers huddled together and seemingly eager for someone to hear their cries and declarations. *Missing parts,* he thought. And as was the case with his dad, Louis could see that Frank and his brother Charley were still oblivious to the noise and action he experienced only a few feet away. They were all guided, as if blind—and they were—to what he and Oona saw clear enough in the dim light of midnight.

Then Louis looked over to Oona, whose charges looked far more formidable.

"Hear me, ghosts!" she loudly proclaimed. "I seek one among you who knows the man called Anton Dietrich." Over the noises of the living night, the witch and seer could hear the loud and long wails of perhaps twenty souls, arms extended through the fencing. "Where lie the earthly remains of this mortal man," she demanded.

Though the wailers could not speak clearly, the expert seer of ghosts and spirits could manipulate the forces of the dead to wring words from their poor souls. These were poor souls for they were neither at rest nor at peace. How could they be? *So many stories. So many petitions.*

"Clausie's deception," cried one. It was a man in the tattered remnants of what could only be a dark uniform. No face. No arms. Another ghost pointed a direction. One more ghost nodded ferociously. The others all wailed on.

"Clausie's deception!" the ghost with no face repeated. The other ghosts pointed and said the word "South."

Oona turned toward the direction to which the ghost pointed. "Frank," she called.

He was at her side before his name had completely left her mouth. His end of the tarp dropped unceremoniously to the ground. Frank was drunk with lust and watched her every move.

"Have Charley continue to shroud me as you move to where I am pointing." She pointed in the direction given by the ghost. "Be careful of the traffic, *mon chéri*."

Frank began to walk as instructed. The sudden thunder of a passing truck caused him to momentarily stop dead in his tracks. "These are…ah…very busy streets," he called. "Are you trying to kill me?" He flashed his smile in the darkness.

"Frank: walk a straight line. As straight as you can, and watch for the cuts of the road."

"And I'll watch the roads too," he quipped as he walked on.

"Count any plot of land you cross, however small, and stop once your path is completely obstructed."

She drew further away and harder to hear over the din of passing traffic and other noises. "Completely?" he asked loudly.

"Yes, and mark your final location," she responded.

The commanding medium turned back toward the cemetery gate. "Come forth, ghosts, and listen now. The world of the living requires more words." Over to the left, Louis was engaged with the phantoms; his arms waved, unsure of the gibberish they spoke. A couple of pedestrians—lovers—casually passed Louis and his father and walked in Oona's direction. She'd ask the boy later what he could recount from "his" ghosts' acts and commotions.

Oona, nearly exhausted from a day that began in Paris and finally approached its end in Brooklyn, New York, turned directly toward the lovers. She stood her ground, and as if by divine intervention, the couple veered off to their right, unknowingly leaving the small group of conspirators and the jumbled mass of departed humanity behind. She drew a deep breath. She arched her back and rolled her shoulders for what was sure to be only a brief renewal. One other ghost tepidly pointed in the direction of Frank. The others had lost their strength, she thought, or for some other reason had now fallen silent. *Great sadness lay behind the wrought-iron boundary.*

And Frank Lowry was safe on the other side.

*T*hey sat at a round table in the corner of the local dive that had served Dad and his cohorts since Tuesday. Whether for breakfast, lunch, or dinner, Mal's Diner had an eclectic menu, huge portions, smiles on the servers' faces, good coffee, and even booze after noontime. Oona was seated in what seemed to be the group's center of gravity.

"I want to know what you did to turn that couple last night?" asked Dad. "You did something, didn't you?" He winked and had, of course, been blind to the paranormal happenings of the previous night.

She gave up a shy smile. "A little trick," Oona said. "Nothing more. Nothing less." She gave a wink of her own to Frank, and steadfastly ignored Dad and the borderline flirtations he had offered her all morning. Then she regarded the young boys, both busily at work on their massive breakfasts, pancakes for one and waffles for the other. The subtle snubs drove their father wild with what could only be envy.

"What can you say about 'Clausie's deception'?" she asked of no one in particular, though Dad believed the question was really directed at him. Oona looked blankly in the direction of the window and the white morning sky beyond it.

He took a long gulp of his black coffee and recounted for Oona the story he was told of Anton's death and his son Nicolaus' efforts to inter him at the Union Grounds. "He must have been

215

known as 'Clausie,' and when his efforts failed, Clausie's subterfuge laid his father in what was likely a shallow grave, within feet of the very spot where we sit now." He thought the witch heard his words. He hoped she was impressed, but got the feeling that she had not listened.

"A vegetable cart served as his caisson," she finally said. Her face was beyond beauty. It was god-like. Her tiny diamond nose stud caught a sharp light from somewhere and glittered for one short moment.

"I didn't know that, but if you say so." If only he could engage the witch more directly. She was cool to him even in the warmest of instances. And while the two collaborated, Dad was left with the notion that his actions, his deeds, and his words were, at best, *tolerated* by her. He hated to feel this way, and while he rarely aspired to be the center of attention, he always felt he needed recognition and appreciation, and especially from young women, in order to maintain his own positive image and self-esteem.

Again, there was no acknowledgment of him directly. Her favors were few and those were directed elsewhere. She sipped her tea and seemed oblivious to her wider surroundings.

His passion stirred and his heart ached. It had been two weeks since he'd been with his wife. No one imagined the length of this ongoing disruption—this escapade. His mind moved to his daughter and his beloved pet, Zupper. He even missed his job, he thought, or at least his air-conditioned office back in D.C. These yearnings hinted of regret, though since the arrival of the witch, he knew progress—real progress—had been made.

"We must return to the edge of the cemetery tonight at midnight," she announced softly.

Louis picked up his head from the half-eaten plate of waffles. He and Oona locked eyes for a long moment, and without a word the boy returned to his breakfast.

"We must be sure before we do any digging. We must not disrupt anything," said Oona.

"I'm on board with that!" Louis' dad exclaimed. He looked to the others seated around him. "You, Frank?" Charley?" Both nodded in mild agreement as their attention was elsewhere.

Oona proceeded to sketch Frank's path from the night before. The men suddenly refocused on the mission. There were three small islands of opportunity for possible excavation of Anton's remains. All were situated in the midst of city traffic, perhaps a total of three to four hundred square feet at most. And as onerous as this scenario was, the possibility that Anton's grave had already been covered by pavement was far worse. But the witch believed that was not yet the case, and their collective need was to move quickly and decisively once they were sure. So little remained of the area that was not already swallowed up by roads and buildings.

The group agreed that they would fan out onto the same Brooklyn streets they had pored over for the last five days. It was a miracle there were still no questions from the law, no admonitions from anybody, and no known allegations of loitering or suspicious activity. While Dad felt they had worn out their welcome in Cypress Hills, there was no hard evidence of it. And if people had tired of his face and those of Frank and the kids, there was no doubt in his mind that Oona's face would dazzle and rejuvenate onlookers and the whole community. That, of course, presented another challenge because drawing attention was exactly what they sought to avoid.

By the time they left Mal's Diner, it was with a renewed sense of commitment, inspired by confidence. Right after church (as Oona insisted they do), Louis and Oona got to work and scoured the three islands together. They looked for any sign of paranormal "chatter." The others diverted attention as best as they could, but the sight of Oona and a five-year-old boy armed with a metal detector, combing the mostly barren chunks of land in between steady streams of daytime traffic, assured those distractions were anything but substantial.

While doubtful, there was a chance, Oona had said, that *Nefesh*, or something akin to a soul could signal a person's burial site, direct from the spirit-world. Other than that, she said she'd reach out in all directions with the young seer, Louis. They'd try to manipulate whatever unseen forces they could muster, for supernatural assistance and to seek advice from unseen benefactors. Still, the validation—the surety—would most likely wait, she had said, till the evening, when the ghosts of the Union Grounds, those departed and mangled meddlers in the affairs of the living, would validate Anton's location for them.

They wandered with purpose and, predictably, they found nothing. Oona had some suspicions, and these, she said, would be born out at midnight. By mid-afternoon, with searing temperatures pouring over the streets, and with their heads pounding from the noises of routine city life, the group retired to the relative comfort of their motel accommodations.

Once Oona and Frank were settled, and Dad refreshed after a brief nap, he called KC. After that, he took the boys out for the rest of the day. It was, after all, a holiday weekend, and though traffic was horrendous, New York had its beaches and parks and places to see.

CHAPTER
54

"*Y*ou know I'd be there if I could," she declared once again.

Her husband listened. The deep voice of his wife was so sexy. It was so desirable. Why *couldn't* she be here, in New York? *Why not?*

"You know with Thankful's ears and…everything else, we'll just have to wait a little while longer. It's Labor Day, for God's sake! You know I'd be there…if I could." *Zupper's dying,* she thought. "You know I can't drive up. And it'd be crazy to fly." She also missed his touch. "And school begins on Wednesday. You have to be here for that."

"No matter what?" he asked.

"Well, yeah. No matter what," she confirmed.

He listened and hung on her every word. Surely this ordeal would end soon, he hoped.

"So honey, I got a call from a friend in New York, and she explained everything we'll need to do once we find Opa. She tried to arrange meetings, but cold calls will have to do on Tuesday. The holiday weekend, end of the summer, and all that…stuff."

"Tell me about it later. I have to get some more rest."

"Loathe you," she said with a smile. He smiled on the other end of the call.

Time passed into evening and then, once again, midnight was upon them. They returned to the fringes of the Union Grounds,

219

and from there Louis served as a conduit and conveyed multiple channels of communication he collected from the ghosts over to the black-dressed sorceress who stood in the night at some distance from him, and who with measured steps moved from one small piece of unattractive land to another.

The boy's fear slowly morphed into something more akin to learning to ride his bicycle for the first time. Communing with the dead was a skill, he thought, that some time and attention would perfect. Once he got past the hideousness of the mangled and decomposed corpses on the other side of the wrought-iron fencing, he was okay with it. He believed he was performing an important task for his Opa and for his dad, who stood beside him and who as before was totally oblivious to the paranormal happenings. He also acted on behalf of the lady named Oona.

Two ghosts were particularly animated. One, with a phantom's voice, seemed to guide the other, who had arms pointing in the direction of Oona and who seemed to have no voice, only a growling noise that reached what remained of his lips. Oddly, to the boy, the two seemed pleased to be involved with the affairs of the living. Other ghosts wailed on in the blackness. Oona, out in the distance, paced one way and then another, with her backside covered by the brown tarp held by his brother and cousin. It was amazing, Louis thought, how all this stuff was happening just as it had the night before, drawing little attention from anyone. There were plenty of people nearby and a constant hum of traffic down Jamaica Avenue and the streets that crisscrossed over it.

Finally it looked like Oona found something. It was hard to see her exactly, but the moonlight helped the streetlights, and he and his dad could see some commotion from Frank and Charley. Yes, it looked as though she was sure. Oona took her place on one precise location and raised one arm to motion them toward her. It was a tired motion.

She was physically and spiritually spent. She'd mark the spot with her foot. There. Right there. *That is where we shall put our spades.* And with all the residue of energy she could muster, she'd share it with Frank later and make sure that what had been a good night would end even better.

The group returned to the Buick in silence, and euphoria best described the mood of the party when her certainty was shared with them. The digging would begin on Monday night, she said firmly.

"Why wait? Why can't we just do it now and be done with it?" Dad asked.

"Tonight is too busy to be digging up Anton. Look around you. We are in the middle of a holiday weekend, and the buzz of humanity is all around us. Tomorrow evening this place will sleep earlier, its residents more focused on returning to work."

"We'll be cutting it so short. The kids go to school on Wednesday," Dad said.

"We need to plan for a Tuesday night departure. We need the boy...and Frank should stay as well. We need you," Oona said, gesturing to Louis' dad. "If someone needs to get to school, Charley can go."

"Oh, can he?" Dad shot back.

"Charley is the only one not needed for Tuesday."

To that remark Charley objected. "I'm not going home alone."

"No you're not. We all stay," decided Dad.

"Talk to your wife. She has the names of the officials you must meet with on Tuesday. She knows what you have to do. And God forbid we should touch private property," she added inexplicably.

"Huh?"

"The point is, we must do everything right. I must replenish myself for tomorrow. It will take great energy, both to mask our operation and to achieve success. The tarpaulin will clearly not suffice. Where we wandered and pointed, we more or less went unnoticed. But digging into the earth in the middle of a roadway island? Now that will attract notice! Exhuming remains? Filling in holes?" She paused and flicked her mass of black hair, and in doing so she created a slight breeze. She was always beautiful, and the dim light cast her features, the full mouth and ample chest, even stronger.

"And what if we're wrong?" Dad said. On those words, there was a sudden lapse in the giddy optimism and sense of accomplishment. There was silence.

"We will not fail," she said.

CHAPTER
55

*M*onday morning came early, and Oona was ready for the beach. The kids were pumped, and the men were okay with it, especially after Oona emerged wearing a floss-caliber red G-string with matching top, and a white see-through "cover-up." Within a few minutes they were in the Buick and headed for Sayville, Long Island. From there they'd take the Fire Island Ferry to Cherry Grove, where they'd spend the day.

Fire Island was always an adventure for Oona. She particularly enjoyed the general store at the Grove, and all the luscious bodies that dotted its beautiful white sandy beaches. This time around, the children would undoubtedly dampen her impulses, but she'd manage to carry out a few brief X-rated flirtations and some daring behaviors with Frank. Before they departed on the late afternoon ferry for the long trip back to Brooklyn, everyone seemed to have enjoyed the brief though hectic respite. And how exactly Oona replenished her body for the night ahead was a mystery to everyone but she.

They hardly slept. Dad, for one, had done all the driving back to their motel. Everyone showed it—everyone but Oona showed signs of fatigue. Wow, already ten o'clock in the evening; it was time.

Navigating the passing traffic, Oona and Louis proceeded ahead of the three others, who carried the tarp, a large Tupperware container, which was to be used for holding Opa's remains, a lantern, and three shovels, all different designs. Leading the group, Oona found the spot quite easily, just as a New York City patrolman slowed at the island. Once he stopped, his cruiser's blue flashers came on. He came out of the car and proceeded toward them. Immediately passing cars that surrounded them drew slower and closer. The boys looked like deer in headlights: Stunned. Silent. Defeated.

Oona faced the policeman, and those around her looked silently on. The officer caught her black coal eyes and after a moment he said, "Be careful." He turned to leave and the group offered somewhat rushed words of thanks. The logjam of cars began to thin out and Oona managed to get to work immediately. She paced around the boys in a close circle and spoke softly in what could only have been Creole. Dad struggled to follow the French in what she said. A shadow seemed to descend around them in a soft cover of what was a hazy curtain and which had the same effect as dark tinted glass.

A minute later Oona knelt on the ground and shifted slightly around, moving her hands in a sliding and circular motion. Again she spoke in Creole. She moved her neck from side to side and rolled her shoulders. Her dramatic face and wild, free hair swirled about in the night. Finally she rose and instructed the men and Charley to begin digging. It didn't matter that she spoke in Creole. Everyone understood. Louis popped the top off the Tupperware and then lifted the lantern to add light for the diggers. The boy smiled broadly. The diggers began to dig. A Haitian-looking onlooker, dark as night, stood against a nearby streetlamp and quickly turned away to avoid Oona's eyes.

She continued to circle the diggers, her hands outstretched now. She held the brown tarp and dragged it along the ground. As several cars slowed—one looked as if it would jump the curb in its approach—each one quickly picked up its pace and moved on, once their drivers' eyes met Oona's black, charcoal eyes. As the diggers occasionally paused to wipe the sweat from their faces, or to glance about their surroundings, the looks of the witch at times had a frightening effect. At other times an intense sensuousness radiated from her body.

Here they worked more or less freely for twenty hard and hot minutes, shrouded in casted shadows and a brown tarpaulin. A few scrub pines littered the site, and their many roots were gnarled. Almost four feet down, the diggers removed mostly soft soil, which in turn formed an uneasy ridge around the ever-widening and deepening hole. *Nothing yet.* The two men dug on and Charley rested on the dirt-covered ground, next to his brother. Two teens looked ominously on and suddenly crossed Force Tube Avenue in the direction of the island. Oona stood like a stone wall; her left hand writhed, as if arthritic and in pain. Then her other hand did the same. There were no words, but some trick was thrown that turned the teens back to where they came. As their images receded into the night, there was suddenly a flash of something at the bottom of the hole. Something shined: the glint of what looked to be a piece of a golden or brass buckle. Frank knelt down as Dad positioned himself over his cousin and looked down in silence. Frank removed an oval-shaped brass buckle with the initials "U S." His mouth widened and he inched about in the grave to show it—to present it—to Louis' father.

Frank exited the opened grave as Dad fell to his knees. Everyone was silent. Oona stood over the hole—arms outstretched again, still with the tarp. Suddenly Oona collapsed onto the ground. Frank reached for her, knelt at her side, and took her in his arms. Charley rose to assist Oona, while his brother, in mid-step into the hole, still held the lantern.

Oona lay motionless in Frank's arms while the two swayed slowly. Victory, proclaimed Dad in silence. Oona's eyes slowly opened. Dad's hands kneaded the soft soil between his bone-dry fingers, which were caked with dirt. He knew she was okay.

Then, with his son at his side, Dad remembered that he forgot to bring work gloves to this job. Those were no longer to be missed, as he needed his bare hands to properly sift through the earth anyway. For now he carefully placed each bit of fragment he could find, whether it was stone or bone, into the Tupperware container. He thought they could find that out later, in better light. Smaller fragments gave way to larger fragments, then to a full skull, whole femurs, and good chunks of other leg, arm, and rib bones. All in all Anton's remains included one leg bone that would be used for mitochondrial DNA sequence testing. Dad kissed it before he placed it in the half-filled Tupperware. The belt plate was wrapped in a bundle of napkins from Mal's, and he tucked that away in a shorts' pocket.

His father reflected on Louis' innocence and those innocent eyes. Having teamed up with Oona's charms and skills, and along with his own persistence and the tireless efforts of his wife, they had won another round.

CHAPTER
56

It was first thing in the morning, and he was on the phone with his wife.

"Okay, we're in the home stretch. Today you have your work cut out for you. And that's assuming you make human contact with some very key people," KC said.

"Yeah, I know," he tiredly stated. "I left my calling card at the grave site, or the former grave site I should say. I'm sure somebody, from the 40 percent of people in this neighborhood who speak English, will come looking for me."

"Don't be a bigot, and don't wait for those people to come after you. You have to get to them early. And for them, especially after a long weekend, I'd start knocking on doors no earlier than 10:30." It was 5 AM.

"Those losers—"

"Losers?" she asked for clarification. "They're the ones with the cushy jobs, aren't they? Hey, you're one of them now too, really. A full-fledged federal apparatchik."

"Yeah, I guess."

"It's time to use that status and its good offices." She smiled, though her mind was never far from her recovering daughter and the dog whose condition steadily worsened. The gravity of Zupper's situation bore very heavily upon her. The true severity of her ailments had still not been shared with her husband, though Zup seemed to be hanging on, if only for her master's eventual return.

How KC hoped for everyone's sake that the dog would just hang on a little longer and not die of a broken heart in the end, as Anton had. "Yes, you are the Assistant Deputy Research Director for the Archives' Civil War Records' Branch. What a mouthful."

"I'll give you a mouthful."

"Pig!" she said. "Listen: full disclosure is a good thing. Go for it! Your bosses will back you up. Everyone is on board in D.C., and your guy Steve even got it in writing."

"So I'll start with the head undertaker, I guess. The one at Cypress Hills. One of his grave diggers told us last week, when we were poking around there, that this guy, whoever he is, always comes to work early. I guess he loves his job. I'll give it a shot and hope he'll agree to store Opa's bones till we get some permissions."

"Yes, that's good. He'll probably have to go to their Board with that request. But good news is that some of the guys who sit on the Board of Directors also have important spots in the City bureaucracy. And let's just hope they don't need to go to the Cemetery Association or directly to the Feds, or the VA. But if we have to, *we* can handle the Feds easier, I think. It's the City officials who can be most difficult for us. You know. Possible turf slash ego issues."

"Yeah, I can imagine."

"Get to the highways' department as soon as you can. Apologize first, profusely. Then give them the federal spiel and let them know that the cemetery has already acknowledged the remains. Hopefully they'll sign off on a waiver for any damages caused by your little excavation and preempt any delays from lawsuits or questions of ownership or control of Opa's remains. And remember, these are historic artifacts, *not* your granddaddy's bones."

"Yeah, right." He smiled.

"You'll need to get to the Board of Health too. They'll bitch and moan unless you get there and, first, say you're sorry. If you can get them to agree not to take issue with the unauthorized removal of a dead body, then you may be good to go. Be willing to pay any fees they say they need, any fines, though be careful with limits on liability."

"Yup." He felt as if he should grow more tired.

"So if the bones are officially in cold and safe storage, and the City that housed those remains for the last 140 years does not officially object to anything, well then, you can probably take a long, deep breath and hopefully come home to take care of the work you need to do on the back end."

"And school," he added.

"Yeah." She looked distressed for a moment. She looked in a mirror and could see the lack of sleep and stress on her face.

"We're almost there. I love you," he said.

"I love you too. Hey, is Oona around?"

"She's with Frank. Fucking, I'm sure."

"You're an asshole. That's like always on your mind."

"You know I only think of you in that way."

"Yeah, I'm sure."

As Tuesday wore on, his persistence and his penance had the desired effects. Questions, demands, and threats were mutually exchanged, as were the usual words of encouragement and acknowledgment, and in the end the actions of one persuasive upper mid-level federal employee, along with the undeniable charms of Oona and the honest eyes of his young son, won the day. Anton's bones were removed to a safe repository, and it was agreed in writing that there they'd stay while a federally-run verification project would proceed with appropriate DNA tests and belt plate analyses. The anticipated results would lead to the interment of Opa's earthly remains in the hallowed grounds of the Old Field Union Grounds.

What the cemetery and the City did not know was the extent to which those tests alone would determine the outcome. The CAAF, the U.S. Court of Appeals for the Armed Forces, had the final say, and would ultimately decide Anton's fate. The conditions and nature of Anton's dishonorable discharge needed to be reversed so as to assure his final redemption. There was growing dread as Dad approached his return to Virginia.

CHAPTER
57

*H*e prepared for the long drive back. It was nearly 6 PM and rush hour was all around them. Hopefully they could make it home within eight hours. He knew he'd be saddled with all the driving again.

Frank, who only a week ago was hopeless and suicidal, loved to drive. But he was technically without a driver's license and, more significantly, doubtful as to what extent he could free himself from Oona. Now clean and hitched up with a beautiful, glowing goddess, Frank had a whole new sense of self-worth. By the time they left New York for Virginia, he required no medications, and generally looked and felt great—like he'd grown a few inches. He was just a little tired around the edges, but relaxed and fulfilled. Yes, Oona had gotten him off his drugs and his addictions. There'd be no need for that clinic in Springfield as he once believed. Yes, it had been one hell of a week for him, and the sadness that crept into his mind now and then was spurred by the likelihood of parting ways with the witch as well as the fear of never finding his wife and son.

Once the Buick Century descended into the construction sites of the New Jersey Turnpike, everyone seemed resigned that they were finally on the road to Virginia. It was agreed that Frank would stay with Dad's family for a while. For Frank, it was equally clear that any quality time remaining with the beautiful witch— as he did not know, though he could expect that she was also an enchantress—would be in the backseat of the Buick. Like a kid eating himself sick with candy, Frank could not resist her embrace even when he was totally spent. There'd be no driving for him this night.

As the traffic picked up, Dad was increasingly anxious and mindful of his two inherited underage, front seat passengers. They were his now so that Oona and Frank could have the Buick's backseat to themselves. Charley's head continued to turn while Louis, seated in the middle, continued to rub against Dad's shifter. The limited space of the car's bench seating grinded powerfully on his mood. *Keep the kids focused on the road, not on what's going on in the backseat.* And he drove through New Jersey. He wasn't sure which task was worse, the driving or the babysitting, or the draw of the sex show behind him, of which he was assured no action. *No relief.*

Oona's charms and enchantments were focused in these hours, and almost exclusively pointed toward Frank. And Frank's own charms and prowess were devotedly and exhaustingly on her. Whether in the front seat or the backseat—it didn't matter where—Oona was the center of attention for all, whether on her back or on Frank's lap or just beside him. More than once Charley successfully snuck an X-rated peek from the vanity mirror embedded in the passenger-side sun visor. The nine-year-old boy, though fascinated with the rear views, many of which he did not really understand or fully appreciate, lamented how Frank's attention had so completely passed from sports to Oona, whose wild hair often completely obstructed his mirror's reflection.

Why don't you just get a room? Dad thought angrily. *I should drop you two off at the next rest stop.* The Buick continued south. "What am I?" he quietly mumbled. "Dog meat?" His thoughts ran wild with emotion. "Why doesn't that bitch ever hit on me?" He had to watch times like these. *Control. Self-control.* "Why hasn't she? Is she afraid I'm contagious?" There she was on her back, legs apart with Frank's head not visible. At that moment, her knees were bent up. "I assure you, lady, all *my* parts still work. Magnificently, I might add." He reflected for another moment. Anger boiled inside. "Yeah, once I was great. Now I'm great once." He smiled wryly to himself. "Hey, KC still loves me. *Just say no.*" He smiled again, more like a sneer, and he looked back again into the rearview mirror. "Yeah, I'd like to play with that gorgeous piece of ass."

Suddenly there were icy stares from the witch. "I can ruin your marriage," she hissed silently. "You don't know how lucky you are." She turned her face from the rearview mirror back to Frank.

Charley and his dad could not disengage, though Dad was badly shaken with that last declaration from the witch. And Louis was poked repeatedly by his brother every time he, Charley, thought he'd seen "something good."

Dad found the courage to make a declaration of his own to the backseat passengers. "You're gonna cause an accident," he said. It sounded more like an emotional rant; a soft-sided, emotional rant.

Frank arose from his place and dreamily sat up and leaned against the side of the vehicle, as if taking a much needed break. The witch put her legs to the car floor and sat up as well. Judging by the look of her black eyes and serious mouth, framed by her wild tresses, Dad feared severe consequences. Then, to his right he noticed both his children slept deeply, one tilted against the other. Then he looked back to the highway and quickly noticed that his eyes were fixed like cement on the road. *Glued to the road!* No matter how hard he tried, he could not move his eyes from the highway, with hundreds of miles still remaining in their long journey back. *Awesome powers!*

What can't she do?

The boys slept on as the Buick barreled down the highways of New Jersey, Pennsylvania, Delaware, and Maryland, and finally, Virginia. About midway down, Dad's eyes unglued. He'd promised to "behave," and she welcomed the arrangement, as the spell required great strength and stamina, two things she preferred to save for Frank. Dad's ears, however, were free to hear the two lovers in the back now and again going at it in a fever-pitch, with periodic climaxes that were as ear shattering as they were coveted. But mercifully Dad's eyes and his stiffened neck found some measure of relief.

Finally they crossed the boundary of Fairfax County, Virginia. And like conquering heroes, they pulled into Dad's driveway at 3 AM. He beeped the horn in celebration. The boys stirred and quickly found their footing outside the confines of the road-worn Buick.

The party quickly entered the house, where KC awaited them in the foyer, lights on and her arms wide open.

Who gets the girl? thought Oona. She was sure of the answer, and witnessed KC and her husband as they kissed like newlyweds. The children rallied around their parents and added the group hug. The witch turned to Frank. She took his hand and kissed it. It was a good-bye kiss. They both knew. She knew she'd be seeing him again, but would never again share the closeness and the convenience of the last few days. That was clearly and completely over.

Then the two women locked eyes for one long heartbeat. Breaking free of her husband and the kids, KC embraced her dear friend. *Sweet scents.* Lovingly.

For one woman there was love. And for the other there was something more. *Turbulence inside.* Something different.

My time will come.

The women slowly disengaged, and frenetic chatting ensued among everyone but Frank, who stood idly by and waited for an introduction, which finally was granted by Oona. She, Oona, politely refused KC's invitation to spend the night and would call for a taxi instead.

Cliona, she cried to herself. *And how that name fitted her so perfectly,* Oona thought.

Dad looked shyly in the direction of Oona and feared additional reprisals. *She looks jealous. Pissed and…jealous,* he thought. He forced himself to think of other matters. "Where's Zup?" he asked.

KC briefed him on their dog's condition. They'd see the vet the next morning, she assured her husband.

Off in the near distance of the second story, Thankful awakened with muffled shrieks. Her father politely took his leave and quickly proceeded up the stairs to see his daughter. "This house," he thought aloud, "fully two and a half times the size of our place in Westbridge, is still not home." *Our home is still in New England. And the warmth of its stark emptiness remains very much with my senses.*

Louis and Charley followed their father.

As he held his baby in his arms, Dad realized his boys were starting school in a few hours. Fortunately they had slept in the car, but there was no telling what the first day of school would mean for them once morning arrived.

With Thankful in tow, their father walked his boys to their bedrooms and begged each one to say his prayers on his own and get some sleep. He assured them that he'd be back to rouse them in just a little while. In Louis' room, Dad glanced up to the trapdoor that led to the attic. Louis was already asleep and had been since his head hit the pillow. His father was struck hard with profound sadness. He was sure what KC had told him was true, that his beloved Opa was gone. Gone somewhere, waiting somewhere for the final acts of this "impossible" mission to play. And utterly heartbroken by the sure loss of his beloved ancestor's company, Dad resolved that once he'd taken the kids to school in the morning, and seen his beloved best friend, Zupper, he'd drive over to Langley to get started with all the sophisticated testing the CIA could muster on the femur and the belt plate that bulged from a pocket of his filthy cargo shorts.

And he hoped he'd also have time to return to work at the Branch. At the very least, he'd call in the morning and start catching up with both his regular job and his "higher calling."

CHAPTER
58

*L*ouis was tired and prone to a little crankiness, but he got right out of bed for his first day of kindergarten. Within minutes he sat among dozens of new faces and noises, and a nice lady—his teacher—stood in front of a green chalkboard and faced the class.

"And what did y'all do this summer?"

The events of summer rapidly flew through Louis' mind like the high-speed train that often took his father to work, or the window shade that, without any warning, suddenly rolled up. The kids around him were blurting out stories faster than Louis could visualize them.

One kid stood and said in his southern style of kid-speak: "I went fishin' with my daddy almost every day." Fortunately Louis could read and he saw the kid's name. Clay proudly sat back down, with a broad, contented smile on his face.

Another one, a girl named Claire, said, "My family took us to Disney World."

And still another girl, Washanda, who was seated right in front of him, said, "We saw President Cheney."

Louis thought and thought of the loneliness that surrounded him now. It was great to finally be in school, and great to see Mom and Thankful again. But since he got up, he knew for sure that his Opa was really gone. And with the teacher and the kids engaged as they were with their stories of summertime, Louis lamented Opa.

But he also missed his once "normal" and usual boring young life, the way things were in Massachusetts, before he ever met the old man. The "old man" who was younger than his dad.

The young boy, seated at his desk, was too polite to admit that those who surrounded him now meant nothing to him, and could do nothing for him to ease his sadness. He longed to be somewhere else. He wanted to return to some kind of normal.

Mom was on the phone as soon as she got home from school. She was livid.

"How could you?" she barked at Oona. Not waiting for a response, she continued, "Sexual encounters with my children in the car? How could you?" Frank was most likely still sleeping in the family room, but she honestly didn't care if he heard her. She was pissed at him too. But it was her friend, her dear friend for whom she reserved most of her wrath, her friend who betrayed every modicum of human decency, having had cheap and multiple sex in front of her sweet and innocent children. And her husband! Yes, he had told her everything. Every detail he knew, from her flying mass of black hair to her exposed breasts, to her clothes drenched in sweat and her parted legs.

Oona was in no mood for reprimands. And with a sharp tongue she shot back, "Do I detect a measure of jealousy in your voice, *ma chère*?" How she hoped that were true.

"You're incorrigible," KC fumed. *Jealousy?* "But why? Couldn't you wait till you got home?"

"Wait for whom?" she asked invitingly.

"Oh, why don't you go and read some palms, you witch." She immediately regretted those words, and the confrontation with the woman who had managed to deliver success to a mission that would otherwise have been impossible.

"I don't do palms." *Restraint and compassion.* "I will speak with you soon, *ma chère* and…I am sorry. I am very, very sorry." She never had trouble with languages, and she could always use the language of love to get what she wanted or needed. She could reach deep into a person's living soul to decipher their words and thoughts when necessary. Romance, German, and English languages, and their many dialects, were rarely a problem to speak. Spanish she'd learned on the fly and it had come in handy in

Cypress Hills. But the language of forgiveness, the words "I am sorry," remained foreign to her, vague in their meaning and unsure of their usefulness in this life. But there, she had said it for KC. If this time it didn't work, she'd say it again, and again, until it did. And with that thought, she softly placed the receiver back in its cradle and prepared for the drive to her office.

CHAPTER
59

*M*elancholia remained with KC's husband, standard fare, along with occasional bursts of anger, depression, and anxiety that followed him wherever he went in the days and weeks following his return to Virginia. Broken-hearted whenever he thought of Anton, and at other times completely overwhelmed with work and the special projects that swirled about him, he was also grieving for the loss of his loyal companion Zupper, who passed into eternity the moment she finally saw him on that first morning after his return.

In marked contrast to her husband's moods, KC managed to make peace with Oona only a few days after their altercation. And the kids seemed tolerant and, at times, even well adjusted at school. Frank, with the help of Oona and KC and the national media, which picked up on his story of hopelessness and rescue from Boston, had managed to make contact with his wife. They agreed to discuss their marriage and prepared for a meeting up in Springfield, Massachusetts.

But for Dad, it was nearly October before his sadness lifted with the good news that finally arrived in two quick volleys from Langley.

Yes, the DNA from the old femur bone was a genetic match with his own. And yes, the old belt plate was not only standard Union Army Civil War issue but, on its reverse side numbers were inscribed, clearly visible now that almost a century and a half of dirt and debris had been removed from its surface, the numbers twenty-nine and below it fifteen. *Anton's regiments.* Furthermore, an additional inscription bore a monogram "A.D." which perfectly matched the style of his initials on Opa's enlistment papers, and unbeknownst to the reviewers, also matched the elegant "A" carved deep in the wood of the attic. *Eureka!*

The Langley files were quickly provided to CAAF, which had agreed to move the review files on Anton Dietrich up in the queue once all testing had been completed. Quietly the Army acknowledged that Anton's conduct should not have resulted in a dishonorable discharge, that he had made good the time he lost when going absent without a proper leave, and that, therefore, in the opinion of presiding officers of the Review Board, the petition to have Private Dietrich rest with his fallen comrades was granted.

As late fall loomed, word was finally received that Private Dietrich would be buried with military honors at the old Union Grounds at Cypress Hills. By Veteran's Day Anton's remains had been moved to hallowed ground. Dad attended the small and touching ceremony in Brooklyn and, by Army standards, the whole process had moved by lightning speed. He waited next for some sign from Anton. It was a sign that never arrived.

Self-talk ultimately assured him that Anton Dietrich had finally gone into the Light. Then Dad moved with great speed of his own. While his malaise had dragged on for nearly a month, and finally seemed to be behind him, and as those around him had managed to do much earlier, it was cause now for celebration, he thought, and more importantly, for a new chapter in the life of his family.

So one day he stood before them and called a family meeting to order. "I am unsure now as whether to stay at my job here in Virginia, and want to ask you all how you would feel about moving back to Massachusetts."

KC and the boys were struck by Dad's words. After all, things *had* returned to a settled state for them. Things had, at times, even gotten remarkably cheery. His wife's friendship with Oona was repaired unconditionally, and her close bonds with Trix—and more recently with her family—were clearly deep and rich as well. The boys seemed comfortable with their surroundings, including school, and at times seemed overtly happy.

There was silence. Surprise.

"My old boss is crying to have me back, and another old boss—Remember Ed Spader? He wants me to work with him too. Work from home—full time. Imagine that? Plenty of alone time for me to work on the family tree and to do some writing and research when I'm not doing venture work for Ed."

"When were you going to tell me all this?" KC asked. She tried to sound upset but was really elated.

"I'm telling you now. I want to go home to my real home-town. Let's face it, we all love Westbridge. And we all love our house there—still unsold. But you know, we'd never fit back there, after living in this place for the last six months. We'll need a bigger place, and Ed's brother just happens to know of one that sounds like the perfect new house for us."

"In Westbridge?" asked Charley.

"Yes," said his dad. "Listen, I also want to talk about things with Frank. You know he's quite the handyman, and he's been floating around in the hill towns of western Mass since he left a few weeks ago. He was a carpenter before Iraq, and from what he's told me, he and his wife are talking about starting over and moving closer to Boston, where the jobs are. They'd be perfect for our old house, and we'd be keeping it in the family, so to speak. Remember how happy we were in that house? Well, their story can be one of a happy young family too, with a fresh new start, and loving each other more than ever in that old red Cape of ours. We can work with him on the financing. I'm not talking charity here, just…family. If he's okay with it, he'll find his feet in no time, while making home improvements to those nagging little issues at our old house."

"Things couldn't be better," KC said quietly and to no one. *We'll be home for Christmas.* "Not here. No way. Christmas down South would never be right for us. It's back home in Westbridge." She paced through their Virginia house. And to think, she'd only just managed to get Thankful's room the way she wanted it. "And I'll be leaving some very special people down here, but *our* lives are not here. They never were. This is not the place for my family. This place, this summer, was an odd detour on life's landscape." She ventured outside facing the creek. "Surely we'll stay in touch. Oona, with all her friends…and lovers in Cambridge and Boston, will be around regularly to visit. Then there are Loek and Trix and her mom, and even some of those characters in D.C. Little doubt they'll be missed, but hey, that's what the Internet is all about." She looked to the heavens and said, "Staying in touch."

"Yes, it has been quite a ride. Now, we'll be home, though smooched together with Frank's family and living at the old house on the floor for a little while." And with the purchase of their new house contingent on the sale of the Virginia one, KC was still confident of a relatively short-term and mostly painless displacement. She had no hopes for divine intervention, of which, quite frankly, she had had more than enough.

EPILOGUE

CHAPTER
60

*H*ow the years had passed.

Here, from the terrace of her Georgetown home, time always seemed to crawl along lusciously. Perhaps it was Erzulie's way to compensate her for how little time was actually ever spent here. Work, family, lovers, and friends were constantly groping for her, coming from all directions. Then there were all the attractions, the world over, like a Disney playground stretching for thousands of miles. The world was a place for parties and fantasies, for sightseeing and for doing nothing, sometimes, occasionally, or rarely as the case might present itself. But now all this was about to change.

This life she had known for what seemed so many years—she was still only twenty-eight—was now about to change dramatically. She knew this to be true. The news was stunning, and terrible, and tantalizing, all at the same time. And like a hard slap to her face, if anyone would ever dare, this event was a wake-up call, as Americans call it, a real game changer. It was an open door to a new room. It was a new page to a new chapter of a new book that was about to resume an old story of which no one, including herself, could be sure of its final outcome. Still, she knew what she had to do.

How everything had changed. She sat back in her glider-chair and took a deep sip of her Blue Mountain blend.

The day began just like any other. The sun rose in the sky and the family rose from their beds. She was already seated in their living room, in her favorite chair, watching her favorite show, *SpongeBob SquarePants*. It was commercial time, and in no particular order, and as she always liked to do, the young girl casually flipped through the cable channels, sometimes slow and sometimes not so slow. She carefully counted the moments till the time she predicted her favorite show would be back on Nickelodeon. It was a little private game she loved to play: She timed herself to "hit" the channel button just as a black screen set to resume the colorful images from Bikini Bottom.

There the young girl sat in the old chair. The children were handsome, cute, and beautiful, and she was the real beauty of the three. But none of that mattered this morning. Thankful was comfortably positioned in front of the TV, as usual, for a Saturday morning.

This morning was different.

"Mommy," she whispered. Then, a little louder, the young girl repeated, "Mommy." Then, rising from her chair, the terrified girl screamed, "Mommy! Mommy!"

These were awful sounds, awful screams. How awful it sounded to KC. Something was horribly wrong with her daughter. She rushed into the living room, and her daughter, as if in shock, stared at the television.

The smoldering wreck of a crashed plane appeared on Channel Five. It showed the remains of a small aircraft and its burned-out carcass. The voice of an unseen, droning newsman announced, "There are no survivors, and the incident is under investigation." The television screen remained locked on the image of the ruined fuselage.

"It's Daddy's plane. It's Daddy's plane!" she cried.

"Honey. Calm down." She was firm in those words, but terrified to ask. But she knew she had to ask. "How did you know Daddy went flying?"

"I didn't, Mommy. Mommy, he's on that plane!" She screamed it. "Daddy's on that plane!" Thankful stood frozen in front of the high-back chair, still glued to the TV, with her mouth and full lips parted. "I know it's Daddy's plane!"

By this time the boys were at their mother's side, and she begged for calm. "There is no reason for...hysteria," she claimed.

She was terrified of the truth being told from the lips of her five-year-old child. And in her heart, she knew the words were true.

Devastation.

When had she seen her last? Nearly two years since she'd been to Boston and over four years since she'd first cast eyes on her. It seemed so long ago, but her heart ached no less now than it had then. Now, a cataclysmic event, horrible and gory in all its details, provided the opportunity she needed to finally reach for and take what had for so long been an unreachable goal. There were times when she even thought to give up on this lustful fantasy, this paramount failure of her young life. And to be honest with herself, she knew it was more than lust. Love, maybe. Love at first sight, perhaps. The shape. *Shapely Cliona.* The manner. *Her voice.* Yes, all these things and more. The challenge too, no doubt. The first time she had not conquered. The first time she'd not cast a little spell or done a little trick when she wanted to help things along. She always wanted it to be totally real, and now, four years later, the supreme challenge of not having her remained so strong. *And now this.*

CHAPTER
61

I t all seemed so perfect. *Now this.* It all seemed like a dream now. Once Anton was properly re-interred, it was only a few months before the family settled back down in Westbridge. Her husband, her dear husband had resigned from the Archives, and everyone returned to Massachusetts. *Like a dream now.* Working mostly from home, he was so happy, happier than she'd ever seen him. How quickly he was consumed with new business ventures. And Ed, he was fabulous to her husband and, by extension, to the whole family. Four years quickly passed, and once Thankful started school, KC didn't hesitate to resume her banking career, though on the South Shore and close to home, and nowhere near Boston.

Now her husband was dead, and before any authority could advise her of the loss, Thankful knew that her daddy was gone. She didn't even know he was flying or that he'd left the house earlier that morning. The mysterious plane crash was no mystery to her daughter.

At one time she thought it had ended. She'd thought the infatuation—the drive—was over. So much and so many, there was hardly time to think about it. But in spite of everything, the thoughts and the longings remained. *The curve of her thighs. The scent of her perfume.* That last Boston trip was both wonderful and heart wrenching. Spending the night with them was the most cruel and unusual punishment. And while she loved the entire family, including her husband, it was KC that meant everything to her. It could have ended back then, perhaps. Oona had had enough of Boston and the frustrations of that which remained so utterly unfulfilled. The pain then was as severe as the news had been when KC told her the family was returning to Massachusetts. *One-sided, uneven desire.*

That morning began so wonderfully. KC was surrounded with the bright and cheery light that flooded into her kitchen. Then, the phone rang. It was her husband.

"I've gotta fill you in on something big, real big," he said. "Once I get there I'll tell you. It's big. I'm so excited."

"Work?" she asked him.

"Business. I'm not going to work today. Not local anyway. I'm flying to D.C. Just for the day. It's real important and I have to fill you in...after I get there and get situated."

"Is it something good?

"Yes."

"How good can it be if you can't tell me?" she asked. "And the way you flew outta here this morning—you were such a jerk—you must be up to no good." She half believed her words. All in all, he was doing the right things, getting the right contracts. "Come on. What is it? What's going on?"

"It's somethin'...big. Look, I really gotta go. I'm sorry, honey. Kiss the kids for me. And please, don't worry about anything. You'll see. I'll call you up later."

"I know." She paused. "Loathe you." Work versus business? What was the difference?

"Loathe you too. Look, I'm gonna lose you, hon. I'm coming into Central Parking now. I'll call you."

It was the last time she'd heard his voice. Now everything had changed. This sudden death was so horrible, so unexpected. Everything changed.

CHAPTER
62

White on white and very bright. "I never knew there could be so many shades of white. Where the fuck am I?" KC's husband continued to walk, to wander, through the cloud-like environment. "Where am I?" He walked on, with no idea of direction or purpose, and then he saw a light, brighter white than his immediate surroundings and quite distinct out there in the distance. He had no idea how far the brighter light was, but for now, he decided to just keep walking. And he did till he froze in his steps.

A sign with a white arrow pointed for "EARTH-BASED ENTRANTS" to the right. He turned as directed and resumed a slow and cautious stride. He knew he was dead and this had to be Heaven. There were more signs: "PLEASE WAIT HERE." "THANK YOU." He could be dead. And he wasn't sure it was Heaven.

A short man approached him, as if out of nowhere.

"Anton?"

"Greetings, *mein Herr*."

"Anton? I must be dreaming. This is too weird. Too fucking weird."

"This is no dream," he said.

"Where'd you come from? I ought to be happy to see you...but...I'm not." He approached his ancestor and the two men embraced. There were some tears, followed by memories of the old Bornheim House in Virginia where they'd first met. Slices of time flashed before his wet eyes. He was suddenly terrified that his life may have just ended for real.

Anton smiled at his great-great grandson. Though now dressed somewhat strangely for Dad's eyes, Anton's looks were otherwise those as before: a kindly, old-looking, and ghost-like man.

"What are you doing here? Where *are* we, Anton?"

"This place is on the fringes of Paradise. As you commuted, I commute here from my home in the Hereafter." He moved his head about and added, "This is where you sent me. Now, I'm here to welcome you, son."

"You mean...I *am* really dead? So you do mean we're in Heaven?"

"Yes and not exactly," he responded. "Well, I suppose it's okay if you want to put it that way—Heaven that is. But this place is more like God's Waiting Room. Come. Follow me. I'll explain on the way to my corner office."

"So I'm really dead. Is that what you are trying to say?"

"I'm not trying to say that. You *are* dead. Your body is dead, mangled and all burnt up, not far from Dulles Airport. Your physical body is gone. Dead. *Kaputt!* Now you are with me."

"So this isn't a dream?"

"Ah, no. No dream, *mein Herr*. I wouldn't fool you with something like that."

"It can't be." He ran his fingers over his balding head.

"Please. It is what it is," he repeated. "Come, please. Let us walk."

"This can't be. Is it a dream?"

"No. It is not a dream. Don't be foolish."

"Or is it something else?" he asked nervously.

"No dream. *Nein!* No dream. Come. Follow me to the office."

"Your office?" he asked timidly.

"Well...yes. You see, I'm a Heavenly Scribe. Officially a number of us share the space, so it is not exactly my own corner office, but my comrades these days are mostly out on assignment. Wait till you see it. You will like it. I know you will."

"A Heavenly Scribe? Those were the guys that got you into Heaven. Right?"

"They helped, but *you* got me here. You know it was really you who freed me from that attic. The Scribes only assisted. What you did, now that was really something. I'll never forget it. And now I can help you get to the Light." He gave a moment for him to digest all that had been shared. "So how's the family? Louis? The baby?"

"The baby's not a baby anymore. Fuck." He stopped in his tracks. "She's only five. Anton, am I really dead?"

Anton slowly nodded. "We have much to review; much to go over." He looked at his subject. So sad, he thought. They usually were. "I'm so sorry," he said.

The men faced one another and embraced once more. Then, they turned forward and resumed their walk.

"Follow me. Come, please. The sooner we get started, the sooner you'll be placed."

"Placed?" he asked.

"Yes. I am your sponsor. It is my job to collect, collate, and sort your mortal life into the Six Chapters for the Annals. Be happy, *mein Herr*, that you are not condemned to an earthly Purgatory, such as the one that I endured."

"What are the Annals? The Chapters?"

"There are six human conditions that comprise the Annals: the annals of your past. The Annals provide an honest compendium of your life. Your past, unfiltered. Everyone who gets this far completes the Six Chapters for the Annals."

"What are they?" He grew edgy. "What are the Chapters," he snapped.

"Chapters? You know all people are different: different lives, different cultures. Different mitigating factors. For the Chapters, let us say for now that it all depends. You—we—need to complete all six of your Chapters in order for you to become a Heavenly Plebe."

"What about your Chapters?" he asked.

Anton did not reply. The men walked on in the direction of his "corner office," and Dad did not repeat his question. Shades of white gave way to familiar shades of what resembled earthly daylight, and both familiar and not-so-familiar colors crept back into view. The colors enriched as the distance to the Light grew shorter. On arrival, the corner office looked more like a large library.

Mahogany bookshelves covered two walls and rose from floor to ceiling, filled with what looked like books, journals, and ledgers of all shapes and sizes. The other walls were marked with floor-length windows, some of which were covered with silky antique-looking drapes. French doors overlooked rich greenery outside, and the Light glowed in the distance. There were groves of birch-like and maple trees, and what was a rich and perfect day was clearly evident through the glass. Back inside, on a large desk sat a state-of-the art computer, complete with a large monitor, a key-board, and various high-tech devices.

Anton took his seat behind the desk. He motioned for his charge to take a seat opposite him, which he did, in a comfortable-looking, velvety wing chair.

"Would you like a beer? Some wine, perhaps?"

Dad said nothing. His mouth dropped open slightly.

"Cigarettes? All the very best. Smoke with no poison, not that it matters now, but no smells. No odors sticking to your clothes. Nothing to offend." Anton looked for some reaction and drew nothing. "But there are no solid foods. No appetizers. Nothing like that. Sorry."

"Cigarettes? Are you kidding me? Like I'm gonna start with that shit again?"

"I'm not recommending them, *Lieb*. But they won't kill you. And please watch the foul language."

Dad could see through one window trees and flora in full bloom, and deer and rabbits that grazed around them. Then, he nodded his chin in the direction of the computer. "How do you like your, ah, system?" he asked.

"Love it. It has the latest Microsoft Office Suite of things, and some in-house enhancements as well." He smiled his smile and added, "And it's a lot better than Vista. You know, it's that over-loaded security-ridden operating system. This," he pointed around the work area, "is much better. A lot better."

"Fuck" was all he could think to say.

"You've got to watch your language here." Anton looked highly serious. "Especially now. It's not going to help you."

"Because I'm not...processed, yet?"

"That is correct," Anton replied. "Once you are in, you are in."

"What about the Light? What's that all about?" He looked down at his hands for a moment and then said, "I guess it's true, huh?"

Anton used his thumb and pointed behind his back. "It's that-a-way." He pointed in the direction of the Light.

"Does that mean...?" He was overwhelmed with everything the day had brought: love, life, death, and now this! *What was at stake here? All eternity?*

"No. Not at all, if I understand you correctly." At times, the men shared thoughts and dialog telepathically. Dad's sudden reaction to that realization was evident. "It means we have some work to do. There is nothing hard. No hard work. A lot is automated. It simply takes time. We have plenty of time, if we need it." Anton stood up and began to pace. "Remember: we don't measure eternity with the same clocks that we used back on Earth." Anton reached into his robe and removed his tobacco pouch and pipe. "So how was the flight?"

"Here? Humph. You must know I'm not crazy about planes."

"I imagine it was very horrible," he said.

"How the fuck do you think it was?" Dad shot back.

"Please, *Lieb*. I am sorry to have asked. But beware of your language issues." He filled his pipe blandly and looked past Dad, at the mass of books behind him. "Watch the language! It can set you way back."

"You want a story for the Annals? I'll give you one. It was the worst fu—freakin' plane ride ever."

Anton slowly drew on his pipe.

That fragrance. Familiar fragrance.

Anton slowly turned toward the window. "Why don't you tell me another story?" He smiled at Dad and Dad smiled at him. "A different story."

251

CHAPTER
63

*P*eople were all about the house. There were tons of people. There were the usual friends and family, and there were people unknown to KC and the kids: people who knew her husband, apparently, and just wanted to pay their respects. There'd be no wake for a while.

"What was there left to bury?" she thought aloud. KC saw Frank over near the back door with his wife, Cathy. The kids were all downstairs at the moment. The house was full of noise. There was the constant hum of sadness mixed with the sounds of television and radio. There were constant expressions of grief, despair, and disbelief, depending on who spoke and who heard. Then, there were words of hope, where there should have been none.

"Look, we don't know for sure. There's no proof he was on that plane."

"He was on the plane," said KC unemotionally to the man she did not know. And she walked on into the study. It seemed all her tears had been shed.

In private. Grief-stricken. Oppressive noise from beyond the closed door. She found tears to cry, and she cried and cried, and then found composure enough to dial up Oona.

"How is it going?" she asked. She knew. KC called her friend shortly after it happened, Saturday. It was already Sunday afternoon.

"Horrible. I still can't believe it," KC said softly.

"I will be there soon. I promise."

"I'd be so thankful. I love you. Thank you." KC was strengthened a bit.

"I love you as well," Oona said.

"Thank you," she said again.

"I will be there as soon as I can finish some business. I believe I can arrive by Wednesday." She listened and heard sniffling and crunching of tissues, but no words.

"Yes, I know. Thank you." KC was devastated by the loss. The boys were finding all kinds of distractions to occupy themselves, while their sister seemed numb and taking the loss the hardest, often doing nothing but moping around the house, oblivious to her surroundings. KC would find a way to get past this tragedy and lead her family out of misery and despair.

CHAPTER
64

There were so many people at the house. Five days had passed since the accident, and plans for a wake and burial were still unplanned. A memorial service was held at the church on Thursday morning, and all those people it seemed were now at the house. Many were formally dressed. Taking the mood to that of a mercy dinner, or a mercy buffet as it were today, sounds of mature laughter finally began to creep back into the house.

There was still much sadness. And then the phone rang. It was Oona.

"*Ma chère.* I'll be arriving tonight, finally. I am so sorry for the delay."

"I'm so grateful. Oh, I love you." She couldn't wait to see her dear friend. Oona would give her strength and perspective. *The perspective of a witch.* Maybe a *shared perspective,* if what her husband wrote about all her very own Salem witch relatives was to be believed. *And somehow I've carried those genes down to Louis and now Thankful.* Oona must love that stuff! Louis the seer. Thankful a witch?

"I will be there soon." She parted her lips. "*Je t'aime beaucoup,*" she said in the loveliest French. "Love you."

"Yes please." She visualized her friend. "The sooner the better, Oona." She was so in need of support. She needed assistance. *Chinks in my armor.* She felt so alone now, alone with three children. *Oona.* Such an unexpected tragedy only proved that no one, including the seer, the medium, the sorceress, the ontologist, could predict the future.

And especially one as the one about to be. "Good-bye, *ma chère.*"

The hours passed very slowly, and finally there was a knock at the door.

The door opened and Oona stood there. For KC, Oona was as intense, striking, and mysterious as she had ever been from that time, nearly five years ago, when they'd first met. The women embraced in the doorway and walked arm in arm into the study. There they took two seats in close proximity. It was after 10 PM. The children were all in bed, and what a week it had been. They would return to school the following Monday.

"I'm so happy you're here," KC finally said.

"I want to stay," Oona said. She looked closely into KC's eyes. Closely. There was nothing there. "I want to stay here." *Still behind that wall of devotion.*

Shock. KC did not expect to hear those words.

"I will be your nanny. I will set up my practice here as well, here in Massachusetts."

Still silence. She did not expect this. Less than one week from the last shock.

"That is, if you will have me." She had never felt so humbled and never recalled ever speaking such words before. And she wanted them to be heard. Acknowledged.

"We've got to reach him, Oona. We have to."

Oona's heart sank for one long moment. She thought of him. He was a good man and a good father. *A good provider.* Annoying at times and married to a woman way over his head—out of his league. "I can help you reach your husband," she said.

"There's so much. There's so much I need right now. Oona, I need to know something."

Oona prepared for anything: any question, any request. "Yes, of course, *ma chère,*" she said. "There. There. I am here with you now."

"There are unknown and unfinished…things. Even Ed Spader, his boss, has no idea why he was going to Washington. There's so much I need to know." The women rose and embraced again. "I have no idea where he left the checkbook." KC sobbed into Oona's shoulder.

"You know I will try to help. I will use all my powers." There were hugs and soft kisses. "We shall séance for your husband." There were more sobs. "I can take care of things. I am here now. I will not be going anywhere until you get what you need." There were more hugs and more soft kisses. "Until you get everything you need. I promise." Oona's eyes blazed as she looked at and gently patted KC's blond waves. "That is, if you will have me as your nanny."

"And not just as my nanny," KC said softly.

"No, of course not."

The women slowly pulled away. "What do you know about caring for children?" KC asked. And they hugged again.

"Nothing, really." They kissed as friends kiss. Oona slowly worked her hands to a sobbing KC's lower back, her very lower back. KC gently but firmly returned her friend's hands to her upper body, and otherwise continued taking comfort from their overall embrace.

"So, you would uproot yourself to become a nanny here, for a cute little girl and her older brothers, a trade of which you know practically nothing."

"Yes," said the young woman and brilliant ontologist, the powerful seer of ghosts and spirits, the sorceress and enchantress, the oversexed beauty who could select nearly anyone or anything in the world.

Just then, Louis entered the study. He was in his jammies but looked as though he had gotten no sleep. He looked very solemn.

Upstairs, Charley and Thankful had been talking about Oona for quite a while.

"Her grandmother was a famous witch down in New Orleans," Charley had said. "If you ask me, she's weird too, and *totally* hot!" He had moved to a mirror where he carefully checked the traces of a shadow—the start of a thirteen-year-old's moustache.

Thankful had said, "She helped free Opa, right?"

"Yeah, Oona was there," Charley had said. "But she helped Louis more, and Mom too. And she is weird, but look at what Louis can do! He's been seeing ghosts since he could talk. If anything, you were just a baby then." His version of events paused for a second and then he added, "Now look at what *you* can do!"

Now, as Oona stood there before Louis, and with his mother, the boy thought, *Will life ever be normal?* He turned around but not before he exchanged a distant "Hello." Then he exited the room and closed the door behind him. He sensed big changes would be coming, and he tried hard to pinpoint which emotion he felt most.

"Oona. Tell me, dear: when do you think you would be…willing to move in? We have a beautiful guest room, as you know. And plenty of room." KC looked at her friend.

"My things are already in transit. Everything should arrive by tomorrow."

KC drew in a deep breath. She could certainly say no. What would be best, she thought, both for herself and for her family? She thought of her friend living here in her house, close by, to help with her kids: help with high-maintenance Thankful, pubescent Charley, and Oona's about-to-be protégé Louis, surely one kid with whom she had connected.

"Please be discreet, especially around the children."

Oona knew she'd fill a void. How exactly remained to be seen. What could she do to make up for a lost father? She was better suited to make up for a lost husband. "I shall support you and your family. I shall remain close and supportive of you and your pursuits for as long as…you will have me." *Seal the deal, ma chère!*

"We can assist each other. We can support our careers," offered KC.

"Yes, absolutely!"

"Maybe I can return to Boston and leave the community bank. That has not been much fun." KC smiled slowly.

"Yes, absolutely." Oona smiled as well.

"And you can practice here. You can have…his home office. It'd be perfect for your…business." KC's eyes were dark with tears and emotions.

"Yes, I am sure it will be." They looked at each other with warmer eyes now, and with matching smiles. Consolingly, Oona continued. "I shall go about my nannying career as my main job, manage your schedules and the day-to-day tasks and chores. I am not happy with New England frigidity, as you can imagine. I am, however, ready for a change, and am eager to revisit my old 'stomping grounds' in Cambridge." *And, Erzulie willing, the void within each of us may be filled by each of us.*

END OF BOOK ONE

Henry G. Brechter
8:23 AM, Sunday August 19, 2012

CPSIA information can be obtained at www.ICGtesting.com
Printed in the USA
LVOW08s1746231113

362559LV00001B/3/P